Number Games

First published in 2019 by
Liberties Press
1 Terenure Place | Terenure | Dublin 6W | Ireland
www.libertiespress.com

Distributed in the United States and Canada by
Casemate IPM | 1950 Lawrence Rd | Havertown | Pennsylvania 19083 | USA
Tel: 001 610 853 9131
www.casemateipm.com

Copyright © Owen Dwyer 2019
The author asserts his moral rights.
ISBN (print): 978-1-912589-06-7
ISBN (e-book): 978-1-912589-07-4

2 4 6 8 10 9 7 5 3 1
A CIP record for this title is available from the British Library.
Cover design by Roudy Design
Printed in Dublin by Sprint Print

Number Games

Owen Dwyer

To Rita

Part 1

Seattle, 2116

'You take the word *quim*,' she said, facing the glass wall and raising a fist, as though she was addressing a rally. 'It was considered offensive by the men of past centuries. Too sharp, you see; too unambiguous. There is something impregnable in its single syllable. *Quim.* To have such a strong word connected with female genitalia was counterculture. To us, it's simply part of the lexicon: little children use it every day, and no one turns their head.'

She paused to watch a swallow which was darting about in the empty sky, like the point of a tailor's needle. When she refocused and turned to face me, her hump became silhouetted against the brilliant blue of outside. And though she looked strangely gnome-like, there was something dignified about her too, as she made her way to the table, where she placed, with deliberation, the knuckles of her right hand onto the polished rosewood. She tapped.

'To us it is a better word than the old, awkward *vagina*, with its intimation of the act of invagination. The vagina was to facilitate, to allow the man to *invaginate* his penis as he would his sword – with the obvious implication of woman as facilitator to his potency. There were other ridiculous words that made you boys giggle – *fanny, beaver, pussy* come to mind – but the word *quim* was no laughing matter. It was the worst word you could use. Almost as bad as the notorious 'c' word, as it was called on the BBC, where it was banned. Which might make us wonder.' She became thoughtful. 'What the "BB" stood for.'

There was a glint of something in her good eye – might have been amusement. Hard to tell with these old Chinese, with their inelastic little faces, when they are joking. I wouldn't have expected the leader of the American Triumvirate to be looking for laughs, at a time like this. Then again, as the leader of the

American Triumvirate, she would feel entitled to look for anything she damn well wanted.

'If we want to understand a society,' she continued, 'we must
look at its taboos. Does not the horror the Victorians showed towards challenges to their ideology tell how intellectually vulnerable they were? How could any society have been stupid enough to
believe that there was a god, an old man with a white beard, who
was intolerant in exactly the same sexist and racist way of their
empire-building forefathers? *Nigger, fuzzy-wuzzy, quim, Chink*,
all words designed to scandalise, and therefore put an end to
discussions in which these subjects might arise. Or, at the very
least, to denigrate the object, make it vulgar, risible even.'

She set off for the water-cooler and I was reminded of a ham-
ster in slow motion: every boardroom had to have its water-hole,
a place for the animals to drink while they considered each other.
When eventually she reached the big blue bottle, she filled with
deliberate fingers a small paper cone, from which she took slow
sips as she considered me. For some reason, I felt a connection
with this old woman, isolated together as we were on the two
hundredth floor of the Ameri-Corpo headquarters, which was itself standing alone in its bed of rubble like a giant glass beehive.
It was all that remained of their government. And here we were,
stalemated in the queen's chamber, with no way out for either of
us. The armed guards outside would stop me, and I was stopping
her. She started talking again.

'These manipulations of language remove moral roadblocks,
which might stand in the way of exploitation and profiteering.
Everybody subscribes to the convenience of it, but lack of debate
leads to chaos, finally. Look what happened to the Victorians:
their ignorance culminated in the First World War, the greatest
devastation the world had known, up to that point. It was their
apocalypse. Their judgement day. The same happened to other
unsustainable ideologies, like fascism, communism and democracy. The disintegration of the terminally named *United* States.
Pogroms, holocausts and the slaughter of millions, culminating
in the mess that was Israel. It was all witnessed and predicted
by the sisterhood, but men wouldn't, or couldn't, listen. And why
not?'

The heaviness of the question seemed to weigh on her, like a
wet cape. Dropping her cup into a wastepaper basket, she turned
back to the endless horizon on the far side of the laser-proof
glass, to the ruins that stood like stumps of rotten teeth where a
city had been. I tossed the sphere and caught it, felt its ominous

weight. I thought about throwing it at her head without arming it, like a baseball: she was so frail, the force would probably kill her. The swallow danced by, then danced away. She looked after it wistfully: swallows were going to survive. Bending one arm behind her back, she continued to gesture with her free hand, slow circular movements now, as though she was waving at an ecstatic crowd through the window of a state limo.

'What matter?' she said. 'How can you learn from a history that has been rewritten? For so long we have refused to acknowledge the truth, and now, we, the isolated and deluded Triumvirate, pace the corridors of our powerbase like Hitler in his bunker or Nero with his fiddle. Now it is the turn of the women to fail. What next? Hand it all over to the children?'

She was motionless for a while. I was on the point of thinking she might have died standing up, when she let go of a ponderous fart. While I searched for something to say to break the awkwardness, she turned and, as if seeing me for the first time, said: 'It's only America now, and I know you might think America a backward and insignificant place, but it is the wound through which the infection will spread. Conversely, treat America, and you cure the world.'

Her attention was caught by something in the rubble below. I stepped over and saw two security cars hovering over a cluster of dispersing people. Shots fired into their midst were followed a split-second afterwards by a muffled crack and violent sparks along the hull of one of the cars, which veered dramatically from the scene. Nothing else happened; no further fire was discharged; the people disappeared back into the rubble; and the cars, following a few cursory search patterns, zipped out of view. The side of her face, tinged blue by the refractor, gazed at the scene.

'Something needs to be done before another collapse,' she said. 'Before another *revolution*. If the rebs gain control of Seattle, a chain reaction will engulf the world, and that will cause annihilation. It really would be . . . how did your friend put it . . . Armageddon. *She* can moralise about the ethics of what we are about to do, but ethics don't matter any more, especially not here. Ethics are a luxury we can't afford. What matters is the collective. What matters is that the greatest number survive. What matters is that *we* survive. No one cares how *you* part your hair.'

She waved a derisory finger in the direction of my hair. I thought this poor observation on her part: I never parted my hair. In this respect at least, I believed in chaos theory.

'Or whether or not you are worth falling in love with. No one cares about or believes in gods unless they absolutely have to. How can they believe in the individual? As long as they are fed and have their creature comforts, the masses will be indifferent. Ideology exists for the oppressed, as a kind of rationale to justify begrudgery, or to give hope. But it makes people, especially men, zealously aspirational. The rebs want to take everything and give nothing. They do not understand balance. Our plan will restore balance to the books.'

Wandering away from the wall, she stopped to stare at one of the high-backed leather chairs that lined the table, as if considering the trouble it would take to sit in it. When she spoke, it wasn't clear whether it was me or the chair she was addressing.

'I know that you are not quite as stupid as either you or we have been making out. I know you have a better understanding of what is happening here, better even than your wholesome girlfriend. She thinks there is still some morality to be salvaged. You and I know different, don't we?'

'What if we do?' I said carefully, not wanting to either aggravate or encourage her. I really just wanted to get away, to another life, where I could go shopping, wash the dishes, take out the garbage, whatever.

'You must put the case to Euro-Corpo, substantiate the data. *Convince* them that we explored every other option and were left with no alternative. They will never believe that you are clever enough to lie to them.'

Suppressing an itch to take umbrage, I said: 'Why should I?'

'Why *not*?'

'But what difference will it make? You've already made up your mind.'

'Oh, everything makes a difference,' she said. 'Small differences, big differences: they all add up. Right now, it is necessary to have as much in our plus column as possible, and the testimony of a boy-slapper, who is incapable of having an agenda, would definitely help. Besides, you would be making a contribution to history: not bad for an insignificant. What is there in the negative column, other than a trace of male pride?'

I could not think of anything, then and there, beyond my discomfort with her ruthless barbarism; it seemed bad manners to bring all that up again.

'You know,' she continued, 'I will not allow anything to interfere with the plan.'

'What about my friend?'

'Friend, is she? Lover, perhaps? *Invaginatee?* She must stay here with us. If you have travelled so far to rescue her, then we already know that you are far more likely to protect her safety than she would yours. She has a nasty streak of the heroic, that one.'

I looked at the sphere and started fingering the coloured panels. I had heard enough.

1

Two years earlier

I stoop out of a taxi and my eye catches the ankle of a woman. It's a swollen ankle, scuffed red where it's been forced into a high-heel shoe, for which it's too big. No Cinderella. Travelling northwards, I'm not disappointed to see that the ankle belongs to a fleshy leg, covered just below the knee with a shiny, shapeless material that passes as a dress. I can see, or at least imagine I see, the curve of a flabby thigh. I think of a squalid, squashed quim, stuffed into a pair of overstretched knickers, hidden from respectable society. Of course I'm drunk. Sober, I'm less venal – or at least better at pretending. Lasciviousness, Emily tells me, is what makes me easy to control. I know it, yet I can't stop being its slave. She's thick around the middle too, Swollen Ankles: stratified fat. Looks like the proud mother of a thousand carbo-rich craps. You can see the self-justification all over her face, like jam. Christ, I want her. She's swaying in the queue with a group of similar gargoyles, being lit with splashes of light from the perpendicular sign over an insulted Georgian door. *Dance Adonis,* it says, like an order. Alongside, there's the shape of a boy, could be two identical boys, flickering alternately from either side of a pole. One flashes turquoise, one pink. Both would look like outlines at a murder scene, were it not for the phalluses, which rise and fall with the neon. Her eyes, moated by ponds of black eyeshadow, are glazed and wandering, attracted to the lights. She doesn't see me pick myself up, or notice me drain and fling away the bottle of alco-pep I've been arguing with the taxi-driver about. They're waiting to get into the nightclub – which, conveniently, is managed by a client of mine. She likes me, this client, likes the way I invest her money without asking where it came from.

There are always crowds at this hour on a Saturday night, outside the clubs on Leeson Street. Women mostly, and mostly married. They're there, ostensibly, to look at the pole-dancers. But looking is not enough for many. They want a taste of boy: a physical indulgence which drugs and arrogance tells them they're entitled to. Their husbands are at home minding kids, or zonked in front of soap operas, where they can exist in the ether of simulated emotion until their spouses decide to come home and tell them what's real again. They're not all like that. Emily is at home, her cool body enveloped between clean sheets, her sacrosanct, sweet-smelling quim, dry and oblivious in its sheath of silk. I'm imagining this; I've never seen it. I've never seen it through dates where we've talked about cinema, or through the painful evenings when I've sat prettily sipping beer with her friends. I've never seen it when she's powdered me with dry kiss-es in her car. Or while I've been hanging on her arm, at one of the upmarket dos where she's shown me off. I've never seen it, and I'm beginning to wonder if it exists.

I sidle to the head of the queue, towards a bouncer. 'Would Amy be there?' I ask. She should be shoving me back into the night, but there's something familiar about me. I've been there before. Muttering something into her headpiece, she tells me to stand back and wait, which I do, until Amy emerges presently from the heaving mess of noise to join us street-side. She does her big-guy act, of welcoming me and remonstrating with the bouncer for not knowing who I am, before ushering me down the stone steps to the basement. I turn to the gargoyles, diffidently.

'Join me?'

#

I get on well with women, mostly because I listen to them with fascination and let them feel in control. You need to know how to surf their moods and react appropriately, or else you'll end up being treated like a cheaper piece of meat than you actually are. I need to work on my technique, because I don't come from money and I don't exactly stick out in a crowd. Amy, now she sticks out a mile, six foot tall and built like a brick shit-house – stuffed into a tuxedo, at least at the club. A thick plait of blond hair hangs right down her back, as far as her muscular buttocks. Her other most striking feature is that she likes young boys. I don't hold it against her. Who am I to judge anybody? She gives me a cheerful slap on the shoulder, plants a free bottle of wine on the counter, then dissolves back into the crowd. I watch her go with the sadness only a drunk can know. Swollen Ankles is speaking to me, and I'm not making her life any easier by being too pissed to talk. I start pursing my lips and nodding like I'm giving a shit about whatever she's saying. In the end, she reaches over and grabs one of my cheeks with a heavily ringed claw. Her mouth dips at the corners; it's full of large teeth, two of which don't quite make it behind the lips when they close. It's talking again.

'You're a cheeky little one, aren't you,' it says, as she leans forward to clutch my knee. I smile and shrug cheekily. She turns and growls at a staggerer-by who has raised an eyebrow in my direction, before reasserting proprietorship by hemming me between the vectors of her knees. Massaging my thigh, she continues. 'Out all alone at this late hour.'

Her breasts, mostly pertox by the look and shape, hold me in the gaze of their perfect nipples, while watery eyes continue to scan me, like I'm some prize she's unexpectedly won. I can't decide where to focus. I notice, clinically, that the focal-point of her ugliness is an upturned snout, and wonder if she should have spent the tit-job money on a nose. The good angel on my right shoulder asks me what the fuck I'm doing, asks what the fuck Emily would say if she could see me. But it is the thought of Emily finding out that charges the situation. If she were to see me now, doing what I'm doing (which, specifically, is reaching towards a pertox tit and feeling its rubbery surface with my fingertips), it would be the end of our sanitised existence. No more trendy restaurants or witty banter or powdery kisses.

Somewhere in my subconscious jungle, I want it all to end, while somewhere else I want it to begin. I want to be a happily married man, wiping his hands on his apron as he goes to greet his wife on her return from a hard day's work. At the same time, I want to have enough control over my life to *decide* whether or not I should work after I get married. To conform or not to conform, this is the question. I'm returned to the scene by the pressure of fingers on my crotch, and put my hand on Swollen Ankles' to squeeze appreciatively. The ugly mouth attacks and grinds itself into mine. Shortly afterwards, we're hovering along in the back of a taxi, where she mauls me relentlessly on the trip to what turns out to be Kimmage. When we fall out of the car, she stabs the cred-pad and returns some abuse by way of a tip.

'Fuck you too,' she shouts as the driver takes off. 'And your fucking stainable seats.'

Turning to search for her prize, she sees me leaning against the wall of a laneway.

'We near your place?' I ask hopefully, but the time for talking is over – which is funny, because it never really began. Her lower lip stretches itself over most of her teeth.

We fuck, fight and fuck again. We make animal noises, to go with our animal behaviour. I become detached, letting her grind and grunt and work me over. Memories come to haunt me, of leather, and the pain of my hair being pulled backwards until the roots burn. I can taste stale smoke and cheap beer, mingling with the faint tang of diesel oil on the breath of a lost summer evening. The sensation of my balls being grabbed brings an involuntary yelp and returns me to the lane: her way of dealing with distraction, apparently. My body becomes a buffet on which she feasts. I wrestle on, gamefully. There isn't much we don't do, and if we've missed something it isn't worth writing about. When I eventually stagger out of the lane, holding up my trousers and ignoring her abuse, it's getting light. And now I'm really in trouble, because Emily will be picking me up in a matter of hours to go to some heavy-duty charity thing.

2

You can see the dome of the Corpo Concert Hall from almost anywhere in the city: it's a great monument to our beloved system of corporatised matriarchy. What you're actually seeing is light. The dome itself is relatively minuscule, inside the gigantic glowing projection it shoots into the night sky when there's a major event. Every city has its Corpo Concert Hall, along with its Museum of Decadence and Forbidden City. The Forbidden Cities are where the Triumvirates live, in splendid isolation, and it's from here that their great philosophy flows to saturate our way of life – shape our thinking. This may be a bit overbearing at times, what with all the marketing, 3D documentaries and propagandised education system, but it's better than anything that went before: you've only got to go to the Museum of Decadence, to see the damage western democracy inflicted. And by 'western democracy', we mean 'men'. You're forced to go to the museum as a schoolchild, and no one's ever been to the Forbidden City. But everyone loves the Concert Hall. You can't help feeling privileged, when your car grips the park-wall and you're slid into the giant glass elevator, which floats you right into the ballroom.

We share the elevator, me and Emily, with some older, Asian couples, stiff with the starch of their clothes, and the uprightness of their position in society. These balls are an excuse for the well-connected to parade their affluence and generosity. But you can't help being enamoured by it all, and you ignore the hypocrisy. Tonight, it's all about raising money for the 'American Unfortunate', but it could be about anything. All anybody cares about, is looking like they care. I mould my face into an expression of concern, as the Mistress of Ceremonies describes the shitty situation at some orphanage in California. A 3D is switched on, and a trickle of fatherless children fizzle into being to walk among

us. Their gaunt faces look ahead or turn blankly in either direction, as they pull aside ragged clothes to show festering sores on
bruised limbs. I'm standing inconsequentially on the outskirts of
a group Emily is talking to, when my ear begins to wander.

'Poor bastards,' I hear some matriarch behind me say. 'Imagine having to live like that.'

'That's what happens when you don't get the numbers right,'
answers another. Her tone is coldly philosophical. I turn, pretending to be looking for someone in the crowd, and see two middle-aged Chinese leaning into each other. If they think I might be
listening, I don't matter enough to worry about.

'But there should be political action,' says the first, a short
woman in a high-collared velvet jacket. Jet black hair furls geo-
metrically from her head in orbit circles. Her face is powdered
white, with the cheekbones light purple: the stamp of the matriarch. 'From the very top. We need policies, not charity.'

'Oh, come on,' says the second. 'Please don't tell me that you
think the Triumvirs have nothing better to do than deal with this
rabble.'

'The question is,' says the first, 'what will happen if they
don't?'

'No,' answers the second, 'I rather think it is what will happen if they *do*.'

I imagine a scenario where I'm confident and socially permit-
ted enough to turn to them and say something like: "Scuse me,
pardon the interjection and everything, but I couldn't help over-
hearing your little conversation there. Mind if I ask you a simple
on the substantive? Why should you girls be doing all the pushing around? Eh? And who's to say these Americans wouldn't be
able to look after themselves, given half a chance? Eh? Eh? Or
that the rebellion that's destroyed their country, is not the product of the very politicians you say should rescue them? Surely
even the most mesmerised disciple of the Triumvirate system
must concede that the world is being run by a selfish elite who
have a greater interest in their own power and wealth, than the
good of humanity. Eh?'

But I could never say this, because I am a boy: I am conditioned not to have the confidence – and even if I did, society
would puke on me for being an upstart.

'No,' the second is saying, 'I think we can safely assume that
our noble Triumvirate are too savvy for interference.'

Tall and patrician, this one organises her body as carefully as
her words, into interesting shapes. She, too, has *establishment*

written all over her, though her style is less formal. They both thumb a generous credit to the charity. The amount of each donation rises and explodes in 3D from the cred-pad before cascading about their contrived self-effacement. This is soon happening all over the ballroom, and the air fills with translucent numbers, dipping or rising, fading or emerging. It is an ecstatic numeration of goodwill, which is accompanied by a chorus of oohs and aahs, while the insensible, forgotten waifs limp colourlessly on.

When the business end of the evening finishes, the crowd, full of its own sense of generosity, settles into a guiltless guzzle of food and drink. The 3D is switched off, dispatching both the ghostly orphans and colourful clouds of numbers to memory. Emily, handing me a drink, smiles the brittle smile she's been spraying around all evening. 'Come on.'

'Fucius,' I say, following her to a balcony, where we look over a roof garden, lit romantically with hovering lanterns. 'I can't believe the number of rich bastards here. Did you see the amount of money floating around that room?'

'Is that all you saw?' she asks, like the whole American thing is my fault. I wonder what answer I should give. She doesn't look like she really wants one: her eyes, blue and cool, search the distance. I wonder why she has taken me to the relative privacy of the balcony, and whether she has something she wants to say. While I'm figuring all this, she moves away and disappears through a gaggle of husbands nattering their way to the men's room. I look at my glass, already empty, and follow. I'm insecure now, suspecting that she has only brought me along to remind her friends that she can actually get a date. It's then that I remember: this whole relationship thing has been manoeuvred by her mother Mianzi for reasons of her own. Mianzi, who also happens to be my boss at Ningbo Digits, thinks I'm a genius because I get results. Tells people about me at the golf club. Is particularly proud about the part where I am a boy, who comes from Carlow. It beefs up her liberal cred. And if this arranged relationship with Emily doesn't work out, it could screw up my career, as well as my head.

Maybe Emily is feeling the pressure of the 'arrangement' from her side, but whatever the reason, she seems to want me to hang around. At the foot of the stairs, she's waiting for me. She takes me by the wrist and continues showing me off to important people. And I begin to believe again, that there might be something going on after all. She avoids William Howe, darling of the tab-vids and slut son of a Corpo board member. This avoidance is no surprise, as they have recently broken off an engagement. Across the room from Howe and his set, Mianzi and her husband Martin are at home in the sea of affluence, as they shuffle amiably through the crowd, towards a table they've reserved. Making our way steadily over, we join them. I've never met Martin, and am struck by his similarity to Emily. It's the seriousness: he has the demeanour of a serious man, with significant things on his mind. Heavily pouched eyes and immaculately groomed silver hair, together with an impeccable grey suit, put me in mind of an old-world politician, with the weight of a crisis on their shoulder. I'm expecting a serious conversation about the state of things in the Re-United States, or whatever, but he leans over and confides: 'See that woman there, with the feathers? Gay as a pantomime. Married with four children too. Very respectable.'

I raise my eyebrows and assume a shocked face. Emily interrupts. 'Let's dance.'

This I welcome. With her stop-start interest all night, I've begun to feel like an engine that keeps turning over but fails to get going. A slim arm slides across my shoulder, as she draws me close and we shamble through a series of techno-funky tunes. There is an aura in her proximity, which goes beyond the touch of skin and smell of perfume. It beguiles me as it defines her. I want her to touch me suggestively, to whisper something inappropriate into my ear, but she behaves so well, I wonder if she's even interested. I catch us in a mirror, and am embarrassed by the contrast of her elegance to my smaller, slightly untidy form.

'You OK?' she asks eventually.

'Mmm,' I murmur approvingly. If she knows how happy being near her makes me, it might encourage her to grab my ass – do *something*.

'Having a good time?'

'Great, thanks,' I reply, with the enthusiasm of a Boy Scout.

'Good.'

'And you?' I ask earnestly, not wanting silence to resettle. 'Are you having a good time?'

'Sure. Why not?'

'You seem quiet.'

She sighs.

'Maybe I'm the quiet type.' And again, the brittle smile. Which brings the dread: she must at least suspect something about last night, about Fat Ankles and the laneway. I can sense contempt. Maybe it's my imagination, because she maintains an impregnable politeness as she leads me back to Mianzi's table, where we resume our place and listen to the senior Corporatist holding court. Specifically, Mianzi is explaining to a group of listening heads how she and Martin have suffered at a recon-spa in Kilrush, where they spent last weekend working on their jowls. A good raconteur, she knows where to draw emphasis and create tension. Emily and I laugh along with the rest. It gives us a break from trying to talk to each other.

Howe and three of his set come over, gallant with alco-pep. Oblivious to the intrusion, they create an extraneous circle on the edge of our table, into which we are dragged. After some time – which Howe spends gushing at Emily – he replies to a polite interjection from me with a slashing movement of his head.

'And who's this?'

He looks smaller in real life, and his voice has a nasal twinge, which doesn't come across on tele-vid. It makes me wonder how anyone takes him seriously.

'I'm Li.'

He glares at me, while I withdraw my untouched hand. Having addressed the question to Emily, he seems to expect her to answer, by way of an apology. But Emily just shrugs. 'Like he says, he's Li. He's a friend.'

Howe huffily switches his attention to *his* friends. They begin giggling through an animated conversation, with occasional looks deployed like missiles in Emily's direction.

Eventually she asks: 'And how have you been, William? I mean really.'

'Fine,' he half-gasps.

'Hey Li? Can we talk to you over here for a minute?' One of his cronies wants to know.

'About what?'

'Hey, it's nothing to worry about. Seriously, we just wanted to ask you about something.'

They're already standing up, gesturing me towards the bar.

'Ask me about what?'

'We just want to, you know, talk. Boys' stuff. What are you so suspicious about?'

They are giggling again, incredulously, looking from each other to me, and finally to Howe, who has edged his chair closer to Emily's. They're smug, these boys. This environment fits them, like a soft leather glove. They'll never question why they're peripheral. Nobody questions anything about the world we all live in. Just as the dead generations of yesteryear would have accepted whatever shit they lived through, I suppose. I don't know why I question things; I just do. It's like I know something that I don't know – which means I must have forgotten it. Whatever it is, it's jumping around inside me, like a Mexican bean. A peppy-pill I have swallowed earlier, with one of the glasses of champagne Emily has been pouring into me, makes me brave.

'I'm not suspicious,' I say. 'It's just, I've never met you before, and I don't know what the *fuck* you would have to talk to me about. The only thing I know about you guys is that your leader here' – I gesture at Howe, who is observing with a sour mouth – 'is trying to mooch my date, and refuses to shake my hand. So, no. I won't join you at the bar, if it's all the same to you. Unless of course' – I turn to Emily, whose face remains as unreadable as it has been all night – 'you want me to.'

'I don't care one way or the other, but if you boys want to have a cat-fight, *I'm* going to the bar.'

I follow, like a dog. We sit on barstools and pass occasional remarks to passing people we know. Though I try, once or twice, to start a conversation, she seems preoccupied. I give up, and begin counting the crystals in the chandelier, which, following another peppy and another glass of champagne, has become fascinating. I've switched my attention to her slender fingers playing with the stem of her glass, when a commotion breaks out at the other side of the room. An auction is taking place, for a person. That's the way it is: everything is a commodity, and everything is for sale, if someone is prepared to buy it. Tonight, the lot is Howe. He goes out on a date with you, sucks your tits, whatever, if you're the highest bidder. The matriarchs converge: they have the veneer of charity behind which to hide. Jumping onto the stage, he makes his way up and down the catwalk, lapping it up. A murmur of approval burbles into a cheer, when he points his ass at the audience and waves it expertly. The MC, who has changed into a sparkling silver jacket, slaps the ass as it passes.

'It's real, all right,' she announces. 'Now, do I hear ten thousand?'

What she hears are jeers and shouts of encouragement, for the removal of Howe's tight trousers. They've caught sight of a fluorescent G-string, and are like a pack of hounds on the scent.

I turn to Emily. 'Nice,' I say. 'Real classy.'

'Eleven thousand,' shouts the MC, impressed.

'At least he's giving it away for charity,' she says.

'Meaning?'

I thank Confucius for the narcotics surfing through my body: I'd never be able to brazen through what's coming otherwise.

'That's twelve thousand to the lady with the pearl necklace.'

'Meaning whatever you want it to mean,' she says, returning a nod to someone.

'If you are insinuating something . . . .'

I find it hard to finish the sentence. Even if she does not know or suspect anything about the previous night, she would know that being 'obliged to oblige' is part of my deal with the Corpo. Mostly it's at Mianzi's suggestion, and mostly just dinner and a couple of hours of being awed by the Corpo's power and influence. I have, on occasion, been tempted back to a hotel room, convincing myself that I find the woman attractive and would have shagged her anyway. It's what's expected at my level, from a man. That is, if he has any ambition.

'That's fifteen, yes, fifteen thousand to Mianzi. Going and gone!'

Martin's been left alone at the deserted table. He's staunch, like so many of his generation, but even he can't take this. Rising slowly, he puts on a pair of grey gloves while Mianzi, in a throng of her peers, is gesturing obscenities, oblivious. As he is making his way to the exit, I elbow Emily.

'Your father,' I say, pointing to the old boy who has hesitated a moment with his hand on the handle.

'Fuck,' she says. But by the time she stands up, he's already gone. 'Fuck. You wait here.' And she hurries after him.

3

I fall out of bed in my apartment and look at a Sunday-ful of sailors playing on Dublin Bay. They pimp up the flat blue, with colourful sails and water-suits, while the boys lay out picnics on the sea-shelf. The dread is back, and I am, familiarly, awash with disgrace. Stuck to the couch like a wet insect, I try to piece together the previous night. There's a recurring image of an ass-cleavage, smiling at me over the stretching elastic of off-white sweatpants. From a barstool in a city-centre flesh-farm, I think. I'm not even sure how I got there, though I do remember hurrying out the side door of the ballroom as soon as Emily left to find Martin.

I hear loud music and see loud lights. Must have been a club. A series of hot burbles floating from my stomach-pit tells me I've been pumping myself with cheap alco-pep. The ass-cleavage morphs into a woman. She develops a face and situates it in the middle of my horizon. Remembering makes my heart sink like a stone, but it's not like I have a choice. The face is heavily made up and enthusiastic. It advances. I see more detail: red blotches beneath the eyes, sloppy mascara. Then it attacks. I taste whiskey on a tongue and remember a stud, hard and round in the swirling slime. I'm on a floor early next morning when memory regains consistency. I creep from a bachelorette-squat Ass Cleavage shares with, I think, a sister. They've both had a go at me. For some reason there's a sense of freedom, infusing with the self-disgust, as I stumble along a pavement. As if I've escaped something.

I make myself a cup of coffee and use it to wash down a peppy. Back on the couch, in the interlude between swallow and kick, I get the familiar, creepy feeling that I'm being judged: that everything I do, say or think is being scrutinised, that I will later be held to account. I get this all the time, when I'm feeling low:

it's called paranoia. But right now it's real, and it scares the shit out of me. I try to blank my mind, to deny the force its fuel, but continue to recollect. I don't want to. I want to forget last night even happened, but my mind is on a roll, seems to be enjoying getting me into trouble. I see myself hurrying through a strange hinterland, after I've escaped from the squat until I find a vac-stop, where I stand and shiver. Eventually one arrives, and I hunch in an empty carriage, like a refugee. When the vac stops at Parkgate, I see through the kitchen window of a redbrick, a woman nursing a child. The white flap of a Corpo-uniform hangs down to release her breast, and a single strand of hair has fallen over her face. Though she glances at her watch, she is mostly intent on the baby. As the vac moves away, a husband comes into the frame and takes the child. The scene reminds me of something, some kind of Madonna-and-child thing, but I can't think straight. So I let my mind meld into the blur of the grey city and the hum of the vac.

The scars from Fat Ankles are still in the circuit mirror. I wonder if Ass Cleavage or her sister noticed, and if so, whether it tainted their enjoyment of my flesh. My skin erupts when I shower, so I step quickly through the drier and apply more ointment. I'm like a fisherwoman mending nets, or a farmer sharpening a plough. We all have to take care of our equipment. I smear antibiotic skin-repairer onto my wincing penis, and gut-lurch when I remember where it's been. Standing by the sitting-room window, with my kimono hanging open, I swirl the dregs of a fourth cup of coffee and look at the sailors. They weave slow patterns on the expanse of the sea, random, free. They can turn any way they like.

#

I'm watching Arsenal, mid-afternoon, foundering against Chelsea in the China Cup, when my irritation is interrupted by Emily's pristine little image fizzing from my sphere-phone, which I've forgotten to switch off.

'What *happened* to you last night?' It wants to know. The oily machinery of duplicity clicks into place.

'I, uh, thought you wanted to be with Martin,' I say, a big look of understanding on my face.

'I told you to wait. I was only gone ten minutes.'

'Well, I didn't think you really wanted me to.'

'And where did we get that idea from? Did I say I *didn't* want you to wait? Did I? Did I?'

I put on a bit of a pout, try to look like I'm about to cry.

'No,' I say. The little head shakes, as irritation dissolves into exasperation.

'Would you like to tell me what exactly is going on here?'

'I thought you, like, wanted to be with Howe or whatever,' I say, letting her think she's unravelling me.

'And what made you think that? I was bloody worried about you. I told Mianzi I'd take care of you. Had to take a real earful this morning.'

Sitting into a miniature armchair, she produces a tiny cup from the invisible margins, which she brings onto her lap. I hope the miniature me she is looking at is holding its composure, or at least losing the right amount of it.

'Well, how was I supposed to know what you wanted?' I say. 'You, like, hardly spoke to me all night, and when you did, it was to make remarks.'

'Remarks?'

'Yeah. About my character. And stuff.'

Even to me, the speaker of these words, they are nauseating. I feel like throwing up, a whole bucketful of the crap I go on with.

'Well, aren't we Mis-ter Sensitive? All I've been hearing about you is how you're holding your own in a woman's world, and how capable you are.'

When I don't reply, she softens. 'Look, I'm sorry, OK? I didn't mean to be ignoring you all night, but you were a bit spliffed, and there are rules about taking advantage. But I would have seen you home safely. Were you OK getting home, by the way?'

'You're checking up on me now?'

'Don't be paranoid.'

'And how was Martin?' I switch.

'Upset, as you'd expect.'

'I ended up running out of that place,' I agree, sensing an escape over common ground. 'It was just so awful, so . . . *vulgar*. Place erupted into a cattle market. So degrading. I don't know how that tart Howe can live with himself.'

'And all conveniently "for charity".'

'Yeah, well anyway, I probably overreacted. Sorry.'

'I'm sorry too, baby. Why don't we meet later for a drink and talk about it?'

A meeting could be perfect. I could tell her everything. About the things I do and the reasons I do them. I could tell her about paranoia: what it's like to live with. I could tell her I want to reform, beg her to take me under her angel wing and make me a better person. Truth is a strange commodity, in a world held together by truism. But I could bet on Emily's morality: the odds would be in my favour with a moral person. This could be it. This could be my chance to free myself from the lattice of secret longings and fears that have been tying me up.

'I can't,' I say. 'Have to go see my parents.'

4

When Emily's image blinks out, I take another pill and decide that I really will go and see my folks. Following an intense hair-gelling and -prodding session, I get dressed, in a beige flannel suit, risqué red shirt (with ruffles) and brown leather shoes to go with my bag. Purposeful and well groomed, I lock the front door and turn to face humanity. The escalator tube from the lobby slides into the city like the proboscis of a mosquito, and delivers me like a drop of blood onto the walkway that moves along the river to vac central.

Ten minutes later, I'm sitting in the Carlow vac, enjoying this time, the surge and suck of its movement. I love the vac, after a peppy pill. There is something exhilarating about the clean buzz and straight vein through which you pulse. Infinite permutation fascinates me. I think of all those tubes, rippling all over the world like capillaries, making Earth look like a brain in those sat-shots you see on the Documentary Channel. A screen sliding from the roof fills with a bald Chinese head, which tells me what the weather's going to be like, and that I should be buying Colgate – that's if I want a winning smile. He produces what must be a winning smile, all teeth and twinkles, then disappears with the screen, when it slides back into the roof. They do that, ad screens, so as to catch you unawares and have a greater impact on your subconscious. There are a few other passengers scattered in the compartment. They don't seem to have noticed the screen, and don't look much like Colgate types. I don't care about them: their glumness is not going to bring me down today. I'm too pepped for that.

Instead, my mind wanders down little tubes of philosophy. I find myself thinking of what journeying on horseback must have been like, when distance would have been a real issue. Or even in later years, when sad bastards sat in cars on ground-level roads and were stuck for hours in traffic jams, pumping fumes into the air – also on the Documentary Channel. But the documentaries never tell you what they were thinking. I wonder why they didn't draw a line, from the past through their present and into the future. Had they taken the time to evaluate the evidence, they would surely have seen what was coming.

#

Elia is in the garden wearing a grubby toga, eating cherries and reading a newspaper. He's in a wicker chair under the Pistachio Tree, legs apart. I can just about make out the shape of a ball in the dark recess of his crotch. Point of origin, beginning of journey: somehow, I can't think of it as home. A warm breeze caressing my boozy face returns me to the scene, and startles the red fuchsias on the gable-end of the house. They create a voluptuous backdrop, against which he sits like a large baby Buddha. Looking up, he smiles.

I say: 'Your balls are hanging out there, pappy-san.'

'I'm letting the air at them. Had a bit of a rash last week. What has you over here so early on a Sunday morning anyway?'

Ignoring it's 2 PM, I say: 'I seek advice from a wise and aged master.'

'Seek away – though I doubt if I can tell you anything you don't already know.'

He folds his newspaper on his knee and waits for me to say something. Cool paper on bare thigh, alien to his warm, soft skin. Laura is at work, and I know that he thinks I'm judging him because of this. He's convinced I'm one of those modern types, who think married men should get out and find a job. I'm not. Who am I to judge? He's happy, that's the main thing. Let him totter about at home, while his wife bends herself with stress in the rat-race. If he minds being a chattel, it doesn't show: he wears his caste like a light summer suit. Yet, if ever I have a problem, he's the one to talk to, for some reason. The fact hangs between us like a scrotum, as he assembles his 'You can talk to me' face. Rising eyebrows send a ripple up the fleshy cliff of his forehead.

'Yeah, it's just that I'm thinking of leaving Ningbo.'

I shove my hands into my pockets and shrug, as I wait for a response to this grenade, rocking slowly from heel to toe like a metronome. The indolent eyes blink.

'Got a better offer, eh?'

He leans forward, and the paper slides from his knee. 'Not as such, no.'

The forehead ripples flatten, then reassert themselves, like tides of thought going in and out. I stare at him while he stares at flashy carp swimming in circles.

'Ah, starting up on your own, eh?' he says, slowly. 'Teach old Mianzi a thing or two. Though there might be a bit of awkwardness there, what with you being boinked by the daughter, and all.'

He knows too much about my personal life. Laura must have heard something in work, or perhaps he has seen the blog of the America Ball. Maybe it was in the paper.

'I'm not starting up anything. And I am *not* being . . . oh, never mind.'

He leans back in the chair and grabs a mound of scrotum thoughtfully.

'Well, I suppose you'd better tell me what's going on, then.'

'Nothing.'

'Well, Fucius, there must be something.'

'No, that's just it. There's nothing. I can't think of anything.'

'You're leaving your good job because of . . . nothing?'

Sitting on a stone toadstool, which I hope won't dirty my pants, I offer: 'I *have* been having problems, with Emily.'

'Ah,' he says, with a bright little smile. 'I thought we might get to that sooner or later. What's going on?'

I could lie, pretend innocence, but that wouldn't stop the nagging discomfort. Besides, it's been a while since me and Elia have pretended that I have a claim on respectability, so I tell him. 'Thing is, I've been playing away behind her back, and she doesn't seem to care. Just does not make sense. You know how possessive women are, especially the Alphas.'

'Does she know?'

'Can't see how not. I've been turning up covered with love-bites and bruises.'

He massages the white bristles on his chin thoughtfully, with his scrotum-tainted hand.

'You're looking for attention. Sounds like you're being a touch resentful because you're not getting it. Attention, that is.'

It does sound like this. But I can't stop thinking that there's more going on. Things just don't feel right.

'Things just don't *feel* right,' I say.

'What do you expect?' he says. 'That's life. That's your problem, Li: you think life is supposed to be more fulfilling. Sooner or later, you're going to have to accept that a man's world is a man's world, and a woman's is a woman's. That's just the way things are. I mean, would it kill you to accept some nice girl with a few bob, like this Emily Bradshaw, and settle down? Eh?'

'Part of me wants to.'

'There's no substitute for respectability,' he says. He's full of these mantras, which he rolls out whenever an intelligent comment is required. Saves him the trouble of thinking.

'But there's another part of me that thinks there should be something more, that there's something wrong. Something I don't understand.'

'There will always be things we don't understand about the world. Why worry about it? Have the common sense and the *maturity* to leave all that to the women: that's how the world works. Understanding that fact is what being a man is all about. These problems with Emily will sort themselves out, if you accept your place and at least *try* to behave yourself.'

'It's not just Emily. It's everything. Everything is too easy. It's like I'm missing a number in the equation. It doesn't make sense.'

His hand moves towards his balls, but I give him a look and he redirects it slowly towards the back of his head, which he rubs with his knuckles.

'Nothing makes sense if you think about it too deeply,' he says. 'If you accept your lot – which is not a bad lot compared to some, believe me – you might surprise yourself by waking up happy some morning.'

'Are *you* happy?'

'Happy? I'm ecstatic.'

His eyes bulge emphatically. I probe.

'Why, pappa-san? Why are you happy?'

'Why? Why am I happy? Fucius, I dunno. Suppose I'm happy because I'm married to a decent woman and a good provider. I like hobbies,' he adds, as an afterthought.

His hobbies are gardening and tinkering in his shed with old radios. I don't want to be insulting, or anything, but have to ask: 'Are you really telling me that you can get all the stimulation you need, from this small garden or from taking old radios apart?'

'Oh,' he says, 'I don't expect you to understand. You are young. Everything has to be hyper-stimulated at your age. But to me, there's a lot to be said for gentle distraction. I have reached the tail-end of a long struggle, in one piece. We always assumed we would end up like the vast majority who were left behind by the booms, doing some kind of menial work, or in service. But we managed to carve out a little corner. And in that corner, we found a little happiness.'

'That makes you happy?'

'*Acceptance* makes me happy.'

The word reverberates between us. We both know what it means: his acceptance, and my refusal to accept. But we don't talk about Zisha; we never do. Instead he continues, his voice barely faltering. 'I didn't have the opportunities you had, but nor did I have the expectation. It was un-thought of for a man to have a career when I was growing up, and even if he did, the Corpo insisted he gave it up when he got married. Seeing you kids getting an education, seeing you elevate yourselves to boomtown, that gives me a sense of completion. And now you want to . . . What exactly *do* you want to do, again?'

'Just get out of the boom for a while. Find myself, I think.'

'Well, only you can find what makes you happy. But be aware, the world is a changing place.' He prods a finger at the newspaper by his ankle. 'This situation in the Re-United States.'

'Won't affect us.'

'Maybe not, but the Triumvirate here are getting antsy, if you ask me.'

'Yeah?' I say, sounding interested. I pick a cherry from the bowl and suck the fruit from the stone. He has no idea what goes on in the real world, but likes to pretend he does. He picks up these phrases from the news, and rolls them out like he knows what they actually mean. I have to pretend I take him seriously.

'They're selling what's left of their Ameri-stock. Something's going on, mark my words.'

But they are the words of a househusband, bandied about with the same groundless conviction as his ever-failing predictions for the soccer tables, or the outcome of a celebrity relationship.

'We'll just have to wait and see,' I say, listlessly, and he takes advantage of the gap in conversation to reach into the pocket of his toga, where he evidently keeps loose fish-food. Retrieving a handful, he throws it over the pond, and when it peppers the surface, the carp turn instantaneously to gorge themselves.

#

Laura arrives tired and uncommunicative. When Elia sits us at the table, I can see the worries of the day playing in the twitches of her eyelids, while he fills our bowls with chicken broth from a tureen. Neither I nor Elia has the heart to start bothering her with my shit, so the only thing that breaks the silence is the sound of slurping. I spend what's left of the meal soliciting grunts from Laura and smiling back at Elia. After dinner, I retreat to my old bedroom where, surrounded by the paraphernalia of childhood, I become, as I always do here, sentimental. Picking up a model Samurai with a broken sword, brings memories of Daisy and the day she gave it to me. It wasn't my birthday or anything, just an ordinary rainy day with weather that made it too rough to play outside. She wanted me to have it, though it was her favourite. Lying with one hand behind my head and turning the figure over in my fingers, I start counting tiny stars on the ceiling. I have long since learned to live with the absence of Daisy, with its pointlessness, and the pointlessness of grief. So I keep counting these tiny stars I drew with black ink in the winter evenings of my twelfth year, the year she disappeared. I get as far as three hundred before I give up.

Waking sometime in a gloomy half-morning, I'm still thinking about her. Whatever dream I've just had has filled me with fresh longing, for the girl I've never been able to shake out of my head. The sense of her presence is always strongest here, and it's getting stronger, like she's knocking at a door. I give an involuntary shiver, like someone's walking over my grave, and I have that feeling again, that I'm being watched.

'Hello,' I croak, but as always, there's nobody there.

Then, I'm drifting back to school, in a kind of waking dream, to when I knew Daisy. She screwed up her nose at me behind an inspector's back, during question time. *How do you feel today? What does that make you want to do?* She didn't trust them. There was an expression room, where you were sent to let your emotions run free, under the eye of a wandering camera. Some kids were encouraged to shout, others to laugh. But we never expressed ourselves at all, because we knew we were being watched. Being children, we were naturally suspicious of the adults who were in charge. We didn't trust the team of Chinese in white coats, who were so interested in a no-boomer school. We didn't believe the teachers when they told us the missing children had been singled out for special education, but we didn't understand enough to question.

Eventually, I asked Elia what was going on. He told me that a certain number of children, showing a certain level of aptitude, were thought to be useful by the Corpo. These were 'streamed' into special schools, where they would be given the requisite education. The Corpo, he said, always had one eye on the future, and used the laws of probability to remove the element of chance from future profitability. It didn't help. I hadn't expected Daisy to disappear so suddenly, and things made even less sense after she'd gone.

5

The following morning, I catch the early express, am sucked away from Carlow and spat back at the city. This time the compartment is crowded, and I have to hang with a bunch of fat women from the plastic handles in the aisle, where I'm bumped around until I feel like a carcass of lamb in a cargo-hold full of bullock. A film of sweat develops under the collar of my work onesie, and I'm thanking Confucius I'm not wearing the beige suit, when an ad-screen sliding from the roof erupts:

Ningbo, oh Ningbo, confluence of financial influence,
Pride of the Irish Corpo,
So join in our happy future,
Here in old Dublino.

This chorus is belted out by a choir of happy onesie-wearing workers, most of whom are young Chinese women, and none of whom I recognise. They're standing on a green hillside in what's supposed to be Ireland, but it's hard to believe, because the sky is bright blue and everything else is spotless. I know the song. We sing it at the beginning of every shift. It goes around my head like a computer virus when the screen disappears, and reminds me of the drudgery that is this, and every other, working day. I'm torturing myself over whether or not to take a peppy-pill, when the *hiss* and *plock* of the door tells me we've arrived at Grafton. I dangle until most of the fat women have barged past, then let go and get pushed out, and on to the escalator, by the stragglers. Topside, I lurch into the shadow of a skyscraper, which I lean against to catch my breath.

I take the damned pill and make my way warily along the upper walkway, waiting for the kick. People-counters hovering overhead flash the delicate greens of their scanners. The Corpo wants to know how many people have disembarked at Grafton this morning. We are like grains of sand, in the runnels between these giant glass-concrete slabs of buildings, which are themselves a composite of sand. Filling with energy, I stroll purposefully, musing on the nature of life. Both the upper and lower walkways are full of mostly women on their way to work. All I can see are masses of heads, in all directions, and this is just one street in one city. Beyond this street, the head-count gets crazy. And the heads turn into limitless dots, being pumped around the world through tubation, along streets or moving walkways like corpuscles in the blood that keeps everything alive. It's mesmeric. I wonder how the Corpo manage to keep count of it all.

I stride into the hulking tomb of Ningbo Euro-HQ, and across the football field of marble that is reception, where I'm greeted by the desk boy. 'Good morning, Li san, what a pleasure it is to see you today.'

I smile and walk on. I'm supposed to think that I'm his hero, and should therefore help him get off the ground floor. To me, he's just another desperate boy in search of a shortcut. The admin pools are full of them. Safely alone in the executive elevator, I examine my work-pad and realise that today's the day I'm to give the talk to the newbies. I've completely forgotten, and consequently have nothing prepared – which, in itself, doesn't present much of a problem. I'm full of what it takes to give an impromptu Lecture: wisdom, jingoes, bullshit, whatever. What does present a problem, is that I'm late.

On the forty-third, school is an auditorium in which are gathered fifty students, all jostling and bantering anarchically as I hurry down the steps towards the podium. Fifty students mean a core of ten, who will be good enough to survive the first month's initiation. We do this twelve times every year, which leaves us with the hundred we need for the vid-screen pool, plus a margin of 20 percent to cover underperformers, systematically shifted out in sync with winners like me, who travel upward. It all works out, provided the interviews, training and initiation are carried out to spec. They will know who I am, the newbies. My bio is in the induction pack, where I am held up as an example, during interview and initiation, of how literally anyone can be successful.

'Money has its own energy,' I announce, clipping the mike to my ear. There is a general dive for notepads, and simultaneous silence, which settles completely when some fool finishes laughing, abruptly.

'It flows like a river into the accounts of the intelligent.' I turn around and wave my hands dramatically, like a river. 'It floods into the lives of those with numerical acumen. But where is the spring?'

They look at me dumbly, a collection of different faces, with the same dumb expressions. They don't know.

'That is what you want to know, is it not? And that is why you are here in Ningbo Digits. To seek this wisdom.'

My pulse begins to throb. I don't believe the words, but can work up enthusiasm for them, especially after a peppy. It's a bit like screwing an uggo: you've just got to get into it. 'The spring is everywhere,' I say. 'It exists all around us, like an invisible energy, in the air we breathe and in the polymer beneath our feet. To find the source, you have to lose your prejudices and open your mind.'

I pause for effect and to give myself time to think – of what the hell I'm going to say next. The faces look like they might be taking me seriously, but you never know what hides behind those blank eyes.

'Accept that you are minions,' I continue, ignoring an impulse to resent them. 'Bustle for your basic, and hustle for the commission. Do this, and you will benefit from world advertising, preferential rates and a proven activity model.'

They're becoming listless, like they're waiting for something practical they can actually use.

'You have joined a long line of ambitious young professionals,' I shout, making those in the front row start. Somebody giggles – probably the same fool who couldn't shut up at the start. 'To begin your futures here. And this is where your future starts. You will be taught to understand your vid-screens. They will be your best friend and wisest counsellor. You will learn efficient responses to all objections and techniques, to erode resistance. Work hard, and you will have the pleasure of watching the gross accumulate: you will earn the *right* to enjoy your percentage. Our operation is a thriving example of the most basic elements of the numbers game. We are streamlined and slick, but are not designed to carry awkward shapes. Oh no.'

Those who survive the first month, will last about a year, before either burning out or being moved up the line. It is as immutable as the outcome of addition and subtraction. We don't tell them this.

'Your functions will be broken down, into simple manageable components, so there is really no excuse. Your vid-screen will do the

bulk of the work. All you have to do is remember the power questions, solicit conditional commitment and get the tone right. Even
the advice you will "individually package" is a pre-programmed
sequence based on common probability. You can't get it wrong unless you are lazy, or stupid, or have a bad attitude.'

They don't like the inference. Some of them begin to shift in
their seats; others look at the floor or the ceiling – reflecting on
their weaknesses, probably. I change direction.

'Every second of every minute, of every hour, money snakes
its way around the world, seeking best returns. It becomes in
fact a snake, with reptilian responses. It responds to the most viable equation at any given second. The snake loves hedged risk;
it loves blue-chip and new technology. It loves proportional spec-
ulation in redeveloping markets, like the RUSA. It does not mind
risking a qualified percentage, despite the lack of confidence by
certain low-riskers.'

This makes them uncomfortable. They will have been warned
against politics during initial induction. Politics leads to independent thought, and independent thought to independent action.
The less complication in the pool, the better, but this is topical,
and the clients are going to be asking, so I continue.

'When the neo-con fundamentalists relinquished their claim
to Section Thirty-three of the Creationist Act, the SEHK bobbed
a digit. The snake watched, and the snake struck. There was a 5
percent chance that this could happen before the event, and a 10
percent chance of a significant bounce afterwards. Tell the clients. Your vid-screens have the rate-cards on future outcomes.
Ask your clients if they love profit more than they fear risk. Shake
them a cocktail of their own attitude to possibility. The trick is
to get the cocktail right. This too can be done with numbers. The
patterns and projections are all in your vid-screen. Your vid-
screen is never wrong, but you won't always get it right. You cannot always outsmart your competitors, or allow for a customer's
stupidity. But you don't have to. You just have to be right one
decibel more than you are wrong, and the snake will slowly lay
eggs in your basket.'

Remarkably, they seem to believe this. I suppose I do too,
in a way. Numbers are credible. I decide to cut the lecture short
and to finish with a good-news story. I can deal with the problem
of Mianzi, if and when she finds out what a joke I've been this
morning.

'Many of the senior people at Ningbo were looking at me
when I was in the pool,' I say, walking around the stage, and

shrugging reflectively. 'And wondering what a *boy* knew about what it takes to be successful. But it was *because* I was a boy that I was successful: I used that very weakness as a strength. I was the most successful trader five quarters running, against all odds and against a tide of prejudice.' I stop, stand square and rotate a penetrating stare at them. 'How did I do this? By understanding those I had to impress. By understanding what they *want*. Our chairwoman, Mianzi, loves profit. Above all else, she appreciates effort, because she understands the direct ratio between intelligent effort and profit. If you give her the effort and get the results, she will show you the spring, guide you along the streams, through the tributaries of success, to the river, and eventually the ocean of wealth. If she did it for me, she can do it for you. If I can do it, you can do it. If *you* want to enough. But you must swim with the river. Add your energy to its momentum. Work the numbers. This is a numbers game, and you are the players. Good luck with your induction, my friends. Good luck swimming with the snake.'

Even with the applause ringing in my ears as the lift-doors close, I'm uneasy. The talk wasn't *that* good.

#

When I get home, there's a message from Emily. There's something important she wants to talk to me about. Can I meet her tomorrow evening, in some retro-bar on the dodge side of town? It's not like I'm given an option or anything, by the hologram, which blinks out with an intransigent little expression on its face. If this meeting's about what I hope it's about, then it's exactly what I've been waiting for. May not be. Folding my onesie into the washer, I throw on a clean kimono and make my way to the window. Heavy clouds are advancing across the bay, and the rain they threaten starts against the window. Leaning my head on the glass, I watch the water spatter like tears in the seagull-shit dried into the windowsill. The sill has been repaired, but the rivets that hold down the patch are rusting around their edges. It's only a question of time before they eat into the aluminium. A gull alighting, right on the other side of the glass, sends me staggering backwards to the couch. It opens its big beak in a threatening yawn. I sit and stare at it, petrified, until it gets bored and flies away.

It takes a while to get my shit together after that, but eventually I make it to the kitchen, where I clip open a ready-dinner.

Activating the noodles with a trembling spoon, I wonder again what this 'something important' is all about. Whatever it is, has to be major – but what? I get tired trying to figure it out. So I eat a few spoonfuls, take a peppy, and lie down on the couch with a headset. Closing my eyes, I try to lose myself in a cacophony of summer sounds, where the happy shrieks of children intersperse with the animated talk of young mothers and the warning monosyllables of background fathers. Birds warble their secret message and a lone dog barks its reply. It's one of those meditation discs – supposed to get you in touch with your inner child. A minute later, I switch on some porn and surround myself with two Chinese uggos, who are more interested in each other's tits than anybody's inner children.

Afterwards I sit, elbows on knees, and look at the message again. I can't tell anything from Emily's tone or body language, but it has to be either break-up or make-up time in the retro. I might not even get the chance to give her my speech, about how it would be a tragedy if we never get to truly know one another. Which is true. What has so far passed, as our relationship exists only on our surfaces. It reminds me of a rich aunt and her nephew, all politeness and modesty. It can't continue, no matter how much Mianzi wants it to. Not unless Emily is a psychopath. I could just ring and ask what's going on, but whatever is going to happen will be better dealt with face to face, I decide. The rain has become heavier, drilling now, smearing my beautiful view, pissing against the glass. A wave of loneliness attacks. I want Emily to be here, right now, in this apartment. I want to be cooking for her and for her to be sitting in the armchair opposite, plate on her lap. I want to be coiled at her feet, being fed delicacies. I want her to scream at me and tell me the truth about myself. I'm so sick of duplicity, especially my own. I want domesticity. I can't handle the wilderness, or any more walks through strange early-morning hinterlands. I want to escape my life, and the way out is Emily.

5

The waiter in Bewley's looks me over as he takes my order. When I look back, his face assumes a conspiratorial smile. Not being particularly gay myself, I look away – which must be awkward for him – but he retains enough composure to generate a self-righteous pout, as he repeats what I've said. I probably look a bit gay in the purple suit. Back at the apartment, it was *de rigueur* in the circuit mirror, and sure to impress Emily. Out on the street, it's a circus. Seems I walk through a sea of rising eyebrows, and I'm pretty sure two teenage boys exploded with laughter behind my shoulder. Adding to growing uneasiness is the tightness of the crotch. My balls have developed a whole other life, as they slide about trying to find space. They're not the only things making me fidget. By the time I've finished my cake, the muzak around the table has graduated to offensive.

I'm expected to leave, to move on and allow another number to take my place. Trying to ignore it, I start strategising about Emily – about how I'd like tonight to turn out. My mind's eye sees a fan of blonde hair on the black satin pillows on my bed. There's an upturned bottle of Champagne in a frosted ice-bucket, and my fingers are tracing the contours of her post-coital smile. Alone in my apartment, we'll have the time and privacy we need. Visualisation . . . leads to reflection. There will be no more uggos, no more flaccid lips, or the sour taste of sagging flesh. No more feeling repulsed by my own yearning – aroused by repulsion. The fusion of images causes me to swell, which borders on masochism in these pants. The waiter comes over, and with one swipe wipes away the crumbs and the coffee ring. He smiles, hovering thoughtfully, perhaps sensing my excitement. They can smell arousal in their own kind, I'm convinced.

'Can I get you anything else?' he insinuates.

'Not at all,' I say, cooling.

Having taken time to scrutinise me judgmentally, he moves away: I'm not worth the effort. I'm watching his back when my attention is drawn to the vid-screen. More riots in the RUSA, this time in Cleveland. A man, standing on a pile of rubble, is holding up a sign that reads 'Freedom'. Tears furrow his dusty face. The scene flickers, and we're looking at a demo for holding mousse. One of the chefs, obviously a refugee, curses from the doorway of the kitchen until her Malaysian over-manager orders her back to her cauldron. The waiter, who has been watching, smirks and returns to clattering dishes onto a trolley. His smirk thinks it knows something – possibly everything. But I know *him*, or at least his type. They load up on peppies at the weekend and lose themselves in the moment, with the first body they can beguile. Man or woman, it doesn't matter. They get their physical comfort where and when they can, because it never lasts. No self-respecting gay would allow himself to be seen with him. I know his type, because I used to *be* it. The only difference now is that I'm richer and better looking. The waiter doesn't quite add up, yet, but he's probably saving for surgery. The music antes up to a panpipe medley of Ronan Keating classics, and it's time to leave the restaurant.

Rain slanting across Robinson Bridge softens the edges of the share-prices floating around the head of the old statue, making it look as though O'Connell's wearing a melting halo. Somebody shoving into my back, jolts me back to the present, where I flip my collar and return my eyes to street level. But my attention is dragged upwards again, by the hum of a people-counter whose pinpricks of colour are sharp and irrepressible, whatever the weather. The Corpo must want to know how many people are walking over the bridge in the rain. Then Howe's giant face is rippling on the river, telling me that Dunnes Stores is still better value: he begins to rhyme off a list of groceries, with amazingly low prices. Deciding I'm never going into Dunnes again, I turn left along the quays, then right into the labyrinth behind Bachelors Walk, where the neon of fast-tofu restaurants glistens on dark cobblestones and makes the place look like something Van Gogh might have dreamt up. A hologram geisha approaches and asks in Chinese, then English, if I would like a happy-hour bowl of tofu and a beer. I politely decline, pathetically making eye-contact. He's programmed to meet my response with a smile, whatever it is: I could be telling him to go eff himself.

The doors at the entrance to the retro swing open like accommodating legs. Inside, I find a heavy red curtain which, when pushed aside, reveals a passageway. Its walls are hung with old photographs, which I review as I make my way along. Though the passage is dark, each photo is illuminated by a small candle-shaped torch. What it's all about, I can't tell. It seems that the women and men in these pictures have done something important, long ago. Stopping to straighten my hair in the glass of one of them, I'm beamed at by a white-haired man in a wheelchair. Whatever he did is forgotten now, pushed into the past by the ever-evolving present. *I've* forgotten him by the time I'm pushing through a door marked 'Bar', where I find a circular bar, just like the door promised, in the middle of a dimly lit room. It's surrounded by nocturnal types who, unlike the geisha, avoid eye-contact. I lower myself, with due deference to my balls, onto a stool, and feign nonchalance. The bartender, an actual middle-aged man, ignores me and continues to wipe the bar, with slow circular movements. He's not programmed to do anything, and glowers at me threateningly when I cough to get his attention. The glower intensifies as he waits for me to decide what I want. If this were another place and time, and I was with Emily at, say, one of her Sandycove comfort cafés, I would be all a-twitter, asking a hologram about their range of consequence-free beer. This place is different. It might have been a replica for the fool or the tourist, but I'm already getting my money's worth.

'Let's see. What kind of beer have you got?'

He slaps a menu onto the bar, and I fumble it open. It's full of drinks the people in the photographs probably drank.

'Er, let me see now. Is there anything in particular you'd recommend?'

'Yeah. Making up your fucking mind.'

'Gosh. OK then. I'll have a Guinness.'

His look tells me that this is probably the worst possible decision, but he proceeds to fill an old glass with black gloop from a tap on the bar. He messes with it for a while, for whatever reason, scooping a knife into its foam and splashing it onto a tray. Eventually he bangs it onto the counter and demands payment. I tap the exorbitant number onto the pad and he shuffles off, to two strung-out Goth-girl types at the end of the bar, where he becomes suddenly dadsy.

There are clumps of people hanging in the shadows, mumbling at each other, probably apologising for coming to a place like this. They might be buying and selling illegal drugs, or weapons, or thermal underwear: it's impossible to tell. The place quietly fills up while I wait for Emily, and is full of chatter by the time I decide she's not coming. It's unlike her to be late, let alone not show up, and I begin to wonder if something might have happened to her, in this shit end of town. There's no answer from her sphere, whose message maintains that she's probably busy, and will get back to me if I leave a message. By now I'm regretting, wholeheartedly, that I didn't make a call last night, but you never can tell the way things will turn out: you can only play the choices in front of you at the time. The messages I leave are relaxed and only amusedly concerned: I don't want to scare away redemption.

On the point of leaving, I'm nearly knocked off the stool by a thunderous explosion of marching music. It's coming from an old plasma screen, hanging previously unnoticed in a corner. The music stops just as suddenly, as old black-and-white images start to flicker from the screen in 2D. At first, it looks like it's just a bleak landscape, but gradually one of the shadows begins to form a shape, and an old horse hobbles from the distance to the foreground. Its legs wobble under its mangy weight, as it plods over what looks like the Russian Steppes. The animal eventually buckles onto its front knees, gives a mournful look to camera, rolls onto its side and dies. This provokes a sigh, from those punters who are sober enough to appreciate it.

'Isn't it beautiful?' A young woman has peeled away from the background, to stand beside me.

'More like pathetic.'

'Yes. Pathetic.'

Her response is unthinking – words to fill a hole before she leaps to the point.

'Want to share an orgolube?'

'Actually, I'm waiting for someone.'

'What? Oh, sure.'

She looks confused: a boy sitting on his own at the bar is usually out for a pick-up. The glassy eyes tell me she's already lubed, out of her head. She wants a good time, and any boy will do. Propriety won't matter; consequences won't matter. *I* won't matter. I should know, I've done enough orgolubes to give a herd of elephants a weekful of happy endings. Sidling against me, she drops her hand onto my penis, like it belongs to her. I remove it, and she looks genuinely upset.

'Come on,' I say. 'I told you I'm waiting for someone. She'll be here any second. What are you trying to do to me?'

She's not bad looking. Has a Chinese tattoo over her left eyebrow, which must mean something. I've no idea what. Her hands wrap around my ribcage, and when she brings her face to within kissing range, I see a tiny pheromone detector, hidden in one of the dots in the tattoo. This will be multiplying the effects of the orgolube. Everything I do or say is going to be triggering tiny orgasms all over her body, causing a mad rush inside her for release. And not just any old everyday, jerk-off type release. This combo promises to be sensational, to be that thing you've been craving all your sordid, rejected, frustrated adult life.

'Why don't we talk about the film,' I say, wriggling out of her grasp. 'Isn't it really moving? Have you ever seen such . . . emotion?'

'I'll show you emotion,' she says, her hand back on my thigh, sliding steadily crotch-wards. 'I've got some French orgos that will tie your little emotions into pleasure knots your tight little body has never dreamed of, baby.'

'Hey,' I say, removing her hand, in a friendly way. 'Why do you women always think you can take advantage of a boy on his own? I said no, OK?'

'You're not *gay*, are you?' she asks. 'Purple boy.'

'If I was, would you leave me alone?'

'No. I don't suppose I would. Though I know you're not. They' – she indicates friends with a careless thumb – 'say you are.'

Returning my attention to the show, I try to look absorbed. There are two peasant women arguing over the horse now, and a small boy hugging its dead neck, crying. Maybe it was the boy's pet. Maybe the girl with the tattoo will just go away. She hovers for a while, then says, as if she's been carrying on both sides of their conversation in her own head: 'You never know, but you just might enjoy yourself. Most men do.'

'Yeah? Well, I'm not most men.' I'm tetchy now. 'And I don't do anything, unless I want to.'

'What are you afraid of?' She laughs. 'Your girlfriend is so *not* turning up. I've been watching you for like, an hour.'

'Maybe not,' I say. 'But no means no.'

The hand's on my crotch again. I take it off again, more roughly this time. She looks affronted. Placing her fingertips on the bar to keep her balance, she turns and searches for her friends, possibly thinking of a retreat with news that I am actually gay after all, but there's one more try in her.

'Well, at least let me buy you another of those drinks.'

I should just go, but standing up in these pants with a full bladder is a challenge, so I say: 'OK, but only if you behave yourself.'

'Don't like behaving myself. Like fun.'

'Don't you like conversation?'

'Conversation boring.'

Her friends have left by now, save for one who is French-kissing the face off a younger boy. Dead-end. There are no other single men around, besides the barman. She has to make whatever's going on with me work, or her evening's screwed. Putting her hands into her pockets, she sighs the sigh of the disenchanted. I say: 'Let's just look at the film.'

She shrugs, like I'm some old husband she's indulging, sits, and stretches her arm on the counter behind me. Wobbling a finger at the barman, she gets him to bring over more drinks.

'Be careful,' she says, when he places another jar of Guinness beside me. 'That stuff has a rough buzz.'

Two jars later, Tattoo has wandered into a sales pitch about this 'Sensations' club she knows in Manchester. We could be there in half an hour.

'Sorry,' I explain, standing up. 'You're too good-looking for me.'

6

The rain has stopped, leaving the alley outside the retro saturated and still. Sporadic drips from the roofs mark time in the silence. It's as though the whole thing is an empty stage waiting for something to happen. When I look down, I see gutters, alive with rivulets hurrying to the sewer-shores, into which they disappear. I'm being mesmerised by the rhythm, when a belt of fresh air hits me in the face and knocks my stomach into my mouth. I take a few steps to steady myself but the reflection of neon, splintering in puddles, makes me dizzy. My shoulder thumps a wall. I lean into it and close my eyes. My mind begins regurgitating images of dead horses and crying toothless crones, and brings on the nausea.

\#

Corpo censorship would never allow the plasma show to be made available to the multi-dudes. Not that they would want to watch it anyway. The Corpo developed Interactive some years back, releasing characters in 3D, to interact with, and include viewers in, the narrative. Elia watches all the time, dishes out advice to distraught Australian fathers whose sons want to join the Corpo, or whose daughters want to give up their careers to raise kids. A surge in my gut forces my head forward, and I throw up a gush of black liquid, which explodes on the pavement, flecking my shoes and the hems of my pants. I'm cleaning my mouth with my sleeve and waiting for the lights to stop swirling, when I hear footsteps slapping behind me. Pinning my back to the wall, I turn to see Tattoo reaching for my shoulder and peering into my face. 'You OK?'
   'Sure.'
   'I told you about that shit.'
   'You did.'

'Here,' she says, handing me a pill. 'Take this.'

Which I do, with the eagerness of an inveterate pill-popper. Whatever it is, I begin to feel a little better, and my head clears.

'Better?'

'Yeah, thanks. What do you want?'

'To say sorry.'

'For what?'

'Being so butch back there.'

'That's OK. I'm used to it.'

'You're a boy, out alone, and I assumed, you know, that you were a certain type. I was out of order, maybe. But I've de-lubed now, and am relatively sensible.'

'Really, it's no problem.'

Helping me away from the wall, she holds my arm while I attempt to stand upright. I want to get home, take more tablets – prepare my lecture for Emily.

'You're not like other boys,' she says, leading me along, slowly.

'No?'

'You're not afraid to speak up for yourself. I'd say you're a career boy, right?'

'Right.'

'Well then. Why don't I let *you* buy *me* a cup of coffee? It'll do you good. I promise I'll try not to be good-looking. I'll leave my mouth hanging open, cross my eyes maybe.'

The ball-squeezer of earlier has disappeared, to be replaced by a woman who is all reason and insouciance. As we stand there, looking pessimistically at each other, we each know that the other has nothing better to do. I need a piss anyway, and like the idea of sitting down to drink something hot.

'Sure. Why not?'

We find the friendly geisha and follow him into the tofu bar. When I come back from the bathroom, she's already eating.

'This is good,' she says, pointing her chopsticks into a carton. *'Dan doufu, lo mein combo*. Want to try some?'

My stomach's beginning to heave again, with the smell of it. 'No thanks. I'm on a diet.'

Though the clump of noodles slithering into her mouth prevent her from saying as much, she makes a face and waves her chopsticks, to indicate that this is entirely unnecessary.

'So what do you do?' I ask. 'Corpo?'

'Me?' She wipes her mouth with the back of her hand. 'Fuck no. I'm a student.'

Taking a sip of tangy coffee from a polystyrene cup, I wait through a reflux for her to elaborate, but she's concentrating on the noodles. Eventually, if for no other reason than to break the sound of slurping, I ask: 'What are you studying?'

'Numbers.'

Pausing, she takes a long gulp of beer and pushes the empty carton away, with a satisfied belch.

'Excuse me,' she says thoughtlessly, before wiping her mouth again. Seeing a container of paper napkins on the next table, she reaches over and rips out a clump, with which she wipes the backs of both hands.

'So,' she says, finding me again, 'what were we talking about?'

The bright light in the restaurant makes her look frail. I can see purple veins through the translucent skin on her forehead. 'You were telling me that you're a student.'

'Yeah, numbers.'

'What kind of numbers?'

'You know, what percentage of people would have to do whatever job, to service whatever percentage of whatever's needed, to keep society going tick-tock. Yaddi-yaddi-yah. Macro-shit, mostly.'

Grabbing the carton, she looks into it for stray noodles.

'Sounds interesting,' I say.

'Not really. What about you?'

'Sorry?'

'What do you do? You know, for a job.'

'Numbers too, actually. I'm in the investment end.'

'Aren't we all. One way or the other.'

'I suppose we are, one way or the other.'

'What type of investment we talking about?'

'You know, what percentage of calls a sales team would have to make to get whatever percentage profit. Micro-shit.'

She starts chasing something around the inside of the carton with her chopsticks. 'Yes,' she says, vague and smiling. 'There's lots and lots of numbers for all of us to play with. Running our lives and telling us how to behave. But what can you do? You either join the equation or you end up in some no-boomer shit-hole, eking out an existence and interacting with soap opera.'

Picking up a piece of tofu that has fallen on to the table, she rubs it into the juice that gathers in the corner of the carton when she tilts it.

'I'm from no-boom stock,' I say. 'And my father lives like that. You might as well know now, just in case you were thinking of proposing, or anything.'

'I'm not a snob,' she explains. 'Just making a point. Anyway, as I told you, you're different. Tell me about this career of yours.'

I'm defensive about Elia, always have been, and sullen enough now to want to go home.

'It's all about investment,' I say instead.

'Investment?'

'Yeah, Ningbo Digits. We're the retail division.'

'Didn't know they had one.'

'Everyone thinks of us as wholesale, but we've developed a retail wing. Boss gives me a nice slice.'

'Fancy you, does she?'

'Has me lined up for her daughter, actually.'

'Yeah? What's she like then?'

'Even more beautiful than you.'

'She the one stood you up?'

'Well yeah, but it's not like her.'

Now I'm defending Emily and wondering why. Why should I care what this stranger thinks about my shitty life anyway?

'Maybe she saw you in that purple suit and made a run for it.'

'She's usually the reliable type,' I say. 'Very good to me, for your information. Seems interested in getting serious.'

'And you? You interested in getting serious, with the beautiful rich girl, no-boom boy?'

'She has a quality.'

'Like?'

'Like, she sees something in me.'

'So, you're actually the one with the quality.'

'No. I mean yes. Not that it's your concern, but as a matter of fact we both have a quality.'

I'm sorry now, that I've allowed myself to be dragged into this, and hope to Fucius she doesn't start asking what I mean by 'a quality'.

'Yeah? Well, what do you mean by *a quality?*'

The face I put on, previously used in these types of situations, should tell her that I don't have to lower myself to being cross-questioned; that she should back off. It doesn't work.

'What do you imagine this vamp sees in you?'

For some reason, I just keep answering. 'Success, maybe.'

She's laughing now.

'What's so funny?' I ask.

Putting down her chopsticks, she takes a sip of my coffee. 'The numbers have already been added up for you,' she says.

'Good-looking kid like you. Does what he's told. You'll make excellent breeding stock. I could do a thesis on you without asking a single other question.'

'Well, if you already know everything, why are you so curious?' I recover some composure – but not much.

'Dunno,' she replies. 'Maybe you're interesting. Maybe you're *intriguing*. You intriguing? No-boom boy.'

'Why are you such a bitch?'

Now she's laughing again. 'You're funny.'

Sleepy eyes find mine, and for some reason, I'm drawn to her. Holding me in her gaze, she produces a small leather case from her sleeve pocket and slides out a thin stainless-steel pinchers. Pushing its tip into her tattoo, she flips out the pheromone receptor and slips it into its tiny sheath. Zipping the case shut, she presses it into my hand. 'Come to Sensations,' she says. 'We'll do it the old-fashioned way. No drugs, no detectors.'

'No way.'

'It's like no other club you've ever been to. You'll want to dance until the cows come home. Matter of fact, you'll want to dance *with* the cows, on their way home.'

I smile, despite myself. Sensing a softening in my attitude, she says: 'Oh, come on. You know you want to. Stop being so uptight, and let yourself have a bit of an adventure.'

'There is absolutely no way you're going to convince me to go to that club.'

7

To me, all women are beautiful. I don't know whether this is something I've trained myself to believe to justify my obvious lack of discernment, or whether I was born with a capacity to see beyond blemish. When I look at a woman, I enjoy searching for the inner child in her eyes, or a hint of compassion in an unguarded expression. Usually I zone in on a detail, something that reflects the woman's personal choice, like a piece of jewellery or clothes. I think of her applying lipstick at a thoughtful face in the mirror, wondering if she's made the right decision. With Tattoo, this is difficult. There is so much going on, from the strange tattoo to the shark-teeth earrings; the gaudy chords of her necklace, which still manage to be tasteful. Right now, I'm concentrating on the curve of her cheek and its outline against the leather collar of her jacket.

'So,' she says, out of the blue, 'do you think the Corpos should have a policy to get men back into the workforce?' Her voice is musical against the drone of the vac-voice, telling us repeatedly that the next stop is Holyhead. Turning to the window, I see, way below, the sparkle of a pleasure raft on the black back of the Irish Sea. It makes me lonely. I'm already guilty, about Emily, though she stood me up and everything. This is a whole other type of cheating. This is premeditated: the puke and pill have left me sober enough to ask myself how I could be so easily led away, by this disconcerting stranger. I'm guessing it's the loneliness again. Its loneliness makes me do most of the reckless, stupid things I do. Loneliness and boredom. And the horror that I might be left with nothing to do with my busy-body mind. That's the way it is in my world: an interminable slouch through wasteland, from one oasis of chaos to the next. Most of the time, what I find on arrival, is a mirage. And I'm wondering, as I gaze through the window, if the thing I have going with Emily, is another mirage.

It's certainly insubstantial and out of reach, just. Maybe this is why I'm willing to shunt fidelity to one side in favour of anything that might offer a bit of substance. Most men I know wouldn't even ask these questions – which makes me wonder, yet again, if there's something wrong with me. Emily said, when she saw me eating ostrich wings once, that I was 'quasi-barbaric'. Maybe she's right. Maybe I'm some kind of throwback, conforming to patterns which don't exist anymore.

'Well?' Tattoo is saying.

I vaguely remember what she was talking about. 'I don't know,' I say. 'Don't really have an interest in these things.'

'Don't have an interest? Oh, come on, career boy. You must have an opinion on the equalisation of the sexes.'

'Nope.'

I need to be a bit uncommunicative, to counter the weakness of character I've shown by allowing myself be dragged on this Manchester adventure. Tattoo is playing her part in the ritual, by working hard at getting me to open up and enjoy myself. The next stop, the vac says again, is going to be Holyhead. A woman in a suit, the only other passenger in our compartment, picks up her briefcase and clutches it on her lap, willing herself closer to home. She's washed out, but not too tired to be tipping her head towards our conversation. Tattoo says: 'You mean to say, you believe men are not responsible enough to seriously take part in the running of the Corpo, that they are driven by their testosterone. All that crap?'

'Didn't say that,' I say, certain that she's trying to tease me in front of this other woman.

'Well, what *are* you saying?'

I decide it will take less energy to get into the conversation than it does to stay out.

'I suppose men would be as capable as women, if they were given the chance. As I said, I really don't care. I'm more concerned with my own shit. Not literally. I mean, with what's going on in my life.'

'Like?'

'You know, like making money, having a lifestyle. Why would I want to change the world?'

The business suit frowns, but Tattoo seems fascinated. 'That's interesting,' she says. 'You're a *pragmatist*.'

My being a pragmatist seems to satisfy something in her, and she shuts up for a while, leans her head against the window, closes her eyes and smiles. And she has a great smile. It fills the

compartment. I like the way she talks to me too: she makes me
the absolute focus of her attention and takes what I say seriously. Something Emily never does. Wanting more, I say: 'Men
did more or less run the world, didn't they? Up until a couple of
hundred years ago.'

'Ran it into the ground.'

She looks up and scrutinises me, before leaning forward and
brushing my fringe from my eyes. 'You've beautiful eyes, Li. You
know that? They light up when you're thinking, like little bulbs.'

'You're patronising me,' I say, glowing. 'Don't you know, men
hate that?'

The woman across the way shuffles her posture. It's a subconscious but noticeable statement, which says that I'm out
of control, and that Tattoo should be bitch-slapping me, right
about now.

'No you don't,' she says. 'You love the attention.'

'And by the way,' I say, 'how did you know my name?'

'Saw it on the screen when you thumbed for the tofu, you
suspicious bastard. And by the way,' she says, u-turning, 'it *is* a
bit of a stretch to say that men are capable of running the world,
whatever about them being involved at some level.'

'And yet they ran it, for thousands of years, didn't they?'

'Look what they did. The old wealth-war-poverty cycle. None
of these things exist any more. Because a group of women had
the sense to stand up and say: enough is enough. You don't have
any of these great social problems, after gradualisation.'

The businesswoman relaxes. They all love gradualisation,
these women. It's the foundation-stone of their dogma, and a
game-winner in every political argument. And the suit knows I
know this. She's pissing me off almost as much as Tattoo.

'Yeah? What about the RUSA?' I say. 'Where's your gradualisation there?'

'America is a basket-case,' she says. 'At the moment. But the
Triumvirates will sort that out in time. *Gradually.*'

The vac interjects, by announcing fatalistically that we've arrived in Holyhead, and that we'd better not stand up until the
vac has come to a complete stop and the doors have decompressed. A group of worker-boys embark, in the uniforms of an
admin pool, clutching their rucksacks on their laps, gabbling
about a soccer match. Both female heads turn in unison. I wait
for Tattoo to refocus.

'As I said,' I remind them both in a loud voice, 'I don't give a
shit.'

#

At Victoria, we catch a local to America-town. On the main boulevard, I try not to look like a frightened tourist, but there's an atmosphere of dissent about the place that makes me uneasy. Tatty Star-spangled Banners hang from windows along the street, which is feebly lit by the flickering lights of old Corpo signs. The names are exotic: *Coca-Cola, Ford, McDonalds*. I've never heard of them, but suppose that at one time they would have held their existence as inevitable. All are oddities now, washed up on the present like flotsam from a dead past. Prostitutes, wearing cowboy outfits and promising to do wonderful things with lassoos, recede into the shadows when Security hovers overhead. They're more like edgy rodents than pleasure-boys.

'Nice atmosphere,' I say.

'It's a touch nervous,' Tattoo admits. 'There've been riots in sympathy with what's going on in their homeland. Security's on yellow alert.'

'I don't seem to remember that little snippet in your sales pitch,' I say, but she just laughs, puts an arm around my shoulder and leads me into a narrow street, where pulsating light from the entrance to Sensations kills the Coca-Cola red, turns night into day. Her thumbprint ensures that we don't queue, and we pass a line of resentful people, to two bald, heavily breasted brutes who lift the ropes for us to enter.

Tattoo was right. I've never seen anything like this club. It's a massive cavern, which might have been a football stadium in a former life. Music and 3D pumps from hundreds of speakers, built into brick and girder. A skeleton of a whale hangs from the ceiling, probably because it can. Beams shooting from its eye sockets, send holograms of naked nubiles to curve around drunks who are stupid enough to pay for the pleasure. As we make our way down steps to the giant dance bowl, tubes of colour fizz across our eye-line and explode into multi-coloured blizzards, lighting the faces of dancers, who lose individuality as they get further way, merging into a crowd that becomes one whacked-out, swaying mass.

'What do you think?' Tattoo shouts.

'I thought it would be bigger,' I shout back.

Grabbing my wrist, she dances her way to a bar, where, leaning on the counter, she explains her order to the bar-droid, like it's confidential information. When two yellow shots are produced, she swallows one and pushes the other in my direction.

'It's called *Yitiao chongzi*. It'll make you dance.'

I'm considering my empty glass, when I feel her hand in the small of my back, pushing me towards the dancefloor, where, brushing away a nubile, she begins an idiotic dance. I try to ignore the scowls of hardened clubbers, as she bounces off them, to create a circle around us. Bouncing closer, she hangs a wrist over my shoulder and gyrates her hips. She's not taking herself seriously. I find myself thinking, as I stand there foolishly, how different to Emily she is, and how exciting this is. It's like there's a ball of something unravelling inside me.

'*Oh come on, baby,*' she mouths, along with the blasting song. '*And let yourself go, and let yourself go, and let me know.*'

When I try to let myself go, she laughs again. At first, I'm stiff and self-conscious, but the music enters my body, and the effect of the shot worms its way under my inhibitions. I wave with the rhythm as she sidles closer, close enough for her breasts to push into my chest. Holding me in her eyes, she sends a hand to gently crawl across the back of my head and draw me in. I'm surrendering, to the music, the drink, and her eyes. Emily becomes a micro-dot in a distant past. I'm drifting towards parting lips, when we're rudely shoved. A beefy uggo and her even beefier, uggier boyfriend have staggered into us, sending us like skittles into another couple.

'What the fuck?'

A sailor suit, whose boy is dressed as a sea captain, though in hot-pants, shoves us back towards the beefies.

'Terribly sorry,' I explain to the uggo, who has grabbed my collar and is staring into my face. 'Bit of an accident there.'

Her face relaxes, and she's on the point of letting go, when Tattoo shouts: 'Get your hands off my boy, you ugly piece of shit!'

The uggo's boyfriend rubs thick fingers over his shaven head in disbelief, prior to grabbing a clump of Tattoo's hair and bringing her face close. 'What did you say?'

'You heard me, butch boy. I told your tit-less girlfriend to get her hands off my boy.'

'Really,' I explain, still in a vice-grip, 'there's no problem here. Whole thing's been a bit of a misunderstanding, that's all.'

But the male uggo is already shaking Tattoo by the throat, with a force that's turning her face the colour of my purple suit. I'd like to help, but the woman, holding me at arm's length with one hand, is bitch-slapping me with the other. I swing a foot opportunistically, and catch her in the crotch. Following an even uglier face, she doubles over and hits the ground. The boyfriend uses the anger this generates to choke Tattoo harder. Encouraged by success, I let go with an almighty kick at his crotch. This has an even better effect on balls. He immediately clutches himself, and falls to the floor, where he lies gurning beside his girlfriend. I'm thinking how they look like break-dancers, when Tattoo drags me away.

'Where we going?'

'The fuck out of here,' she says, pushing oblivious dancers roughly out of our path.

Bouncers, making their way from the entrance, cut off our escape route. I turn and run directly into captain-boy, who, obviously a quick learner, catches me in the testicles with a knee. I fall to the floor, white lights in my eyes. When they clear, Tattoo is beside me and we're being kicked by a combination of seafarers, uggos, the bouncers, and one or two others who get into it, to the rhythm that's pumping from the walls. Instinctively, I throw myself on to Tattoo and hold her, with all my strength, in a foetal clinch. I can smell the perfume of her neck through the pain. Its musk, strangely familiar, makes me forget I'm being kicked around a dance-bowl. We're grabbed by the bouncers, dragged through the crowd and dumped into a lane, where more beating seems on the definite side of likely. We're not the only ones. Two other bouncers are at work on a slick gangstery type, who looks at us imploringly from a mess of blood, as if we could help. She's wearing a blood-spattered pinstripe suit and silk shirt; she must have loved herself in it that morning. Then there's a heavy thud across the base of my neck and a strong Chinese voice cutting into the mess, as I make my way to the ground.

'Enough.'

8

Zisha used to make boats. With his large, capable hands, he could whittle a shape out of the clumsiest lump of wood: refine it, with precision, into a detailed pleasure-craft. Our home was full of his models. He used to paint them, in the colours of their particular Corpo. Tiny insignia on the hulls replicated the exact lettering and registration of some larger, oblivious double. Me and the tattooed girl are miniature details lying together on the deck of one of his boats, sailing in isolation across an endless sea. The sun is beating on our naked bodies, and the taste of sake – or is it blood – warms our mouths. Now we're under the glow of sunset, stretching to the position of Vitruvian Woman, arms and legs extending in perfect proportion, fingers touching. The sky is sliding across our eye-line, its infinite dull-blue merging into the orange gash of a sinking sun, where a small scattering of clouds dissolve. I don't know if there's a crew on board or anything; the boat seems to be taking care of itself; you don't need detail in a dream. We are alone, alone and going nowhere, under emerging stars.

'Li.'

Laura did not discourage him from making boats. A happy hubby meant for a happy home, she said – possibly thinking of the hours Elia spent distracted by his hobbies. Elia, with an eye on a predestined future for at least one of his sons, agreed. No, it wasn't strict parenting that drove him to that terrible decision, one Tuesday afternoon in his twentieth autumn.

'Li.'

I was on my way to meet him, when it happened. But whatever it was he had to tell me, I'll never know: his appointment with destiny was more urgent.

'Li.'

The tattooed girl is a giant shadow leaning over me.

'What?'

'You awake?'

I nod and smile – still on deck.

'You OK?'

I shrug, and a darting pain registers along the keel.

'She's gone to get a doctor.'

'Good,' I hear myself say, then. 'Who's gone?'

'Fucius, what were you doing back there? You could have got yourself killed.'

I try to move towards the voice, but my body is heavy and non-responsive. The sky and sea blow away like cirrus, revealing her elfin face, chinked with concern and haloed by light.

'Why did you do it?' she wants to know.

I want to be back on the boat, and resent being plucked from the warmth of my dream, to where I'm going to have to start dealing with shit, like these questions. But I'm glad, in a way, because now I can look at her face and realise that she's real. I reach to touch her cheek, and she moves away, but that's OK too, because now I can see a lantern. It's so pristine, so multi-faceted: each tiny glass reflects light in its own particular way. I've seen this before. Most Corpo lobbies have something monstrous cling-ing to their ceiling. This is the first time I've seen one this small. Or really looked at one, and from directly below – which, I've real-ised, is the perfect perspective. It might be vulgar or beautiful to have one in a room of this size. I'm too fucked to care. All I know is, I like the shimmering distraction of its complex beauty.

'Li?'

Her head between me and the nice light again, blocking my view of detail.

'Li? Can you see me?'

'Yes,' I say. I can make out the spikes of her hair in the light; the rest of her is fuzzy.

'I said, why did you do it?'

'Do what? Where are we?"

'We're in her apartment. Why did you throw yourself on top of me, protect me? I mean, I'm not hurt at all.'

As she comes into focus, the shark-teeth earrings swing ep-ileptically.

'Good,' I say. 'That's good.' Then: 'Whose apartment?'

She rubs her hands up and down her bare arms, shivering, though the room is not cold.

'But why did you do it? Why did you jeopardise yourself to save me?'

'Didn't really think about it.'

I touch her arm. 'You cold?'

'Don't,' she says, standing and stepping away.

'We not friends any more?'

'You could have got yourself killed.'

Kneeling, she takes my hand. 'You need to tell me. Why did you throw yourself on top of me like that?'

'I don't know.' My mind is beginning to clear. 'I just did it, OK? What difference does it make?'

There's a large painting on the wall opposite. It's of a mountain, blanketed in red foliage. A waterfall threads its way into a glassy lake, and ancient houses, made miniature, speck the mountainside. I want to lose myself in that painting, to become tiny and make my way along one of the paths to the door of a house. I want to be let in and hidden under a bed, where I can fall asleep. I fall asleep.

The bleeping of locks makes me turn my head towards the sound of a door being opened, but my view is blocked by the back of the couch I'm lying on. There are murmurings, which sound like questions, then a Japanese with tired eyes appears. Waving Tattoo away, she sits beside me. Puncturing me with something, she makes the pain subside. Reaching delicate fingers into her bag, she produces a spray and sprays me with something else, which makes my skin tingle.

'You'd want to control,' she says, as she lifts my lid and peers into my eyeball, 'those animals of yours.'

Another voice says: 'Tell me about it. So hard to get good staff these days.'

Though I'm groggy, I recognise the voice I heard just before I lost consciousness in the laneway.

'All the same,' says the Japanese, 'some day they will go too far. It's hard for me to keep tidying these *incidents*. You should at least give your sluggards their anti-testo before they start work. This is barbaric.'

'Please, do not trouble yourself with my problems. You would be better employed remembering that you will come here anytime I call you, *yisheng*. And you will attend to any business to which I require you to attend.'

The doctor's hand, which has been moving a scanner along my forehead, freezes. 'I did not mean disrespect.'

'I am glad to hear it.'

'I merely sought to give you the benefit of medical advice.'

'Your advice is duly noted.'

'I take my medical responsibilities seriously.'

'We all have our responsibilities, doctor. You have yours, and I have mine.'

'Understood.'

The doctor, half turning her head, bows in the direction of the voice, before reaching into her bag for a bottle of pills. She picks up my wrist to take my pulse, and looks at me thoughtfully. 'He is young and healthy: there should be no residual. All is well that ends well?'

'If you say so.'

'Here, handsome,' she says, turning to me. 'Bite on this, and when you wake, you'll be a new boy.'

'Will he be OK?' Tattoo's voice wants to know.

'Yes, of course.' I see the doctor look at her watch, and then the world goes black.

#

I'm dreaming again. I must be in Carlow, because I recognise the bridge in Bagenalstown. I'm wandering drowsily, along familiar tracks, through the countryside of my childhood, past the rape-seed plantations and paddy fields to the squares of bok choy and millet advancing from Kilkenny.

'It's all part of the Corpo's agri-expansion,' Elia says, looking up from an old radio he's been soldering. 'And you can't stop the Corpo.'

But there's a wasteland, where I'm running barefoot. It's fenced off in preparation for the bulldozers. We've found a way under the beams and run from fence to fence, leaping over the uneven surface, pretending we're war-cars or flying dinosaurs. It's a wonderful freedom. You can shout, or scream, or sing, and no one can hear you. I'm with Daisy and we're creeping along the periphery, running like freed animals across the scrub. There are kisses: hurried things needed to establish something we don't understand. We hold hands, jump over a stream. One falls, both fall. Over and over again, we leap, one saving the other. We're screaming, falling, laughing. Then I'm back on the boat, still naked and still in the Vetruvian position. Emily is standing over me, fully clothed in the uniform of a Chinese school inspector.

'We're all the sum of our parts,' she's saying. 'What are yours?'

I look up, gormlessly, because I don't understand.

'What are your parts?' she screams, slapping the rail with a teacher's pointer. 'You have to tell us.'

Tattoo is standing beside her, they're shoulder to shoulder, both dressed the same, and waving their pointers.

'Tell us. Tell us.'

#

When I wake, the apartment is quiet. A grey slit of a window, which runs the length of the wall, is the only source of light. It reminds me of a pillbox. I feel alone, more alone than I ever remember feeling, and I want Emily. I need her strength to guide me home. I sleep.

'You awake?'

I'm waking again. There's a warm glow in my hand. It creeps up my arm and spreads pleasure to every part of my body. Tattoo's face comes into focus. She's holding my hand.

'You awake?'

I nod shyly, ashamed of the pleasure.

'How you feeling?'

'OK.'

Balancing a tea-bowl under my chin, she says: 'Here, drink.'

When I've dutifully sipped, I sit up slowly: stiff and sore, but better. Now that I'm up, I see we're in a long rectangular room with white walls and ceiling. Most of the furniture is classical Chinese, elaborate, probably expensive. There's a print of a panda chewing bamboo hanging on the wall opposite the mountain painting. Tattoo is wearing a black silk *quipao*, which clings to her like skin.

'They've taken our vids and wallets.'

'Fuckers.'

'Yeah.'

Putting her hand behind my head to help me drink the tea, she creates an intense wave of pleasure, which causes me to splutter.

'I've been lubed.'

'Yeah, me too. Doctor thought it would help us relax.'

The curves beneath the silk tell me to forget everything else and initiate reckless fornication.

'Fucius, whatever they've given us is strong.'

'Apparently it's some Japanese herbal shit. It's all I've been able to do to keep my hands off you while you were asleep.'

Reaching an arm around her waist, I try to draw her towards me.

'Better not,' she says, moving away. A chasm of disappointment opens in my chest.

'Why the fuck not? It was all you wanted at the retro.'

'I know, but . . . .' She looks uncomfortable. 'That was before I knew you. Knew what you were really like.'

'Yeah? Well, let me tell you what I'm really like: I'm, like, really horny. And if I don't get some, in, like, the next three seconds, my testicles are going to explode. One after the other.'

Slowly, she pushes fingers through her hair.

'I know. I feel exactly the same, and I don't even have testicles.'

'You can have mine.'

'Behave.'

I can't.

'Please. This stuff is driving me insane. We've got to do something.'

It's at this point that I realise there's something in my forehead. Reaching up, I feel a tiny nub.

'Doctor stuck my pheromone detector into you. Said it would help.'

'Fucius, no wonder.'

Grasping for her with both hands, leper-like, I fall off the couch and lie, weak and bruised, feeling every dancefloor kick. Tattoo, tantalisingly close, keeps her distance. The smooth softness of her thigh calls to me through a slit in the silk. Sitting into an armchair, she folds her legs under herself, but by now, the bulb of a breast is visible, where there's an undone button.

'I'm going to stay here,' she says. 'It's safer. If I try to help you up, our touching will drive us both crazy.'

'Just, please,' I gasp. 'Help me. Do something.'

'How bad is it?'

'It's insane. Please, I'm begging.'

'It wouldn't be right. I'd be taking advantage. Remember what you said to me in the retro? Women have no right to take advantage of men the way they do.'

'What? Fucius, I never said *that!* Just . . . please, take fucking advantage.'

'No means no,' she says.

I try to move toward her. If I can at least touch her, the lube effect might take over. But my body is battered, and moves slowly.

'Tell me how you feel,' she says. 'I mean, emotionally.'

'What? I have an erection that's about to nail me to the floor, my whole body is a mass of bruised craving, and you want to know how I feel *emotionally?* Well, let me tell you. Emotionally, I feel you're a bitch.'

'You're angry now, but you'll thank me afterwards. And you know, how you feel now is more or less how I felt when we met – when I was the one who was lubed up and pheromone-high. I had to control myself to respect you. Why can't you do the same for me?'

'You weren't on this Japanese shit. And anyway, I don't use this stuff: I'm not used to it.'

When I inch within range, she moves to another chair.

'You're in denial. You're refusing to accept equalisation of culpability. That's a real male thing, you know.'

'Equalisation of culpability? What the *fuck* are you talking about? I'm being turned inside out here. I've never known a craving like this.'

'You're playing the blame game now. That's all. Everything is everybody else's fault. You are *such* a man. And I thought you were different. Talk about scratch the surface.'

'I'll scratch your fucking surface.' I make a lunge for her ankle. Standing up, she folds her silk-dripping body onto the couch. I can see right up her inner thigh. Barking like a seal, I change the direction of my crawl.

'Don't you have any respect for me?' she wants to know. 'Can't you see beyond your physical cravings?'

'What kind of a monster are you?' I'm weakening now, barely able to talk. 'Why are you doing this?' I start to cry.

'Hey,' she says, down on her knees and cradling my head. 'It must be something they've given me too. I'm all over the place.'

The orchestra of drugs, pain and pleasure sounds louder in my head, until it becomes an unbearable crescendo. I'm on the ceiling, looking down at myself and being reminded of a *pieta*. I try to find a better place, but there's nowhere I can hide, no wasteland to run through, no boat to lie on. I have no control, and there's no logic or direction to anything. I'm in hell. After I've ejaculated uncontrollably, I lose consciousness before the shame kicks in.

#

Maybe it's the next day, or maybe it's the next week. When you're coming to terms with disorientation, you don't really care. All this in and out of consciousness, is really screwing me over. Things like timelines are incidental, when you're watching houses in a painting slide down a mountain. I'm alone again – if you don't count the panda, whose jaws are actually moving, slowly, on a bamboo shoot. I went out like a light. The girl with the tattoo must have punctured me, with something psychedelic, judging by the panda's expression. A quick fumble confirms that the detector has been removed, as does the absence of insatiable yearning. Someone has had the decency to clean me up: I'm wearing a fresh kimono.

Hauling myself to a sitting position, I look around. A teapot and cups have been set on a nearby table. I totter over to examine them. The tea is cold – which is good, because the pot starts to jig when I try to pour, and most of it goes over my hand. By the time I sit into the armchair, the bowl has calmed, but tea continues to jump onto my lap and all over my chin. With nothing better to do, I sit looking through the slit-window, glumly counting the bulbs and spikes of the Manchester skyline. After some time, huffing and puffing, and trying to persuade my limbs to obey, I feel brave enough to try standing. As I rise, my head begins to spin, and I have to grab the chair to keep myself from falling over. Equilibrium returns sluggishly, and I begin a kind of slow dance, to examine the different parts of my body. When it's established that I'm still, remarkably, more or less in working order, I sit back down and begin to wonder where everybody is.

They will be wondering about me at work. Mianzi will probably assume I'm on, or recovering from, some binge. That is, if I haven't already been replaced. That's what they do: the centipede grows another leg. They won't care enough to be suspicious, or to come looking. Will Emily, I wonder, or, having jilted me at the retro, will she be glad of no contact? It occurs to me, in a detached way, that I should be more concerned, but the inside of my head is an echo-chamber where thoughts reverberate in a meaningless way. There are probably as many questions I should be asking as bamboo shoots in the panda picture, but asking them would take energy I don't have. So I sit and stare through the window, an empty bowl on my lap.

The cityscape is relentless. At one stage, you could probably have seen mountains or at least trees from this height, but progress devoured it all. Even the sky has surrendered to concrete and polymer. Nothing is free any more. Space itself has been measured and sold to the highest bidder. I shuffle the chair nearer to the window. Outside, cars are buzzing around buildings like flies, entering, leaving, sticking to walls, as their passengers do some other thing, which might add to their credit column, while all the time, people-counters hover unnoticed. I sit back, tired. Perhaps I should be more afraid, but I'm still of the opinion that

things can return to normal. I accept that the situation is some-
what more extreme than my usual weekend frolics, but cling to
the hope that it's just somewhere further along the spectrum,
from being chased over a garden wall by an angry husband.

The door opens, and a Chinese enters. Carrying a slim briefcase, she's wearing a tight robe, which squashes her cleavage to
the shape of a baby's arse. She's well put together, though, for a
woman her age, and might be attractive were it not for the eyes,
which are cold enough to make a shark recoil. You just know
that this is the voice everyone's afraid of. She sits opposite, and
crosses her legs.

'It is Li, is it not?'

I nod. There's no point in lying. I'm too afraid to, anyway.

'And you work for Ningbo Digits?'

'That is also true. Where are you getting all this information,
anyway?' I ask politely. 'And where's my friend?'

'In answer to the first question, it is none of your concern.
And the second, is the reason I want to talk with you.'

The eyes, as calm and cold as the voice, tell me that she's not
accustomed to being argued with.

'OK,' I say. 'Just wondering.'

'You're quite comfortable, I trust?'

'I've been beaten, held against my will, lubed up to my gills,
and now my friend is missing. I would say, with respect, that I
am very *un*comfortable. I could do with a peppy, seeing as you
ask.'

The baby's arse rises and falls, with a sigh.

'You are quite an insolent boy.'

I shrug, already regretting the outburst.

'Which I find appealing,' she adds, causing me to look up. A
finger is tracing her lower lip, thoughtfully. Involuntarily, I imagine myself wrestling with that cleavage, and a tide of testosterone
washes hopefully over my body. Catching something in my look,
she says: 'Unfortunately, we do not have time for that now. There
are one or two pressing matters on which I would request your
assistance. Firstly, my name is Haichu, and I am owner of the
club in which you and your friend caused a riot.'

'I'd hardly call it a riot,' I say, modestly.

'Well, Security are comfortable with the description. And now
they are carrying out a very *uncomfortable* examination of my
business, to establish its cause. I'm convinced they will not leave
me alone, until they can justify their existence by establishing a
culprit. Do you wish to be put forward for that position?'

'Well, I hardly think that's fair. I'm seeing myself as more of a victim, at the moment.'

'I agree. Your friend, however, is a different matter. Though she has told us *you* started the fight, our cams confirm you as an innocent party. A fact corroborated by my staff and by other witnesses – of which there are plenty. If you could also confirm this, Security need only hold the girl to be charged. The whole matter can be expedited with the minimum of fuss. That is, if you would be so kind as to join the other witnesses and thumb this statement.'

A pad is produced from her briefcase and pushed across the table.

'Statement?' I say, stupidly.

'Yes. We can add your testimony to the others, and have a watertight case against this troublemaker. And then, maybe, you and I can have . . . lunch, before we pay your compensation and send you on the next vac to Dublin.'

The fact is, Tattoo has been largely responsible for the 'riot'. In thumbing the statement, I would be telling the truth. Notwithstanding the fact that the bitch tried to stitch me up. *And* all the prick-teasing. Then there was the compensation. The number on the pad is generous, and I might even enjoy a *lunch* with this Alpha-Chinese: the whole fear thing is, I'm finding, erotic. I'm still residually lubed, and her raised eyebrow promises an aggressive release: one of my favourite types. I could be back in the arms of Emily in time for supper, telling her my story, letting her in. All the reasons, all the different aspects, all the simple numbers add up to one conclusion. I reach over the table, but stop short of taking the pad. There's something about this situation I don't trust. I say: 'Seems reasonable. But can I talk to her first? I would like to look her straight in the face and tell her why I'm doing this.'

Her eyebrows flatten, but she can't accuse me of anything. I feel I've been clever.

'But of course.' When she's finished smirking, she stands up. 'She's with Security now, but as soon as they finish, I'll have her brought in.'

Clipping the case shut, she moves towards the door, but stops behind my chair. 'Oh, and Li,' she says, 'there is nothing else that we may have omitted' – I feel her hand on my shoulder, where her fingers squeeze, like emissaries of future pleasure – 'from our report, that you can think of now, is there?'

I think of the rough treatment we've received from the bouncers, and of her conversation with the doctor. I think of the gangster in the gutter, and the terrified look on her face. I think of how I have been forcibly lubed, and of the locks on the apartment door. I think about how neatly Tattoo is being stitched up.

'No,' I answer innocently. 'But if I think of anything, I'll let you know.'

#

A dam has burst, and a valley has flooded. On a corrugated roof of a hut you can't see, sits a woman, her husband and two small kids. A close-up brings her right into the room. I can see the lines on her sun-beaten face, including deep ridges pulling down each side of her mouth. It's like this flood is just another biblical disaster, which she'll have to deal with. *This too will pass*, her face says, but if not, she will die, and get it over with. The camera begins to pan slowly outward, and the children huddling on their father's lap, come back into shot. This cluster at the far end of the roof, leaves the woman alone and weakly defiant, giving her something else to endure. As the camera continues to back away, more and more roofs come into view, dotted all over the valley like bits of debris, to which ravaged people cling like insects.

'The dam was sabotaged by rebs,' the voice-over says. 'And many families were below the waterline when the wave hit. The authorities are doing all they can.'

Though there are several news-pods hovering over the valley, I see no rescue cars or boats. Too delicate for this, I switch to the channel that loops *Neighbours* twenty-four seven – to the familiar soapy warmth of predictable plot-lines and attractive young bodies.

#

It's towards evening, judging by the leaden colour of the window, when a bowl of noodles and a tea-tray are brought in by a woman I recognise as one of the bouncers. She's innocuous now, out of her black suit, almost human. I miss her when she's gone, though she only sneered at my effort at small talk. I eat, gratefully, then make the tea. It goes cold as I watch 3D and wait for Fucius knows what. Finally, the door opens, and Tattoo is shoved into the room by the bouncer.

'If you try anything like that again, I will have you butchered,' the bouncer says, closing the door.

'Winning more friends?' I say. Tattoo glares at me, rubbing her arm where the bouncer has been mauling her.

'Tried to make a run for it.'

'A run for it? And what about me?'

She looks at me blankly, as though she doesn't know what I'm talking about.

'Well, of course . . . I was going to come back with help.'

'What help? The American cavalry?'

'OK, OK. So I went for it. Thought, if one of us was free, it would leave us both in a better position. You would have done the same.'

'Ha!'

I'm at my least articulate when I'm upset.

'Don't tell me you're pissed off?'

'*I* was offered a statement to thumb – would have left me completely off the hook. But, oh no. I just couldn't do it. Couldn't leave you here on your own to face the music. What a bloody idiot.'

'Yes, you are a bit of an idiot, aren't you?'

Smiling thinly, I turn, with a shake of my head, to the teenager arguing with his father on the 3D. Tattoo says: 'Don't pout. It makes you look like a queen.'

Something occurs to me. 'Were you offered a statement, as a matter of interest?'

At first, she looks as if the very suggestion is an outrage, then shrugs, apathetically.

'I may have been given something. But it was hardly what you would call watertight legal testimony.'

'Yeah? What did it say?'

She hesitates, tries to conceal the guilt in her face – which is as obvious as forbidden chocolate around a child's mouth.

'That things may have been *slightly* more your fault than mine.'

'Did you sign?'

'Well, at first I absolutely refused . . . .'

'But . . . ?

'Well, what would *you* have done?'

'Oh, great. Now everything's going to be dumped on me.'

'But after I thumbed, they told me that you hadn't, and that you wanted to see me. At that point, I knew we were both screwed. That's why I ran for it. Would have got away too, if they hadn't shut the security screen. Bitches.'

'How inconvenient,' I say, coldly.

'Fucius, Li, why didn't you just thumb your statement? With both statements signed, there would have been contradictory evidence. We could have had them both discredited. That was the reason I signed mine: I was protecting us both.'

'How noble. I didn't sign, because I didn't trust her.'

'Then you're a fool.'

'Probably.'

She looks at me thoughtfully, then asks: 'Were you trying to protect me again? Is that what all this is about?'

'Certainly not. I just played the odds. A little better than you, by the looks of things.'

'You *were* trying to protect me,' she says. 'That's the second grenade you've thrown yourself on for me. You're a chivalrous little fuck, aren't you?'

I turn back to the teenager, who is now remonstrating with his mother, and try to disguise a feeling of nervous exuberance.

'You tried to protect me,' she sings, her voice creamy with insinuation. I refuse to answer. 'Ooh,' she says. 'We're a little bit touchy about the whole protecting-me thing.'

'What is your problem?' I snap. 'I just didn't feel right about it, but I'd thumb it now in a heartbeat. Haichu!' I shout at the door. 'Are you out there? I'm ready to thumb. Bring back that statement.'

Raising the volume of the 3D, she bitch-slaps me sharply. 'Calm the fuck down.'

I put my hand to my cheek, shocked.' 'What the . . . ?'

'Don't be a child. You must realise there's something going on here.'

'That really hurt.'

'Are you completely stupid? We're being held here against our will. If this was a simple case of peppied and disorderly, we would have been handed over to Security last night.'

'What are you talking about?' I try not to let my voice crack, as the heat of my cheek cools to a sting.

'We must have seen something they didn't want us to see.'

'Like what?'

'Like that woman being beaten outside the club. Dead. I overheard the doctor talking on the vid to someone.'

'Who?'

'I don't know. I said I *heard* the conversation. I didn't see it.'

'Who was the woman they killed?'

'How am I supposed to know? But it sounded like she was someone important.'

'Fucius.'

'Those testimonies might implicate us as accessories.'

I wait for her to elaborate, but she's busy in her own mind.

'Well, what do you think will happen now?' I ask.

'I don't know. I think we've witnessed some serious crime, and I don't exactly see this Haichu giving us our vac-fare back to Dublin, while telling us she hopes we enjoyed our visit.'

I'm too sick to be dealing with this. At the best of times, it would have been disorientating, but in my present state, between the drugs, the beating, and now this slap . . . .

'I really am *not* feeling very well.'

'Pull yourself together,' she says. 'We don't have time for your shit.'

'*You* might not have,' I say. A sudden gust of panic hits me, and I run to the door, where I pull at the handle uselessly. 'But I do.'

Then I'm at the window, fumbling at the catches. Tattoo comes over and gives me another unmerciful slap across the face. Same side: she's a southpaw.

'Sit down. We're thirty storeys up. What are you going to do? *Fly* back to Dublin?'

I stand rubbing my face, bewildered.

'Stop *doing* that. You're more dangerous than any of these bitches.'

'Look at me,' she says, holding the sides of my head, so I'm looking straight at her. 'We've got to get out of here, sure. But we can't panic. OK? Now, I know you've taken a bit of a hiding, and that you're disorientated . . . .'

'A bit of a hiding? Disorientated? No, I wouldn't say I was disorientated. Since I met you, things have been so calm . . . . No, I tell a lie: *serene*. I really feel that I'm beginning to get in touch with my inner chakras here.'

'You can't possibly mean that you're blaming me for all this?'

'You're the one starting all the fights. You're the one slapping me around the place. I don't know what kind of boys you're used to associating with, but I can assure you, I am *not* accustomed to physical abuse.'

My eyes fill, and I look away.

'Oh, for crying out loud.' She reaches over and puts her hand on my shoulder.

'I've tried so hard,' I say, turning my whole body, and batting her hand away, before retreating to the armchair, where I curl into a snivelling ball of resentment. The Australian teenager from 3D-land is standing with hands on hips now, gazing lovingly at both parents, who have taught him some life-lesson I've missed, in all the excitement. I look back at Tattoo spitefully. 'All you can do is blame me for every little thing. Then slap me.'

'I'm not *blaming* you,' she says, coming over and sitting on the arm of the chair. 'Neither of us is to *blame*. I'm just saying that, you know, you have to keep your shit together. That's all.'

Ignoring the opportunity to point out that she is clearly to blame for absolutely everything, I stiffly say: 'I'm doing my best, under very difficult circumstances.'

It's important for her to know this. If you don't point things out clearly to a woman, they simply won't get it. I was therefore happy to dispel a little pride in order to make the point.

'Come here, baby, and stop behaving like a big boy's blouse.'

The dam finally bursts. I melt into her, and sob frustration onto her shirt, as she pats my head consolingly.

#

I flip the 3D when Tattoo's in the shower. There's more from America. Riots, this time in Chicago. A delegation of diplomats and higher Corpo servants are being sent out from Somalia to try to sort things out. They're at the vac-port in Mogadishu, all smiles and hopeful gestures. Then it's back to Amanda Plunkett in Chicago, hunkering in her flak-jacket, pointing to ruins and explaining.

'Local government has completely broken down here, and the city is in the hands of the rebs. Now that they don't have Security to deal with, it seems they've turned on each other. Various factions, including the Grand Old Oprys, some Liberals, and The Freedom Fries, have been firing at each other's positions, since about oh-nine-hundred this morning. It's not clear what anyone's objective is at this stage, but it would appear that there is a power-grab at play. The problem is' – she cowers behind an anti-laser barrier, as a slice of white light tears overhead, to carve another chunk out of what used to a skyscraper – 'the Triumvirate has fled HQ, and now there's nothing around which a conglomerate can be built. This, in turn, has led to increased and more intense competition.'

There's more laser-fire, this time in the distance. Amanda's voice becomes bolder. 'Things in Chicago have deteriorated to the chaos we've seen throughout the rest of the subcontinent, and Seattle is now the last stronghold of Corpo control. The Africans are going to have to somehow piece together a board of directors, if they are to succeed where Europe and Asia have failed. When Mrs Omogi and her delegation arrive in a few short hours, they will have to locate, and regroup, what is left of the city Corpo. It is thought that she will then try to bring these together, with the exiled Corpos of other cities, which have relocated in Montreal. Once there, she will attempt to piece together a multi-Corpo board of directors. The last surviving triumvir from Chicago, Mu shi, has said, in a news-release, that it is her hope that a strong central board, with a viable Triumvirate, can be re-established in Chicago. This will allow, she says, international Security to join what's left of the local force, in order to establish an ally for Seattle, and take back the north-west. This would, according to Mu shi, form a base from which to re-corporatise the rest of the country. The inclusion of the rebs in any discussions is not an option, as Mrs Omogi has made it clear that she will not negotiate with terrorists.'

Tattoo is standing beside me, rubbing the side of her head with a towel, while wearing one of Haichu's *terry-cloth* robes, in which she looks diminutive. 'Hard to believe,' she says, 'that we're talking about the birthplace of Corpocracy.'

'Yes,' I agree, watching a droplet of water snake down her neck.

9

'It's a question of proportion.'

Tattoo's hair is being messed around by the breeze and needs to be re-spiked, constantly – which she does with her idiosyncratic finger-sweep. 'You and I might think we have problems,' she goes on. 'But if you consider us as components in the overall matrix, we're nothing. I mean, look at the millions who are dying or starving in the RUSA. Who are we, and who really cares what happens to us? We're just integers. And no one cares about integers.'

We're sitting on the broad back of a mountain, which ranges above us, while below, it dips into the hazy distance of ground already covered. There's plenty of sky here, behind mountains, which push up the horizon. Clouds are racing, dissipating into new patterns. I'd forgotten what a theatre the sky could be. Bursts of untainted air, cold and immeasurable, fill our lungs and flatten our voices. The highlands are preserved as a national park – probably because there's nothing worth mining or otherwise exploiting that cannot be found more easily elsewhere. The Scot-Corpo uses the land for deer or bear hunting – irresistible pastimes for Asians with a taste for adventure, according to an ad on the vac. But that's only during certain times of the year – which I hope isn't now. The ads were interrupted by breaking news. Omogi's vac was blown up over Nova Scotia. There were no survivors.

'Yes,' I say, 'but to us, you have to admit, our problems are pretty freaking enormous.'

Tattoo, intent on cleaning her nail with a twig of heather, makes no reply, and my point is lost in the wind. Standing up, I wave my arms. 'I mean, what the hell do we care about whether anyone cares about us or not? Or even what's happening in America? The whole shit-heap could descend into communism, for all I care. Right now, you and I are on a bloody mountain. And we can't even contact anyone, in case our call is traced.'

When she looks up, her eyes are the colour of the landscape. 'Perhaps *Emily*' – she laces the word with sarcasm – 'would be worth a call. *Emily* should be able to use some of her super contacts to help us out.'

A crow, which has been caught in a gust, tumbles, gathers its wings, and soars on the current. It seems to be struggling to find its original direction. The tips of its wings tremble against the wind. Its small body strains towards some intrinsic thing.

'OK,' I say, 'maybe I will call her. As soon as we reach somewhere where there might be a phone.'

'Make sure she doesn't stand you up again.' She laughs, then becomes serious. 'You heard what the doctor told us. We can't take the risk.'

What the doctor told us, was that Haichu's tentacles reached into the Brit- and Irish-Corpos, as well as the underbelly. We would have to be very careful, she said, as she led us down the fire-escape in the apartment block. We would have to lie low, at least until the investigation into the pinstriped gangster's death cooled, and Haichu cooled off. Pushing two vac tokens and a homing chip into our hands, she told us to go to her holiday place in Scotland, which was well stocked and out of the way. We would be safe there, until she contacted us. We were to take her advice and not try to contact anyone. She was sick of being party to brutality and criminality, the doctor. Would be reporting the whole operation to Security, if Security was not riddled with corrupt officials on the take from Haichu. She wished us luck, and assured us that she was in no danger, before quietly shutting the steel door and leaving us at our old picnic spot in the lane.

#

'Come on.' Tattoo pulls me up by the armpit and we continue lumbering in the direction the beeps are telling us to go – which, inevitably, is up.

'Screw this,' I say after about half an hour, dropping onto one of the boulders that push through the heather like exposed knucklebones. 'I'm going to stop at the first house we come to, and phone Laura. Get her to pick us up.'

A crow, moving at extraordinary speed, slices across my eyeline. Is it the same one? The sky has paled by now, and darkness is spreading from the east.

'We can't.' Tattoo stands over me, panting. 'Phone anyone. We have to keep going.'

'No,' I say. 'We don't. Why should we believe anything that doctor told us, anyway? She could be in it with Haichu, for all we know.'

'Yeah? Well then, why did she help us escape?'

My silence brings a flicker of victory to her face. I consider her slyly as we plod on. Her cheeks are flushed, and she's as tired as I am, but more determined. She has lost, for the time being, interest in me: I can tell. Which reminds me why I never stick around for 'mornings after', with their cold reprisals and reintroduction of reality. Sooner or later, the woman wants to go back to work. I'm more at home with the foamy intensity of flirtation, than the drudgery of sober interaction. I tried, on the vac ride northwards, to sustain a little sparkle by telling her about Emily: at the time, she had not seemed that interested. Yet as the day wears on, it seems that this snippet has caused an undercurrent. I feel sorry afterwards, that I've opened my mouth – which I'd only done to fill the void of her silence. Nor was there any need for me to talk up Emily's strong-silent skillset. I don't know why I did. Maybe I was showing a bit of vulnerability, as you would a bit of shoulder, as an enticement. But I was wasting my time: she didn't care.

She doesn't seem to care about anything. Usually, the more time you spend with someone, the more you get to know them. Their habits and idiosyncrasies give them away, sure, but mostly two people who spend a bit of time in each other's company begin to open up, voluntarily. Not so with Tattoo. The more time I spend with her, the less I know about her. I always seem to be telling more than I intend, while she gives nothing away. This is what keeps her in control of the dynamic. But just in case this isn't enough, she has another skill. A way of twisting things so that everything that's not my fault, is at least my responsibility. It's as though she already knows everything I might think or be feeling, so further discussion is pointless. I should just do what I'm told. The really infuriating thing is: this is what I usually end up doing. And we both know that, if all else fails, she has a slap in her locker. Here I am again, being dragged along. Being encouraged and congratulated for every reluctant step I take. We crest a hill, and the homing chip goes berserk. Below us in the valley, fading into the dusk, there's a low stone cabin.

After we shower, we dress in clothes which have been left conveniently in a wardrobe. (My balls drop gratefully, when I remove the purple pants for the last time.) We eat, generally establish our presence in the place, then sit staring into a fire Tattoo has lit with logs from a heap in the yard. Although the cabin is single story, there's a cellar, half of which has been converted into a freezer. There's enough food down there to see us through an ice-age. The ceiling is low, and has all sorts of useful things hanging from its wooden beams, like battered brass pans, antique firearms, and something that turns out to be a riddle for sorting wheat from chaff, according to a sticker on its rim. There's only one bedroom – an issue which we're both too tired to discuss. I'm managing to do too much talking again.

'Tell you the truth, after a hard day at the numbers, there's nothing like a nice uggo to help you work off the tension.'

She says nothing.

I continue. 'A lot of people would look down on an ugly woman, but I say that their enthusiasm and lower maintenance level, make up for any physical abomination.'

I don't even know why I'm talking about this stuff. My intention was to get her into the seduction zone, by dissing Emily and highlighting my liberal views on sex. But I seem to have taken a wrong turn somewhere, and now sound like I'm opening at the Perverts' AGM.

'Are you always this inane? she asks, crossing her legs and turning towards the fire, her skin reflecting the amber glow.

I've been called this before, by Emily – which makes it sting all the more.

'Just trying to make conversation,' I say, quietly.

'You've got to admit, it is a bit strange. Good-looking boy like you porking all those uggos.'

When I don't reply, she loses interest and starts rubbing her arm, as is her habit when she's thinking. She's full of habits, like those impatient tussles of her hair, or that disbelieving wobble of her head, to indicate that I've said something stupid, again. Emily, who's still doggedly playing on my mind, has her own habits. She too is a head-wobbler, but her hair, flat and long, is not suitable for tussling. Emily is far away now, and the image of blonde hair on black satin is losing its potency. I'd still like to know why she stood me up, though: unfulfilled curiosity lingers, like an interrupted argument.

I'm pulled back to the cabin when Tattoo says: 'Well?'

'I'm going to pay the good doctor for this,' I switch, waving my glass at the clutter of our eaten meal. 'When all this is over.'

'When all *what* is over?'

We look at each other, and realise that neither can answer the question. Tattoo leans back on a futon sucking a prawn shell, which she throws into the fire, before putting her hands behind her head, interlocking prawn-smeared fingers in her hair.

'OK,' she says. 'Let's recap. We go to a club, witness a murder, get entertained by the murderer, get aided in our escape by a Jap doctor, leg it northwards, and end up here together, under instruction, from said Jap doctor, not to attempt to contact anyone, for fear that our pursuer, assuming that we *are* being pursued, will locate and do Fucius knows what to us?'

'That's about the size of it.'

'While,' she says, 'we know *what* has been happening, we don't yet know *why*.'

'What do you mean?'

'Well, we're both students of the numbers. Doesn't it all look like a bit of a coincidence?'

'What else could it be?'

'What do *you* think?'

But I don't know what to think, beyond an urge to kiss those sardonic lips and push her into the futon – this, despite the hairy armpits and prawny fingers. Her eyes shine in expectation of an answer.

Demurely, I say: 'If there is something behind all this, beyond coincidence, then why don't you defy the laws of probability and seduce me? The ripple effect would probably sort out this whole mess.'

#

Was never going to work, I conclude, lying on the futon by the dying fire. I went in too cold. Should have worked in eye-contact, a longer preamble: a bit more innuendo, perhaps. Too bloody tired. Rejection is always cruel, and she has a flair. Laughing in my face, she stood up and went to bed.

Watching one of the doctor's movie-vids to distract myself, I listen as Tattoo's preparations for sleep fade to silence in the bedroom – which she took without discussion. The movie, which really is inane, is about some lower-ranking Corpo worker who has discovered a high-ranker surreptitiously building up a competing conglomerate. The doctor should have better taste, but her library is full of populist mulch. The villain looks a bit like Mianzi – which sets me thinking. About her advances. About how she propositioned me less than a week after I was summoned from the pool. Dinner at her city pad? This, I laughingly dismissed as the mischievous joke of a witty superior. Then there was the crawling hand around my waist, and the meaningful looks when we worked late together. Would I rub her shoulders? I thought of the artificially high breasts she seemed to be pointing in my direction, and the reconstituted skin of her face when she rubbed it against my cheek at my vid-screen. Almost new; almost like a young woman.

I remember what it's like to capitulate, the feel of her arms, the nuzzle of her neck, and the smell of pheromone perfume tinkering with my senses. I remember, too, being slapped on the bare buttocks and told to get off and go back to work. Her veiny ankles sat one on top of the other, under the desk, where I scrambled for my underpants. I think of Emily, and daughter supplants mother. I think of golden hair and slender shoulders, lithe arms and clear eyes. Then she and Tattoo are locked in a serpentine embrace, crawling, sliding around each other's bodies, as one. I feel myself harden, flick to a porn-vid, and three minutes later there's a damp tissue-wad hissing on the embers. As I listen to those millions of carriers of my genes being burned to death, I think of the trillions of ancestors that made it possible for them to exist, however briefly, and of the incalculable loss of tiny life. There's an inevitable brutality in natural selection – a simple justice that has no reason beyond survival.

Tattoo is right: integers don't matter.

10

I wake early the next morning face down on the futon, like I've been trying to fuck it all night. The fire, by now a cold Pompeian mound, is being ruffled by a draft from the chimney. Tiny avalanches trickling down the slopes of a miniature Vesuvius entertain me, as I watch, heavy-eyed, with my cheek in a pool of drool. There must be millions of granules, all perfectly formed by the fire: to the human eye, they're just dust. It's only when I haul myself to a sitting position, that I notice that Tattoo has thrown a duvet over me during the night. Her gallantry is poor consolation. Looking around, I suppose I'll have to tidy before she gets up.

This reminds me of Elia, who always reminded me of the White Rabbit, on those weekends when he hurried around the house picking things up, and repeating: 'She'll be up in a minute. She'll be up in a minute.' It's the same with millions of fathers in millions of homes all over the world. No respectable woman would allow her husband to keep a sloppy house. There was always low-level tension, in the hour before Laura either got in from work or out of bed, with Elia rushing from room to room, muttering to himself. The punishment for sloppy housekeeping in our house was 'discussion' – something Elia feared more than the beatings you heard other fathers were given. I don't have to wonder what type of wife Tattoo would make: I already know she's a beater. When I blow gently on the Vesuvius, I injure its shape and redistribute its essence around the grate, and up the chimney.

#

'You know,' she says, when she's finished breakfast and joined me by the back door. 'Who's to say men aren't really the ones in charge, and that they have deviously manoeuvred their women-folk into doing all the work?'

I stop what I'm doing, splitting logs.

'You mean, in the same way that humans could be the reproductive vehicle for jiz?'

I'm trying to be clever; the analogy, having occurred to me the evening before, seems to have found its appropriate moment. An expression, which flits across her face, tells me she doesn't know whether I'm joking or insane. 'No, seriously,' she says, sitting on a stump. 'Take you as an example. You'll probably settle down with this Emily, or someone like her. And when you do, it will be perfectly respectable for you to stay at home with the kids, while she assumes the yoke of responsibility.'

'Well, it's no fun being at home all day, is it? Being a nonentity.'

'Easier than trying to deal with the pressures of the day-to-day in some heartless Corpo.'

I spit on my hands, lift the axe, and swing it into a log. It splits neatly.

'Depends which way you look at it.'

She looks like I might have said something meaningful, for a second.

'What's your deal, anyway? You want to be with this Emily, don't you? Settle down; all that crap.'

'I would like to think that there's slightly more to me than that.'

'Why? Because you spend your time getting peppied out of your tree and chasing uggos? Why do you do that, anyway? You trying to punish yourself with these ugly bitches, or what?'

I shrug. There have been so many. Since school days, they've always been there, lurking. Most of us boys in Carlow were drilled by our parents in the art of self-respect. There were always fathers at kerbsides with kids, giving their faces one last wipe before they pushed them on to the school bus, telling them to be good for their teachers. Although Elia did occasionally bring me to the bus in the morning, he was never in the village square, where we were dumped in the afternoon. Nor did he ever seem particularly interested in me when I arrived home. He was forever and obliviously tinkering with some obscure, uninteresting thing, which left me with what turned out to be too much freedom, once school ended. Hunger was the only thing which could encourage me to come home. Though I usually made some effort at homework, it was not uncommon, once dinner had been eaten, for me to wander back into the streets, looking for distraction. What I found was, the streets led nowhere, and the wasteland was just a wasteland in the absence of Daisy.

There were however, the mechanics: a bunch of low women, leathered up and lurching around the Square at the weekends. They sped around on their impressively flashy hov-bikes – removed silencers turning the swish to a scream. They were always quick to whistle when I passed, though I considered myself too young to be on their radar. There was something in their indifference to the future which made them exciting. More so, because the future itself was as dangerous as they were. The future had been impressed on us kids as a threat – one that could only be tamed with sacrifice, hard work and planning. We would have to scramble onto the lowest rung of the Corpo-ladder, or preserve ourselves intact, for some well-familied girl. But the mechanics were living in the moment. I was intrigued by the image of them, standing in a doorway, slowly wiping their hands, remarking at the boys who hurried past – exuding marginality. At weekends, scrubbed and greased with different oils, they would drape themselves territorially around the monument to Lao Shi in the village square, partying late into the night, sometimes breaking an empty alco-pep bottle, sometimes singing.

They could otherwise be found in pool-halls, or bars, or anywhere seedy where they could use filthy language, peppy-up, and leer. To them, life was now: life was smoking in the sunshine when the boss was away, or twiddling with phase-drivers under the hood of some yokel's car. *Rev it up, rev it up, right right, knock him off.* Life was swigging alco-pep, thoughtfully, as they discussed the possibility of married men. They would tell you anything. And they could be persuasive, whispering commitment, promising the freedom of the open road. They were at their most lethal in summer, when rich boys were sent away from the city for a holiday. A wife could quickly find her husband being consoled under the glow of the sky-cinema, and be challenged to a knife-fight if she objected.

It was under the whizz-bang of a midsummer firework display that I first discovered the pain and pleasure of flesh. I was fourteen, and standing casually with my friend Bernard, watching florescent swirls dance in the night sky, when we were accosted by two mechanics with whom we were on blushing terms. Did we want alco-pep? What did we think of the fireworks? Had we ever been on a hov? Bernard, forever in terror of new experience, hurried away to be pursued by one, while I, too shyly fascinated to object, was whisked into the night by the other, clinging to the leather pockets on her studded jacked, pushed back by the acceleration.

'Relax,' she said, dragging my arms around her waist. 'I'm not going to bite you . . . yet.'

I resisted her pawing and stroking for as long as I could, on that riverbank where we stopped to drink more alco-pep. Inevitably, I gave in to her strong hands and surrendered to her mouth. She worked me over for what seemed like hours, laughing every time I came, and making me do things that filled me with shame. Afterwards, she drove back to town at a more leisurely pace and, leaving me in the square, said: 'Remember, bimbo-boy, you're mine now. Any time I want, any way I want, you come running.'

For year, I avoided the street where the garage was, had to go home from school by a convoluted route. Getting home that night, I found Laura snoring softly in her armchair, and our house otherwise dimly silent. My body was burning, my mind confused, but nobody knew, and nobody cared, where I had been, or what had happened to me. No one would ever know how I could not get the mechanic out of my mind. I was hers any time and any way: I was to come running. The thought of her, looped relentlessly, filling me with shame, and a druggy sense of lecherousness. Something not understood at the time left a spore in me, which continued to grow and fester.

#

'Well, the uggos belong to the empire of the rejected,' I say when I return with her bowl of tea. I'm playing with the idea of honesty, but the trust isn't there, so I don't tell her about the mechanic, though it might help her seduce me: I've known women use sympathy like a tyre-iron to get into a man's pants. But it can bounce the other way too, and I'm not risking pity. Assuming an aura of intensity, I try to sound interesting. 'They have to push the boat out more. They have less shame, more enthusiasm, and are generally more experimental. Probably because they're grateful for any little bit of attention, and don't know when they're going to see action again.' Though I'm saying it, I don't believe it. My thing with the uggos is something primal. I don't know what, but I do know that it was born that night by the river. I feel an itch to forget about trust and tell Tattoo – to throw myself at the mercy of her sneers.

'Uggos are more fun,' I say, instead. 'You don't have to work as hard.'

She's quiet for a while, like she's bored with the whole thing, then wanders into the house, leaving me swinging the axe. When she re-emerges, it's ten logs later and she's chewing a string of soy-curd.

'OK,' she says, 'forget about these uggos. Tell me, where do you stand on equalisation?'

I stop swinging, and straighten.

'What?'

'I mean, shouldn't men take more civic responsibility?'

A cool breeze, coming from the mountain, meets hot sweat rising through the thin cotton on my back, and causes a shudder. 'Never really thought about it.'

'Come on, you must have an opinion. It's one of the biggest issues this generation is facing.'

'I suppose. But it's pointless trying to stand up to the Corpo one way or another, so why let it bother you?'

This is another lie. These things *do* actually bother me. The thought of so many starving and displaced people makes no sense, on a planet of plenty. I'm also secretly sickened by the blatant double standards of the Corpos. Even *I* know that greed is not as good as they're making it out to be.

'Fucius. You must care about something.'

Having inadvertently piqued her interest, I decide to push on with the point, though I'm making things up as I go along.

'I'm basically a sociopath,' I tell her. 'I've seen enough bureaucrats and profit-bullies to be disillusioned about people.'

'Why would you hate people?' She waves the butt of her soya string at me. 'That makes no sense whatsoever.'

'Look at the disregard people have shown towards the planet,' I say, leaning on the axe-handle. 'And towards the other creatures that lived here. Lions, tigers, elephants, and so on, have all been made extinct, except for clone zoos. Great complex creatures, evolving over millions of years, have been wiped out through indifference or greed. And what we do to animals is nothing compared to what we do to each other.'

'So, you do care.' She smiles, but I'm in no mood to be patronised, and rant on, bullishly.

'And all done in the name of Corpocracy. It's enough to make you sick.'

'Then why don't you speak out against it? Do something, instead of wasting your life on pills and women.'

'Because there's so much logic, so much evidence weighted in favour of the Corpo-system. Only a fool, or a raving madperson, would speak out against irrefutable facts.'

'You mean the windies?'

'That's exactly what I mean. And you needn't tell me those debates aren't stage-managed either.'

Windies are regularly presented on the media to debate with and be torn patiently apart by intellectual Chinese. Though the setup is contrived enough to be preposterous, it's accepted. No one wants to look ridiculous. Ridiculous is the worst thing to be, in a society that makes a religion of being smart. She nods and shrugs, looks like she's on the verge of taking me seriously. I might actually be nearing a breakthrough.

'I've always been uneasy about the way you're greased into the Corpo's groove,' I tell her. 'But as I've said, there's nothing you can do about it, so why bother?'

'Yeah, but you're a shareholder,' she says. 'You have a vote at the AGM. And every vote can make a difference.'

My torso is beginning to shiver under a layer of cold sweat. I pick up the axe before I cramp. Intelligence looks like it might be turning her on, I say.

'The agendas at the AGMS are controlled. Everyone knows that. The whole voting system is only there to placate.'

'You see? This is what I'm talking about. You have the smarts to see what's going on; you just don't have the guts to do anything about it. Typical male cop-out.'

Thumping the axe-blade into a log, I lift the whole thing shoulder high before letting it fall. It splits neatly. She's right, of course: men are too distractible to do anything properly.

'They say that before the Great Reckoning, most of the woes of history came from man's inability to control his emotions. Which may or may not be true, but just because you women have the ability to manipulate the weaker sex, does that mean you should?'

I'm wishing she would. Wishing she would put her hands on my chest and push me into the cabin – on to the futon, which I primped when I went to make the tea. She moves instead to the fence behind, where she sits and watches me with the axe. I wonder if she's checking out the muscles on my back; I wonder if I *have* muscles on my back. If so, they must surely be visible under the wet shirt. The axe is getting heavier than the conversation, and it would be nice to stop swinging at both. I stick the blade into the stump, and leave it there.

'My back is so *stiff,*' I say.

But she just says: 'Windie.'

And walks into the cabin, leaving the word hanging in the rain-promising air.

11

'You are interesting,' she says, as we finish lunch on the third day. 'When you actually open up and give your opinion. Instead of all the homme-fatale crap you go on with.'

'Yeah?'

She points her chopsticks in the direction of my head. 'Not as empty as it looks.'

There's a smile, vague enough to be incomprehensible. A shred of beef, stuck between my wolf-teeth, makes me want to just put my hand in there and yank it out, while a bulge in my lower bowel wants to release itself as a fart. These things I cannot do, not in front of her. Proximity, following several days of being holed up in a cabin in the rain, is becoming irritating. *She's* becoming irritating.

'Do you think democracy is a viable alternative?' she says.

'I'm not really into politics.'

'Democracy is just manipulation of the masses. Any snake-oil saleswoman with enough money can sell them the lies. Get the multidudes to lap it up.'

'But isn't that, in effect, what the Triumvirate system is?'

I say this absently – thoughtlessly. It's an old argument, and I'm just repeating it – not really caring about what I'm saying. She cares, though – has the troubled look that goes with a busy mind. Looking straight into me, as if plumbing the depths of my shallowness, she says: 'It's been proven, for generations now, that a world run by intelligent women is the best possible world. Better than anything that went before. They make the decisions that need to be made, based on empirical evidence and without the distraction of a self-serving opposition. The whole population benefits.'

'And America?' I say, hoping to shut her up. 'Is that the best of all possible worlds?'

The table is post-meal messy, and I instinctively begin to gather up the plates.

Sitting back in her chair to allow me space, she puts an ankle on a knee and looks up at me. 'America needs time. And patience.'

'Whatever.'

Returning from the dishwasher, I gather the rest of the table-crap in silence. I'm happy to accept defeat, if it helps the interminable conversation go away. It's the asexuality of the situation I don't like: the clinical analysis of dull things. She's been at this for days, and I'm beginning to feel like a panellist on a current-affairs blogathon. Tattoo, unaware, it seems, of her profound physical attraction, prattles on, like the host. Questions, questions. All eye-contact and intelligent hand-gestures. It's a delicious agony, to be within touching distance of the untouchable, irritating thing. When I sit back down, I can see downy hair on her jawline, and tiny ripples of goosebumps on her arm: my interest in her body has gone microscopic. I see it all: a fleck of blue in the brown of her eye, a tiny laser scar on the side of her nose, where she's had something done. This type of connection, I've never experienced before. I can sense her essence, and somehow know that she's feeling as isolated as I am. It's like I'm calling in to her loneliness from mine: there's no answer.

'What are you looking at?' she says.

'Nothing much.'

'Why don't you answer my question? You never answer a difficult question.'

'Why don't you stop asking them?'

'Because I'm interested in your opinion – in what you have to say.'

'I don't have anything to say. You need to accept that.'

'Don't denigrate yourself. It's such a male thing to do.'

'Don't patronise me. That's a female thing.'

'It's because I *don't* want to patronise you, that I want to know what you think. Why don't you talk to me? The poor-little-lost-boy act is getting you nowhere. Not with me.'

'Whatever.'

This is one of these conversations that keeps going round in circles, so I shut up, pout, and become semi-foetal on the chair. While devouring, slyly, with my eyes, what I want to take with my body. My whole body. This is no caressing-fingertip-from-erogenous-zone-to-erogenous-zone thing, no Emily-style lip-pecking. With frustration stoked beyond the point of return, this is consummation. For the first time, I realise, there's a profound connection between the emotional and the physical. It's an uncomfortable feeling, one without control or direction. My senses are finely tuned. I can hear her breathing, and my heart is beating to the rhythm of hers. I can smell the musk from that part of her neck behind the ear, where shreds of black hair meet translucent skin.

'Ah, we're back to the monosyllables.'

And on we go. On and on, in smart-arse orbit of something too real to be confronted. I play along. Abject, weary: the unfulfilled fool.

'Actually, *what-ev-er* has three syllables.'

'Whatever,' she repeats.

The rain, pattering against the window, is the only thing breaking the silence. It's been three days of watching her move around the cabin. Three days of lousy vids and pulling the stomach out of myself when she goes to bed. Boredom itself should have been enough to drive us to sex. And she wants to talk about politics. I go to the fireplace, where I start to make a wigwam out of shards of log. We'll need heat; we'll need this rug or this futon, or both. Everything I do, or think, can only travel in one direction. Destination sex.

'Why don't you want to talk?' she says, following me as far as the futon. Grunting from my hunched position, like an injured animal, I say: 'About what?'

I'm hoping there's a change of subject coming. Something like: *What's going on between us? There seems to be a lot of sexual chemistry in the air. Can you sense sexual chemistry?* Now, there's a subject I could talk about all day. This is what I want. What I get is: 'Politics, or the state of the economy, or America, or whatever? It has to be better than all this, sulky silence.'

Knees about fifty centimetres apart, hands behind the head. If she were naked, instead of in combats and baggy sweater, she'd be in the perfect position. Is she aware? It's all I want to do right now: make that most intimate of connections. Forget Michelangelo's finger-touch on the Sistine ceiling. *This* is the communion of the physical with the spiritual: the joining of the organs of communication and continuation. The kiss at the doorway of eternity. The motherload of motherhood. The source of all that has been created: all that drives the pulsing life of the planet itself. And I want to be down on my knees before it, worshipping, adoring – serving. Right now, I cannot understand how she could be thinking of anything else.

'Well?' she says, nudging me with her toe.

'Not in the mood for another heavy conversation.'

'Why not?'

'Dunno.'

'Oh, come on.'

'I'm not in the mood. Right?'

'You can tell me.'

'What do you want to *know?*' I say.

'I want to know what you think. I want to know what you feel. I want to know why you push me away.'

In the pause that follows, I notice three buttons, left carelessly open at the top of her shirt, allowing me to see most of her neck and shoulder. A hemisphere of breast brings the ensemble together, and raises the picture to a masterpiece. Desire and contempt smoulder together, creating a super-charged erotic feeling that even designer drugs don't give. Demands I make love to this woman, now – as often as possible, for the rest of my life. I'm worn out masturbating. Tattoo nearly caught me the night before, when she unexpectedly came out for a glass of water, left me fumbling my penis into my pants, like a hot potato. I study her face, but she's illegible. The thing is, I know I should be subtle, send a signal and wait for her play. But the urge is too strong, that contemptible male urge, which sends good sense to Jupiter for a holiday. Boys are not supposed to make the running: I should be all demur. All smile and suggestion. This innate urge, older than humanity and deeper than propriety, tells me, with its rumbling voice, what nonsense I am, what nonsense this situation is. There is no such thing, it says, as the nonsense. There is only the urge. I plunge. I splurge. I spread myself like butter on her toast.

'I push *you* away?' I say. 'You're the one keeps pushing me. Ever since I've met you, I can't think straight about anything. You lead me on with all this . . . flirtation and these . . . meaningful looks. You literally *threw* yourself at me in the retro. But when I try to get close, you just shove me away, and behave like you have no idea what's going on. And the sad thing is, the more you mess with me, the more I want you. All I can think of, is getting as close to you, as quickly as possible, for as long as possible. It's getting so I get dizzy even looking at you. And you keep reeling me in and casting me away.' I hang my head, red and pulsing – savour, momentarily, my great moment of shame and release. It's an ejaculation of sorts, and we men just love to ejaculate. 'You've tattooed yourself onto me,' I say, quietly. 'And I can't wash you off.'

I walk outside before she has time to spoil the moment with one of her comments. Standing under the porch, looking at the rain, I fart, rip the shred of meat out of my mouth, and feel, for a few seconds, like a man. When it's clear she's not going to follow, a sickly feeling of having played all and lost, takes over, and I become hollow and pointless again.

#

The following morning, with the rain finally stopped, I lurch off on a solitary walk to indulge my sulkiness. I'm drawn over the sodden heather and guttered tracks by a desire to escape the emotional complexity and self-examination that constitutes a simple conversation with my cabin-mate. Of course, there is self-justification and defensiveness in the mix – who does she think she is, and all that. Mid internal rant, I discover a lake and stop in my tracks, struck by its calm beauty. My heartbeat slowing to the pace of nature, I throw my jacket onto a rock, where I sit soaking in the insinuation of eternal peace.

When I do eventually look at my watch, I see that it's approaching twelve: time to return to the cabin and start preparing lunch. Residual sulkiness tells me not to bother, pointing out that everything I've been doing so far hasn't worked, and that what I really need is a little dignity. In other words: let her make her own fucking lunch. I'm happy where I am. By the time Tattoo finds me, I'm sitting on shale, trousers rolled to my knees. And I'm shivering, having gone, recklessly, for a paddle – where I found eternal peace freezing. When I hear the crunch of her feet behind me, I don't turn around.

'Hey,' she says.

Since my emotional explosion the previous day, our conversations have all actually been monosyllables. 'Hey hey.'

She sits beside me, and we stare across the water. 'Nice lake.'

'Yeah.'

There are ducks in the distance, circling. Flies dancing near the surface disappear from time to time into the solemn glop of a fish. The sun, which is high in the sky, brings some translucence near the water's edge, but this dissolves into the impenetrable black of the centre. Reeds bearding the shore are trampled where I've made a gap, and water foams quietly near our feet. Tattoo hands me a crude sandwich.

'Brought you something to eat.'

'Yeah?'

'Thought you might be hungry.'

'Thanks.'

'Save you killing one of the ducks.'
'Yeah.'
'You're like the lake,' she says presently.
'How?'
'I don't know what's going on beneath your surface.'
'You're like the ducks.'
'How?'
'You never stop squawking.'
'Nice. Good thing one of us is not touchy.'
'What do you want from me?'
'Maybe I'm not looking for anything.'
'What does that mean?'
'Who knows.'
'Eat a sandwich.'

When I flick a piece of crust towards one of the ducks, they change course in unison. Slowing to examine us as they approach, one dips its head and snaps up the soggy bread, while holding us in its nervous eye. Tattoo throws another piece at a straggler.

'Losers need to eat too,' she says. We relax into the moment and feed the ducks. The summer seems to fill the valley and press back the mountains, which are looking greener in the mid-day light. There's a lonely feel to the place, like it's just us and nature. No one's trying to sell us anything, and there's nothing to be enumerated. Unless you start counting ducks – and that doesn't even make sense. What the scene adds up to, is isolation: blissful, undemanding isolation. Spreading herself on the shale, she leans on an elbow, holds me in her eyes. I'm expecting her to say something – she usually does – but this time she just keeps looking. It's one of those pregnant moments, full of mystery and possibility. I get drawn into her brown eyes, and find a history of emotion. I'm like an art lover studying a masterpiece. There's amusement and confrontation, along with a sardonic glint – as you'd expect. But behind the conscious expression, I see flecks of concern and sadness – which fuse, in my mind at least, into a cry for help. It's irresistible, and I edge nearer, opening myself like a flower.

It's the perfect moment for a kiss – which I think she's on the point of delivering, when something frightens the ducks. They rise suddenly, collectively, clattering their wings and squawking just over our heads. Tattoo, laughing like an excited child, stands up and throws a piece of bread into the air after them. There is always something to kill a delicate moment, some banal fucking thing that has to happen at exactly the wrong time. Tearing her sweater over her head, she plunges into the lake before I can stop her. She rises out of the water, still laughing, and throws her head back, sending a plume of droplets into an arc. She screams, and her voice reverberates in the empty valley.

'You better get in here,' she shouts. 'I'm not going through this alone.'

I don't know why I should follow, but I do. Perhaps I'm trying to catch the last breath of a dying moment, or even give birth to a new one. The male animal will never quit. And the male animal must live with the consequences of its single-mindedness.

The freezing water grips. I struggle to make my grimace into a smile as we splash maniacally around each other. We should be graceful mermaids, in a post-coital electric atmosphere, gambolling – toying with each other. Dancing the dance of celebratory courtship. But it never works out like that. For some reason, the numbers conspire against you, and you seldom get what you want. And on those rare occasions when you do, you find that you don't want it. Maybe Tattoo knows all this as we splash each other in the cold, dark water, which sucks our breath and blotches our skin. Because she bobs beside me, holds my hand beneath the surface and whispers: 'Nothing easy is ever worth having.'

Then she's laughing again.

13

Tattoo doesn't seem surprised when I return from a morning stroll and tell her about the camper-vans at the side of the lake.

'Well, it is only Scotland,' she says. 'Not Tibet. There's bound to be tourists knocking about, at this time of year. Come here.'

I'm distracted from further thoughts of campers for the rest of the day by sex – for which she's developed a voracious appetite. Evening comes, eventually, with the mountains turning shadowy before dissolving into murk. The stillness that follows, with which we are companionable, is broken by the distant sound of singing and carousing. Tattoo wants to ignore it, and tries pulling me back beside her, but I've had enough of sex: my testicles are burning and my penis limp – the air in the cabin acrid. Besides, I need someone else to talk to, even if only to tell them about all the sex Tattoo and I have been having.

We finally got it together when we returned from the lake. In the end, she did, actually, put her hands on my chest and push me onto the futon. Not a great believer in foreplay, she straddled me as soon as I fell, asking vindictively, and repeatedly, if this was what I wanted. Which I found disturbing, because the last thing I want is someone even more screwed up than me, expressing sex through pain, or pain through sex – whatever. Though we both relax a bit after three or four epic shags, she still fucks me as though it's an act of revenge. I tried to get her to tell me about herself, during a brief post-coital recuperation, but she's having none of it – which leaves me thinking, as I shower, that sex to her is just another bodily function.

Though it might look, to the undiscerning eye, like I've made progress, I know I haven't – not really. I'm being used. And my inner paranoia tells me that I am also being scrutinised: this latest development will be used against me at some future date, as yet another example of an inability to connect with other people, or some other dull human failing. Those judges in the chamber of my skull, will point to my vanity and to how it blind-sided me into thinking I was somehow worthy enough to deserve the glory of a relationship. The hope of being loved, like so many of my illusions, has evaporated in the broad daylight of reality. Fact is, even the uggos of Dublin's cattle-marts made me feel better about myself than she does. Tragically, her indifference has made her more intriguing, and as I gingerly soap my balls, I want her love – more than I remember ever wanting anything. She's this great new country whose interior has to be explored in order to be understood. And I'm the Boy Scout for the job: dejected, confused, yet trekking on.

'Come on,' I say from the doorway. 'Let's just say hello. What harm can come from it?'

She snorts, as if she knows the answer, but comes along anyway. A few minutes later, we're making our way towards the noise, when she says: 'Let's just check things out first. Before we announce ourselves.'

This makes me uneasy but, too drained to argue, I bottle up and follow, as she circles the camp to the ridge of a small hill, where we lay on our stomachs to observe. The vans are in a semi-circle around a fire, above which you can see the tattered remnants of some animal clinging to a makeshift spit. A small crowd hunch around, drinking, and though I can't make them out in detail, I can tell they aren't pretty.

'What are youse looking at?'

A child's voice makes our hearts jump. We turn to see a girl standing in the gloom. She's wearing a dirty dress and holding a golf club, a driver, the head of which she cradles in her hand.

'Who the hell are you?' Tattoo hisses. 'You frightened the shit out of us.'

'Who the hell are *you?*' she says back. 'You're the ones is spying on our camp.'

She has a slurring Scottish accent, which modulates to the rhythm of the club bouncing on her palm.

'Did we frighten you?' I ask. 'We didn't mean to. It's just that we're staying at a cabin nearby, and were wondering what the noise was.'

'Ye didnea frighten me,' she says. 'It'd take more than a pair of poofs the likes of youse could frighten me.'

Her defiance is highlighted by a bent smile. Though the kid looks as if she's never had a decent meal, she acts like she's Chief of Security.

'OK,' Tattoo says, with a respectful eye on the club. 'Now that you've discovered us, we'd better go down and say hello to the family, eh?'

The girl walks behind us, as we make our way towards the camp. As we near, I shout: 'Hello the house.' For fear we would catch them by surprise and get shot.

'Shut *up*.' The girl spits on the ground. 'With your fucking *Hello the fucking hoose* – ye'll frighten the dogs and wake the bairns.'

As we walk into the camp, the figures, who turn to face us, come into focus in the firelight and we slow our steps. It's like we're walking onto the set of a horror-vid and everyone's ready for the shoot. Fiery shadows dancing on ravaged complexions make me think these characters can't be real. But there's more than theatre here, there's pain: the faces are sliced with scars, and their hanging mouths are scattered with broken teeth. Everyone's been beaten up at some point, apparently. There's an assortment of styles: some wear kilts; others, combats; one or two sport hi-viz waistcoats over naked torsos. They're thin, stooped figures who hang their heads like vultures and glare up suspiciously. They're gross, swollen people, with inflated bodies and massive, immobile limbs. None seem to have normal proportions. They make the uggos I've been chasing in Dublin look like beauty queens – like Emily. Their children slouch or hunker, sucking bones, looking more dangerous than the adults. Bottles and flasks lying around the site, add to the debris of whatever has been on the spit. We stop, instinctively, on the edge of the circle of firelight, and fidget. They look us over, while a pup yaps and the fire cackles. I'm about to say something by way of small talk when one of them, a large man with enormous female breasts, stands up.

'Who the *fuck* are youse? And what the *fuck* are you doing with our wee Jinny?'

'Found them spyin', so I did. Up above there on that there ridge,' Wee Jinny says.

'We're staying at a cabin nearby,' I say, trying to sound urbane. 'And we heard your singing. We just came over to see what was going on. That's all.'

'To see what's going on? So, you're a pair of bastard spies all right.'

'Oh no, absolutely not. We were just wondering what the noise was, that's all.'

'You tellin' us now that we can't have a party under the freedom of god's sky? That we're dis*turbing* you?'

Pagans, I think. With their 'god' mention, and wooden crosses hanging around their necks on leather straps.

'What? No, anything but. Glad of the break, actually, and to meet new people. We've been on our own a lot, you see . . . .'

A soft shoulder-poke from Tattoo tells me to shut up.

'Then what the fuck are you doing way out here?'

With eyes bulging in the firelight, he looks ferocious, as though he would think nothing of shoving his ham of a hand down your neck and reefing out your heart. Tattoo, gripping me above the elbow, edges me away.

'Hey,' she says. 'If you're going to be all pissy, we'll just fuck off back to where we came from.'

'Yes,' I say. 'We'll let you get back to your party. Sorry again for disturbing.'

There are already three of them blocking our path. One has a squashed red socket where an eye used to be. Another, as far as I can make out in the shadows, has a scar running diagonally from her left ear to her right nipple.

'You going to stand there and let your man do all the talking?' Big Tits wants to know.

'Why not? He's so good at it.'

The face winces as he tries to comprehend the joke.

'Why don't ye just sit down and join our party?' he asks, suddenly cordial.

When I look at Tattoo, she's holding his eye in a way I don't like: brinkwomanship – the cause of so many inter-female problems.

'You can stick', she says impolitely, 'your . . . *party* up your . . . .'

'We'll be on our way then. If that's okay with you,' I say, hoping to neutralise her insane antagonism.

'Ye talk stupid,' Jinny says, peripherally.

'Well, ye see, it's *not* all right by me,' Big Tits says. 'How do I know that, soon as ye get back to yer cabin, ye'll no be calling the local security to have us moved on?'

He, or she, or it, becomes even more menacing, looming over us like a bear with tits, daring another contradiction. I can see that he's irritated by Tattoo's attitude. *I'm* irritated by Tattoo's attitude – which has a talent for getting me beaten up.

I say: 'Well, if you insist. Of course, we'd love to join you.'

'There he goes again, Jem,' says Jinny. 'Talkin' like a poofter.'

Twirling the club expertly, she holds me in a stony stare, sensing that I'm the weaker one, the easier prey. She, I decide, is a dangerous little bitch. I can see her breaking my knees with that club, then smashing my head as I'm crawling away.

'As a matter of fact, we're glad to have a bit of company,' Jem says, putting his arm around my shoulder, his mood taking an implausible swerve to affable.

Over the following hour or so, the fire's warmth, together with the hooch I've been respectfully gagging on, slides me into a relaxed mood. The woman with one eye is not so bad – once you've drunk enough to be able to look at her directly. She's telling us the story of the knife-battle that turned her into Cyclops.

'I was in refo-camp in Glasgow, and this monster from Oslo, Ossie, wanted my endy-smokes. Well, when you're locked up like that, the only pleasure you've got's your smokes, so I tells her to piss off. So she challenges me to a fight. It's like that, inside. Ye have to fight for everything. She's way bigger than me but I dinnae care. I'm prepared to die for them smokes and she's got to know that.'

'Aye,' Jem says, enhancing with insight. 'You never know until you have nothing, just how important the wee things are. Gertie's right, them's the only things worth dying for.'

'A few smokes?' I say, not getting the point.

'So,' continues Gertie, 'we fought non-stop for weeks, me and Ossie. Ye cannae get away with long fights in refo-camp, so we fought with days between each blow. That's the most vicious fightin'. You have to keep your hatred up for weeks. She hit me with her teapot in the queue for dinner. I stabbed her in the ribs with my fork at supper. The next week, she punches me in the throat, and the week after, I knees her cunt. And it just keeps goin' and goin'. All the other prisoners kept sayin': "Just give her the smokes." They already had, and was gettin' her stobies in return. But I wouldnae. I was only a poor woman, with neither share nor stock, but my dignity was worth more to me than my life.'

Her sunken face becomes remorseful, and you can read the history of hardship in its lines. I've never thought about people being *this* dispossessed. Those who've been left behind by the great booms –and there are plenty – are thought of more as shirkers than victims. The privileged elite rationalise that the numbers are the same for everyone, and if the dispossessed only put in the effort, they would take out the reward. Yet good people – people like my parents, who lack connection and therefore opportunity – are never given a chance to partake in the rewards of the Corpo-society, not really. They still worship at its altar, and play their part as customers or non-franchised workers at the lower end, but they never really belong. No-boomers. Laura has fought hard for her children: every day has been a bare-knuckle fist-fight, and every night she staggers home beaten up and spent. Do this drudgery for a lifetime, and you just might scrimp enough to get your daughter to Corpo-college, where it all begins. Despite the obvious injustice, she's bought and paid into the Corpo-ideology, and no one's going to take it away from her. She might be in a gulag, for the hours she works and the holidays she doesn't take, but the dream of success is there, backed up by the proof of numbers. Sometimes I believe that clinging to this is the only thing that keeps her going. The Corpo-dream.

Back at the campfire, the gargoyles remind me of the mechanics in my hometown, the way they live by a different rule-book. Only, the campers seem to have torn up the rule-book and wiped their arses with it. Looking them over, I wonder if they are contemptuous of corporatism, or if they even understand enough to be bothered. They look like they're more concerned with where to find the next tin of beans, than the rights of the individual in the face of the collective. Maybe they're free, or maybe they're just poor. I look from face to battered face, trying to figure it out, until I come to Tattoo. She's sitting on the ground with her elbows on her knees, dangling an empty bottle of hooch ruminatively. There's something about the way she's hunched that makes her look edgy, like a coiled spring. Sensing my gaze, she glances over and, seeing what I suppose must be my unfocused drunken eyes, turns away.

'And when the bitch came at me with her spoon,' Gertie drones on, 'I knew the last thing I was ever going to see with that eye was that spoon. I was in surgery all night, but they couldnae save the ball.'

There follows a silence, because no one knows what you add to this. The silence develops into an inebriated acceptance of the hardships of life. Even the dogs have settled, resting mournful snouts on front paws, in the fire's hinterland.

'Well?' I ask eventually. 'What happened Gertie? Did she get your smokes?'

'She did, aye. There was nothing more I could do. Didnae want to lose the other eye. You see, Ossie knew I had something to lose after all. My sight.'

'Did you get even?'

'I wish I could tell ye I got her afterwards, that I tracked her down and killed her when we both got out. But it doesnae work like that. The strong finds ways of making the weak give them what they want. That's the way it's always been, far as I can see. With me one eye.'

A collective snigger inspires Jem to lighten the mood. 'We're all afraid of something, me lad,' he roars, giving me a hearty slap on the back that sends me lurching forward. 'And d'ye know what scares the crap out of me?'

'Newborn babies?' Tattoo says.

'Newborn . . . ? Whaa? Ah, ye mean the tits?' He gives a loud laugh. 'That's very good, that is. No, no, it's no so much the bairns. What scares me is that this evening will end without us having had a song from our honoured guests. Now come on, yer Irish, yer notorious fer yer singing.'

'Well, I'd hate to offend you, Jem,' I say, because he's looking directly at me. 'But I don't really know any songs.'

'Oh, for Fucius' sake,' Tattoo says impatiently, before erupting into the entire thirteen verses of the Intercontinental Corpo Anthem, her face hard with patriotism.

'*Let the numbers set you free,*' Jem says afterwards, repeating the last line. 'That's what it all boils down to all right: freedom.'

There was a general mumble of 'Aye aye' and 'Wi' the grace o' god' – which amazes me, because I can't imagine that any of these have done a day's work in their lives. The song is so ingrained, I suppose, that no one really listens to the words any more. Jinny turns to me and, nodding towards Tattoo, says: 'Are you her bitch, then?'

'Yes, I'm her bitch,' I say, glancing at Tattoo – who returns a look which says: I'm the sad-bastard mayor of sad-bastard town. I crawl over unsteadily, and whisper: 'Don't be always putting me down.' Before I collapse heavily with my head on her lap. She leaves it there – probably out of pity – and I lie listening to the long rambling songs of the campers, something about some dude called Lord, who has a shepherd. I don't know if I've fallen asleep and am therefore dreaming, when I open my eyes and see Haichu, sitting cross-legged at the far side of the fire.

I hadn't noticed the terracotta floor of the freezer before, but I watch now with detachment, my blood edging along the channels between its tiles. The floor, which is at eye-level, turns into an interesting mix of reds, as my blood reaches, and blends with, a pool of urine. The matt of the tiles is complimented by the gloss of the blood, and appeals to my sense of colour-coordination. The pool continues until it meets a glutinous pond of puke, which it encircles gently, sending exploratory capillaries into its interior. It's this detail that dominates before I lose consciousness. I can feel it going as though it's being dragged away on a wave. I can see, in those seconds, the soles of my assailant's bare feet, her twitching heels disturbing the surface harmony. There might be someone calling my name, as if from a distance, before the wave crashes and encloses me in darkness.

#

The first thing they do is separate us. I don't know where they've taken Tattoo, but I'm dragged into the cellar.

'This is Martha,' Haichu says. 'She's . . . a memory therapist, and will be helping motivate you into recalling . . . any information that may be of interest.'

The way she carefully removes and folds her jacket onto a case of the Doctor's wine, tells me that this Martha considers herself a flash butch. But she has her useful side too. A hoofing thump into my stomach has a number of effects. Some, like insensibility and instant pliability, I'm sure were expected; another, a gush of hoochy puke which explodes over the gloss of her shoes, comes as more of a surprise. It doesn't perturb her, though, beyond a muttered curse, as she motivates me out of my clothes and onto a chair, where I sit with my hands tied behind its back. With professional adroitness, she lashes my ankles to the legs, exposing my bollocks. As she kneels to check the knots, a fat tongue emerges, to slide along her lower lip.

'There,' she says, with a last little tug on the cord before she stands up with the pride of a job well done. Unbuttoning her cuffs, she rolls up her sleeves, glancing from me to Haichu and back to my bollocks. Her eyes have that hair-trigger alertness that goes with violence. Martha will have ideas about herself; ideas about entitlement.

The cellar has previously been such a friendly place, a place where I could peruse frozen food as a prelude to the ritual of Tattoo-pleasing meals. Those same sacks and stacks are ominous now, like silent witnesses. A lamb carcass is swaying, like a pendulum, following earlier contact with Martha's shoulder. I decide, in my infinite optimism, to brazen it out.

'Information?' I say vaguely, as if unfamiliar with the word. 'I'm sure I have no idea what you mean.'

'Oh, but I think you do,' Haichu says, like a villain in one of the Doctor's vids. 'Yes, that little mouth of yours looks perfect for blabbing.'

'Well, I'm sure I don't know what you mean.' I try a distant expression, as though I'm struggling to recall some forgotten detail. 'I don't know what you think I might be *blabbing,* or who exactly I might be blabbing it to. But I can assure you, I'm no blabberer. I've had no opportunity to blab anything to anybody. And I don't know anything to blab about, anyway. Really, I don't. For Fucius' sake, I can't believe that a little misunderstanding about blabbing is what this is all about.'

'You can stop blabbing now, for a start,' Haichu says, with a backward swish of her hand across my cheek – which stuns me into silence. 'And I will reiterate what we both already know. You saw that woman outside the club, the one my women were . . . restraining.'

I shrug, and survey the rest of the cellar, cloudy now through my tears. Try to look anywhere but her eyes. I hate that they can see me naked.

'Woman?' I say. 'I don't seem to recall . . . .'

'Turns out,' Haichu says, 'She was some kind of undercover operative, sent to infiltrate my organisation. I mean . . . please, what did they expect? And now Security is looking for witnesses, making a thing out of it. They have it in for me, you see, for various reasons, only they're finding it hard to get evidence. They caught you and your girlfriend on hele-vid, and now all the little busybodies are searching high and low, buzzing around like insects. You've been on every screen, you know. You're quite famous. The missing witnesses.

'I can save you a bit of trouble there,' I say. 'Yes, I did see a woman in a pinstriped suit, and yes, I was aware your thugs murdered her. I've already passed on a detailed account, including a full description of the victim, to my advocate. I've instructed her to send this information to three of her colleagues, and those three, to three more. Each one has been instructed to release this information immediately to Security, if any harm comes to either myself or Tattoo.'

Assuming an interested expression, she looks at Martha, who jerks the corner of her mouth in amusement.

'Who,' Haichu asks carelessly, 'is Tattoo?'

'Tattoo. You know, Tattoo. The girl I'm with.'

'Ah. Is that her name?'

Now I feel terrified *and* stupid. I've never actually asked Tattoo her name.

'It's her nickname.'

'And what's her real name?'

'You know, I've never actually asked her,' I say conversationally, proud of my composure. Not bad for a boy spread-eagled on a chair with his balls exposed.

'Well,' Haichu says, 'if you do not know her name, then how will this great team of advocates know who it is they have to protect? No, if you had done as you say, you would have to have had her name. I think this is just a little bluff on your part. But to make sure, I will go and ask . . . Tattoo, her side of this story. It will not go well for you if your stories do not match.'

She turns to Martha, who now holds a cosh. 'Don't let him freeze to death.'

Martha sits with a buttock on a crate, when Haichu leaves, fingering the cosh. My bladder, never much of a friend at the best of times, collapses, and a stream of urine pours down my thigh and pools around my ankle.

'Animal,' she says quietly. Grabbing a handful of my hair, she raises my face to hers and repeats: 'I said, you are nothing but a dirty animal. What do you say to that? Pretty boy.'

Staring at the snaking blood-vessels of her eyeballs, I sense the close physical presence of a man-hater. To her I'm a piece of meat, as all boys are, and like all boys, I am exploitable. Her slick composure is fragmenting, now that there's no one worth impressing. I was already shivering; now I begin to shake.

'Please. Don't.'

This she acknowledges with a flick of gratitude in her greedy eye: my abjectness is making this more interesting. Slowly, she walks around me, patrolling the perimeter of her prey. When she stops behind my back, there's an excruciating pause, before I feel the pressure of a hand mauling my shoulder, followed by an examining slap on my thigh. The hand slides thoughtfully up my back, as though it's examining horseflesh.

'No. Please.'

In front of me again, she says: 'You say no, but you mean yes. I've seen your file. I know what you like.'

'No.'

Her cosh, glancing off my ear, slaps my head aside and leaves it limp on my shoulder.

'You like uggos,' she says. 'You like it rough. I know what turns boys like you on. You pretend to be afraid, to be all pure and innocent. But you love it.' Grabbing my chin, she kisses me roughly. 'Don't you?'

There's a brief respite, as she fumbles in the pockets of her jacket for something. Her expression lights into a leer when she finds and arms a small hypo, with which she pierces my thigh. Following fast on the initial pain, a river of warmth washes through my body, from the frozen tips of my ears to my numb ankles. It surges onwards, through my blood, into every vein, before settling on the confluence of my penis, which miraculously and immediately stands erect. When I look up, Martha has removed her trousers and stands naked from the waist down.

'No, please.'

But words are useless. They're feeble things in the face of a physical situation. Words are for dinner parties, or for arguments in controlled environments like work, or a café. I know that words will not make any difference, but I say them anyway – adding to my erect impotency. From far away I hear Elia calling, telling me dinner's ready and that Laura will be home from work soon. I want to call back, to tell him I'm in trouble and I need help. I want the reassurance of his lap. I want his smile, his lumpy stew and his boring stories about his childhood. I want to be four again, and for someone to come into the cellar and carry me away, for me to be someone else's responsibility. Martha holds my head between her hands, like a melon she's about to squash, and forces her lips onto mine.

'Kiss back,' she says driving a fist into my kidney. I slump, too weak now to support my own weight. She pushes her thumb into my neck until my jaw drops. I feel her tongue slither like a lizard into the cavity of my mouth, to probe the dead weight of mine. She grabs my balls and squeezes, sending streaks of pain through what's left of me.

'Kiss back,' she says, into my face. Tears stream, as I will my tongue to flip around hers, and the pressure on my balls relaxes. Fumbling open her tunic, she releases a large breast and pushes it into my mouth.

'Suck.'

Its spongy texture makes me gag; my stomach wants to crawl up through my mouth and make a run for the door. Using ball-pressure for control, she keeps me sucking until she's ready to slam me into her. When she does, her weight sends us crashing to the ground. Me and the chair are hauled upright by my hair and she punches me in the face, causing my nose to explode. Wiping her bloody hands on my chest, she remounts, more carefully this time, and begins slapping my ears, like a bass drum, to the rhythm of her thrusting. Whatever she's given me means I can neither come nor lose my erection, so Martha has all the time she needs in the slow-moving shadow of the lamb carcass. With her own ideas about what she wants, she alternates between licking the blood on my face and beating it.

I drift in and out of consciousness, considering, for the first time in my life, what it would be like to die. The cellar becomes a rollercoaster: bags of frozen shrimp fusing with bare light-tubes, merge with wine crates and Martha's jacket. It becomes one mess, as though I'm looking into a washing machine. Then a force, cleaner and more definitive than the mess, intervenes, and our bodies judder. Her heaviness becomes flaccid and peels away. Then I fall too, in slow motion, to where terracotta fills my horizon.

14

When I open my eyes, the terracotta has disappeared, and I'm encased in the cool blue light of a car cabin. Tattoo is driving, her face intent on the instruments.

'What's going on?' I say, with a voice that sounds like a bugle. Reaching to my face, I find my nostrils packed with cotton wool. But there's no pain, just a disconnected numbness.

'We're heading back to Ireland,' she says, peering at the sat-nav.

'What's going on here?' I parp, indicating my face.

'You were bleeding all over the place. I gave you something for the pain. Don't you remember anything?'

There's no concern in her voice, just irritation at having to explain. I try to remember, not wanting to appear brain-damaged.

'Parts,' I say, disjointedly. 'The cellar. After that . . . .'

What I *do* recall, makes me shudder. Laura once told me that a woman who has had a baby can never have the neck to be precious about her body again. But I never truly understood that whole tenuous link between self-esteem and body. Not until now. Now I realise, for the first time, what a spendthrift of my physical sanctity I have been. What happened in the cellar has turned the volume up on all my secret issues, and splayed me like a dissected frog pinned to a wooden board in a laboratory. Martha, having read my file, has turned me, with brute force, into the person I was pretending to be. The fantasies have been dropped on the lab floor, along with other entrails, like self-respect and choice. I have now actually become the piece of shit I always pretended to be.

'Try not to talk too much,' she says, sounding as though this is more for her sake than mine.

And for a while, I am quiet as I put together the fragments of recall. There's still a lot of fuzz.

'What happened to Martha?'

'I smacked her with the cosh.'

The way she puts it, it's as though this is ordinary, everyday behaviour.

'Oh,' I say, equably. 'Think I remember that, now you mention it.'

Pushing the throttle-lever forward, she sends us into a dive, before banking dangerously onto a lower road. There's something going on. I'm about to ask what, when I realise I'm naked save for a blanket that has been thrown over me. This, I pull about myself nervously, as the car steadies. I need time, and sit looking out the window, trying to straighten garbled thoughts. But all I can do is stare dully at the orange lights of a cross-channel turnpike, streaming against the black of night. Rain drumming at the windscreen is pushed aside by frantic wipers, whose persistent burr becomes the only sound we can hear. Tattoo starts fiddling with a sphere-phone she's not supposed to have, sending messages.

'We over the ocean?' I say.

'Yeah. About twenty clicks out.'

'Where we heading?'

'South-west.'

'Who you messaging?'

'Friends.'

There's determination on her face – which makes her look like she knows what she's doing. This, at least, is reassuring. The weight of my head becomes too much for my neck, and I drop it gently onto the window, where, without any warning, tears begin to dribble *from my eyeself-respect going nowng and hnd* that hardly deserves to be called a response. I continue, my words *tumbling . . . o the cabin. I ne.*

'Thank you,' I say, hoarsely.

'For what?'

'For rescuing me. For caring enough to take the risk to get me out of there.'

She grunts, not unpleasantly.

'And I thought I was so independent.'

But this plaintive cry for attention is lost in her preoccupation. Checking something in the rear-cam, she opens up the throttle and the car surges forward, narrowly missing a freighter, before dodging between several cars.

'What's going on?'

'Those fucking campers ratted us out to Haichu.'

This isn't what I asked, but at least it's interaction.

'For the reward?'

'Yeah. They jumped us, but I managed to get away. Double-backed to the cellar, where I discovered you and Martha.'

'Did you kill her?'

'Don't think so.'

'You should have killed her.'

'Martha?' She says the name like there's something familiar about it, like Martha's some old codger who has to be known, to be appreciated. I'd like to know where exactly this is coming from, but Tattoo doesn't elaborate: she's too busy swerving violently under, over and around other vehicles. By now, I'm terrified – would be pissing myself, if I wasn't so dehydrated. I need to talk, to be reassured by her. Meeting her, for all its difficulties, has interrupted the isolation. She's entered me like a light, and shown me parts of myself I've never seen before. For some reason, she makes me feel almost whole – which is something I find I desperately want. Battered as I am, I'm beginning to understand what it is I've been chasing all these years. Intimacy. Everything else is just fluff.

'Am I badly hurt?'

'You'll live.'

'I don't feel too bad, considering. There was a time there when I genuinely did not think we would be seeing each other again.'

Another grunt. I continue, words tumbling out. 'I knew you'd come for me, though. No matter how bad things got, I just kept saying to myself: she'll be here, she'll be here.'

Nothing. I try to reroute the conversation through her, in the tradition of the awestruck male. 'How did you manage to get us away? There was such a big gang of them.'

'By putting one of the vans onto automatic pilot,' she says, studying something on the dash. 'And sending it through the campfire, while I stole another.'

While this isn't much, at least I'm getting some attention out of the moment – and moments are important things to me. I have always preferred the gratification of a moment, to the sacrifice of the present for some dreary future that might never happen. Clicking something on the sphere, she causes two metal antennae to click from the its base. This is no regular phone.

'Where did you get the phone?'

'Stop talking, will you.'

Removing a panel from the side of the sat-nav, she places the antennae into the connection and fiddles with the keys. There's an electronic hiss, a few sparks, and the sat-nav goes blank.

'What are you doing?' I say. 'We'll never find where we're going now.'

'If we can see the satellite, they can see us.'

I'd like to know who exactly 'they' are. I imagine, absurdly, Haichu sitting on a satellite with a pair of binoculars. Tattoo is getting snippy, so I surf onto safer ground.

'How did you get me into the car?'

'I'm trying to concentrate. Keep quiet.'

A horn screeches nearby, as we drop off-road, into the empty black night. We swerve into space, away from the turnpikes, until they become thin fluorescent ribbons, shimmering in the distance. Though still terrified, I work up the composure to say: 'I'd just like to know what's happening, that's all. I think I have a right to know what's going on.'

'OK, OK. Fucius. I dragged you out of the cabin and you came around after a couple of minutes. You were able to walk and all. When I was doing the camper-van thing, you went wandering around naked with a huge grin and this ridiculous erection – totally out of your tree. But you did what you were told, and got into the van when I asked.'

Her voice is cold, in the pale glow of the cabin. It feels like there's a distance growing between us, in the small space. But my inner-self dismisses this unpopular thought, like a head waiter waving a street urchin from the back door of a fancy restaurant. Whatever bit of common sense I had, has been knocked out of my head by Martha's cosh, and I don't want it back. The car dips suddenly, in a pocket of turbulence, and she leans forward to examine the Altitude Indicator before making adjustments to the ballast. We level, then climb, but we're still going fast enough to be in trouble if we hit another pocket.

'Slow down, will you,' I say. 'You're making me sicker than I already am.'

'We're in a hurry.'

'Why?'

'Haichu and Martha are a couple of clicks behind us.'

'What? They *followed* us?' I say, like it's some kind of an affront. Looking around, I see two pinpricks of light in the distance.

'That them?'

'Yep.'

'For shit's sake, put your foot on it and get us out of here.'

'Relax.'

'That's easy for you to say. You have no idea what they did to me. What they put me through. I was raped, you know? Have you any idea what that's like? You don't seem to care much, from what I can see. You haven't even asked me if I'm all right. Well, I'm *not* all right. Thank you for not asking.'

This last part I semi-scream; the rest has been a mere anguished sob. The thought of seeing Martha again zaps me with terror. Tattoo, leaning over, gives me one of her incisive slaps. A back-hander this time.

'Calm the fuck down. You're not helping.'

In shock, I sit with my hand covering the stinging patch on my face. Although I don't know why I should even be surprised any more.

'It's OK for you,' I say after a while. 'You weren't the one who was raped.'

'Not the time, Li.'

'Not the time? Is that all?'

My voice begins to quiver, though I'm careful to avoid another slap. She doesn't notice, is too busy configuring the manual navigation system with quick fingers.

I repeat: 'Is that all you have to say about what happened to me?'

'What?'

'I've been raped, in case you hadn't heard.'

'Look,' she says, 'now is not a great time for drama.'

Unable to restrain an offended tone, I say: 'Is there anything I can do to help?'

'Yes. Shut the *fuck* up.'

I feel like telling her to pull down immediately and let me out of the car. There's no way anyone should be spoken to, let alone slapped like that. But we're a half a click over the Irish Sea, being pursued by dangerous criminals, and I'm wearing a blanket. Now, I have to concede, is *not* a great time. I determine, however, in the silent safety of my head, to have this out with her at the first opportunity, and make my point in a calm, rational way – which will leave her no option but to apologise. And I'm pissed off about being slapped, pissed off at the ease with which she uses violence as a means of control. I mean, women are always preaching about how they're the great listeners, the great communicators. This hypocrisy pisses me off too.

I could hit back, but this is something men just do not do. Not using our physical advantage, has become so ingrained as to make the idea preposterous. This doesn't stop me thinking about it, though. Closing my eyes, I can hear the swish, and feel the thud, of hitting Tattoo with a blunt object. This gives a flicker of satisfaction. There have been lots of occasions and reasons over the years when I've felt like clouting somebody, but never has the old impulse been as strong as at this particular moment. But hitting Tattoo is not possible – not when she's driving, and not when she hits back – so I settle on a pout and decide to restrain myself, until we reach that safe place in the future, where I can make my point.

'Can we stay ahead of them?' I say, when ten minutes of silence has crawled by on its hands and knees.

'Hopefully.'

'Where are we going?'

'Ireland.'

I try to remain patient.

'Where, in Ireland?'

'Later.'

My ribs begin to burn, and my left arm to ache. I groan. Whatever she's given me is wearing off.

'Here,' she says, handing me a small pill, which I gratefully swallow. Soon I'm all dizzy and happy again. Though I already miss our cabin in Scotland, I imagine another Shangri-La, this time Irish, where we can continue our lives together. Her shitty attitude is most likely a result of the pressure she's under. Let's face it, all of this can't have been easy for her either. Everything will work out. She dips the car over the lights of Ireland's eastern conurbation and into the heavy traffic of the lower zone. Having zig-zagged up and down through screeching cars in the City's busy roads, for what seems like an hour, we come to a rugged stop over my apartment block. I wonder how she knows where I live, but drop the question: add it to all those others I mean to ask at a more opportune time.

As the car powers down to the roof park, she turns and takes my hand. 'Will you trust me?' she says. 'I realise this has been a bit of a shit-storm, but I know some people who can sort it out.'

'Who are you?' I say, but she just smiles – a soft, endearing smile that sends a harpoon through my gut to snag on my heart. Right now, I'll do anything for her, and anything she's ever done to me is forgiven. That's the type of gratitude you get from a man in love.

15

I've never been to Athlone. Hovered over it, maybe, on the way to the Galway Races. It never registered. Has this reputation, like a lot of midland, that it's to be avoided. And now I'm powering towards a parking lot on the outskirts, having finally received instructions from Tattoo, who wants me to meet her in some joint called the Random Inn. These instructions take several days to arrive – days spent in varying stages of perplexity. At first, I'm convinced Haichu and Martha will come knocking. This terror lasts for a while, but gradually melds into the lesser fear that I will be hauled in by Security to answer questions. When scans of the news-blogs reveal nothing about a murder in Manchester, let alone WANTED posters of me and Tattoo, fear dilutes into anxiousness.

Stubbornly cautious, I venture out only when it's absolutely necessary: once to buy provisions, and once to get my hair done. Being mindful of their safety, I make no attempt to contact my parents. Nor do I turn up at Ningbo Digits for work, having become, by now, entirely indifferent to that institution and its utilitarian demands. When word finally arrives from Tattoo, it's in the form of a vid-text. The one-way message, which can't be argued with, tells me to go to Athlone.

The town is built around the Shannon, and I see, as I lower the car onto a graffiti-splotched multi-wall on the outskirts, a shanty, spreading like a rash from the banks of the river. Nobody speaks about poverty. Because it's not supposed to exist. Though people concede the existence of 'the poor', they're referred to like another race, one that has *chosen* counterculture. Real poverty is a real bitch when I meet it in Athlone. It's the smell that gets you. Smell penetrates, and tells you this is no 3D or Corpo day out. You're on a high wire, and there's no net, so you'd better tread carefully. That's what the smell says. It's burnt rubbish and sewage. It's a mess of other effluents you don't want to think about, as you walk around pot-holes on the bridge, which leads from the car park over the river. It begins to rain, looks like it's been raining forever, as I kick through sodden litter on the main drag. Blank-eyed children appear, flocking around, blocking my path and nudging me with battered print-machines.

'Few creds?' they ask, reasonably. Insolent rats, their wet fur slick, loiter along drains, unhindered by bony dogs more interested in nosing around split trash-sacks. Trash-sacks don't bite back. Old women in chairs outside corrugated huts, look through me, while men wander purposefully, carrying bundles or attending to shacks they call home. Others shoulder children too young for the print-machine mob. Further along the street, younger women clump in apathetic groups, drinking or chewing endo-smokes. A group outside a bar leer as I pass, but like most no-boomers, they live in fear of the things money can do and, making me for a boomer, leave me alone.

It's not until I find and enter the Random Inn that the kids piss off. I watch them wander away in disconsolate groups, as I brush the rain from the sleeves of my jacket. I've given them some money but it's never going to be enough. Looking around, I see that the bar is lit by a single bulb, the green blush of which makes the four patrons hunched along the counter look like they've just returned from their own graves. There's a musty smell floating on the general stench, which seems to originate from a sodden jacket draped over a chair in front of the glow-heater: someone else has just come in from the rain. The heads look me over before making a point of ignoring me.

A stooped Chinese behind the bar must be the owner. It's unusual, but not impossible, to find Chinese running business-es outside the Corpo. Some are retired, others disgraced – for reasons we will never know. She says she's busy, when I ask to speak to her, so I order a small beer and tell her I'll wait. This amuses the clientele – who look like they're easily amused. I feel their eyes burning into my back as I make my way to a table, where I start the waiting. The only other occupant of the bar is a succulent bluebottle, which swerves drunkenly between the light-bulb and the heater. It seems at home here and set-tles on the next table, to show off its glistening green waistcoat. From time to time, following a fart or a painful burp, one of the other bar-flies glance in my direction, with triumph or apology – it's hard to tell from their cement faces. These are old-fash-ioned women. The type who believe young men should not be unaccompanied in a public house. When they're not scoping me, they gaze at a vid-screen where Chinese cart-races play to the incomprehensible squeals of a pep-fuelled commentator.

Time passes slowly when you're in a bar on your own. Eventually, the beer in the bottom of my glass warm, I make another sortie at the Publican, who tries to repel me with the broadside of her hump.

'Look,' I say, 'I'm supposed to ask you about someone.'

'Yes?' She's evasive – polishes glasses and rubs beer-nozzles to underline her indifference. It's not really acceptable, never mind wise, to be rude to a Chinese, but this one's old and alone.

I've already asked her to look, so I try a different approach. 'Listen, grandma, this is important. I'm looking for a woman . . . .'

'I'll be with you in a few minutes,' she says with a rasp, reminding us both of her station.

With inborn obedience, I bow and retreat to my seat.

'Stand you up, did she?'

One of the bar-flies swivels towards me. There's a shadow of brutality on her face, which reminds me of Martha and sends a shudder through my sphincter. Another man-hater. Someone else laughs, a brief nervous giggle that both acknowledges the swiveller's dominance and pleads with it to go easy. When I try to look them over, all four have turned back to the screen and resumed a protective hunch, where they start muttering among themselves, as if I never existed. I try to make them out, but they're just shapeless lumps of people, as perennial to in this bar, and all bars, as the grey sky that hangs over Athlone. I let them get on with their farting and return to my head, where I'm putting the final touches to the conversation I'm going to have with Tattoo. There are lots of questions in there, and the list keeps growing.

#

'Please,' I say to the Publican, following another half-hour of pretending to be fascinated by my sphere. 'I need to talk to you. It's important.'

'OK,' she says, with the strained patience you'd reserve for a five-year-old. 'What do you need?'

'I'm looking for a friend.'

'Was there someone in particular, or will anybody do?' the Swiveller says. Though I try not to show it, I'm filling with fear. A tremble creeps though me, and warns that my bladder's going to do its thing if she keeps this up. I'm not as over my Scottish experience as I thought: I'm glass – see-through, and ready to shatter. Somehow, I stand my ground as I wait for the ripple of supporting laughter to sigh to a close. I want to walk out, to wait, hidden across the road in a cardboard box, and hope for Tattoo to arrive; to be in my own company, with only the rats to worry about. Something anchors me – some stubborn instinct.

'Young woman, tattoo over her eye,' I say.

'Ah, a tattoo over the eye. Bit subversive, is she?' says the Swiveller, prompting a snort of dutiful sniggering. They're being entertained: *I'm* entertaining. It's a real novelty to see a pretty boy like me in a bar like this.

'Has she been in?' I say to the Publican, as calmly as I can.

'No,' she says, heavily. 'She has not been in.' Glancing at her customers, she adds: 'Why don't you hang around. We can talk in a while.'

The quiet that follows is broken only by the hysterical commentator, brought miraculously close through the technology of 3D. It's a sophisticated system. You can see the foamy spittle of the frantic horses dribble in ropes from their mouths, and the steam of sweat rising from their scarred flanks. And still the jockeys work them over, cracking, slapping, driving the dumb beasts. I'm sitting there, entranced by the violence, when the door opens and a boy – must be about twelve – enters. He stands for a few moments in the doorway, eyeing the bodies along the bar, before approaching the one that has not turned to look at him. Tugging her sleeve, he says: 'Daddy says you're to come home. *Now.*'

This delights the others, who simulate whip-movements. The Swiveller laughs. 'That's right, go home now, *mammy,* before *daddy* comes in himself to drag you out.'

She looks at me, presumably for affirmation, but I've already turned my head towards the woman being dragged out by her shoeless son. I can see them through the open door as they wander down the street, the boy easily dodging the clumsy cuffs of the mother. She makes to double back once or twice, but he has a determined grip on her sleeve. He's daddy's boy, on a mission that nothing's going to stop. The bluebottle follows them out, zigzagging into the gloom, before the Publican walks over and closes the door.

'Can you at least tell me if there have been any messages?' I say.

'No,' she says. 'No messages.'

An amused groan from the Swiveller discourages me from pressing the point. A while later, another of the patrons, announcing dinnertime, peels herself off her stool and waddles into the street. The clientele, now reduced to the Swiveller and her main sidekick, order another beer to assert their dissidence. I order tea and sit sipping it, not wanting to be tipsy in a dump like this.

#

'This your first time in Athlone?' the Publican says, sitting opposite, with tea of her own. The Swiveller and her friend frown, before deciding to return their attention to the racing. The pantomime is over, at least for now.

'You could tell?'

Up close, her skin is like filo pastry.

'You can always spot a boomer.'

'The clothes?'

'The nervousness.'

'Where's my friend?'

Already lost in the ritual of tea-pouring, she doesn't answer.

'Please,' I say, when she has filled and sipped from her cup. 'You know something. You know why I'm here, don't you?'

'What I know,' she says, between bird-like sips, 'is that you are out of your depth.'

'How do you know that?'

'Well, aren't you?'

This is difficult to disagree with, when I think about it. I've really no idea why anything is happening. A bit of enlightenment – if that's what she's offering – would be welcome, but I've no reason to trust this ancient woman, with her papery skin and gluey eyes. She looks like a walnut, and seems as hard.

'What makes you say I'm out of my depth?'

'You look like you belong in a Dublin nightclub.' She eyes my *shimao* jacket. 'For young men of questionable sexual orientation.'

'What does that even mean?' I say, knowing exactly where she's coming from. It's not only the jacket, it's the whole thing: the hair, the strides, and the mud-spattered calfskin boots, which will have to be chemically cleaned. A boy can't take pride in his appearance, in a place like this, without being accused of this shit.

'We get boomers visiting us here from time to time,' she says. 'Some are sent by the Corpo to assess our situation. Others come on charitable impulse. Either way, they look around, take their notes and move on. We never see them again.'

'I'm not here to take notes,' I say. 'I just want to see my friend. I'm not trying to cause any trouble. And really, I don't give a shit about the Corpo.'

'Yet you dress and smell like one of their whores.'

Right again. The old bitch seems to have a real handle on me.

'I'm nobody's whore,' I say. 'You don't even know me.'

'What's there to know? You're a boom-child. A bottom-liner.'

'You've made your mind up about me very quickly.'

Uninterested in defending her opinion-forming methodology, she continues: 'Most of you don't even know places like Athlone exist. You can't believe that it's possible.'

'That's unfair. You don't know the first thing about me. I'm from Carlow,' I say, like it's a badge of honour. 'I'm as no-boomer as they are.' I indicate the slouches at the bar. They sit obliviously limp-jawed, mesmerised by a yapping jockey giving a post-race interview.

'No,' she says, 'you're a boomer all right. You might be first-generation, a lucky boy, but you're still a boomer, just as they would be if they were given six months of luxury and money. When you have something to lose, your attitude changes.'

'I've worked hard for everything I have, so forgive me if I don't feel I have to apologise.'

Her face crinkles into a dry smile. 'These two,' she thumbs towards the bar, 'would tear you like a piece of meat between dogs, if they got you on your own.'

'I can handle them.'

'No. No, I don't think you can.'

'How do you know? You don't know anything about me,' I say. I'd like to remain cool, but she's really good at goading. I force myself to remember my reason for being there. All I want is to meet Tattoo, make a few valid points, ask a few justified questions, and generally tee her up to a level of respect that will allow me to throw myself at her with a fair chance of getting a response. I don't know why this old bitch is breaking my balls, or where she fits in to the mystery that buzzes around Tattoo.

'On the contrary,' she says. 'I know everything about you.'

16

We walk into the night together, back along the street, past the old castle and towards the river. It's quiet now. The children have dissipated with the dusk, like the dogs and rats. Most of the huts are powered by shards of solar-pads, hanging from wires, on makeshift scaffolds nailed to the roof. These provide the juice for the only light on the street, which leaks through open doors, along with cooking steam and the sound of people eating or arguing. Part of me – the part that makes conversation at cocktail parties – wants to creep over and spy on them. Another part is wary of the reality, afraid of what I might see by looking it straight in the eye.

The Publican, recognising my unease, gives a self-serving grunt. It's the first sound she's made since we left the bar, save for the metronomic clicks of her walking-stick. I'm walking like someone behind a hearse trying to keep *down* with her pace. The texture of the street-smell has changed: thin night air has fused the tang of stewing animal with burning trash and ubiquitous, raw sewage. If the locals mind, it doesn't show. Those who are still about, pause conversations and scrutinise us from plastic beach-chairs as we pass. You can't help wondering what goes through their minds, in the face of the undeniable rottenness of their environment. Though I imagine, like people everywhere, that they would have their spectrum of preoccupation. Food or smokes would be the likely currency, and they would spend their time haggling for one or both of them. Success is relative: same game, different numbers. Tramping conspicuously along the strip with the Publican, I'm overdressed, overfunded and, judging by their looks, deeply resented.

'It is generally better to keep walking as if you know where you're going,' she says.

'Then why don't you tell me?' When she doesn't reply, I say: 'We'd better be going, to meet my friend.'

'We'll be there soon enough.'

There's a couple shouting at each other, somewhere in the clutter of huts, but it's distant, and I can't make out what they're saying. A man seems to be accusing a woman of something; she's hitting back with mocking retorts. A dog barks, punctuating their vitriol. The dog stops when a loud, peculiar laugh resounds in the deserted street. It pitches to a hysterical crescendo, then levels to a mournful keen. There's something empty in the mania, as if the joke is not understood. It's as though the laugh has an afterlife of its own, fuelled by some deviant energy. It belongs to a woman who is sitting on a tin drum in the shadows, hands on knees. She stops abruptly when we near, and stares at us with vacant eyes. A purple tongue lolloping out of her open mouth rests heavily on her lower lip. When we've walked on a few steps, the laugh starts up again. Then stops again.

'Down syndrome,' the Publican says. 'You don't see it Corpo-side because they're killed before they're born. All abnormal foetuses are. But down here in the wilderness, anything grows.'

I've never seen anything like this before, and have to look back to convince myself it's real. When I do, she's still staring at us, opening and closing her mouth slowly.

'It hardly looks human.'

'Of course she's human. She's just different, and you're conditioned not to expect difference.'

'But who looks after her? Shouldn't she be put somewhere?'

'Like a zoo?'

'That's not what I meant. How about a hospital of some sort?'

'Oh, she's able to look after herself well enough. Life is not so complicated here. And besides, we don't have basic medical facilities. Only an idealistic fool would think that we were in a position to provide a specialist service.'

'Why not? This is Ireland we're talking about. Not Florida.'

'Problem is,' she says, 'we can't build anything here. Every time someone shows enterprise, the Corpo moves in and buys them out. They take what they want for their own projects. What we're left with is a husk.'

'Why would they even do that?'

'You really don't understand, do you? The Triumvirate are not beyond scavenging in a dump, if there's profit in it – and they always find profit. Besides, they don't want something to grow out of the weeds that might blow seeds into their flowerbed.'

'Flowerbed?'

She sighs the deep sigh of the exasperated. 'There has to be a loser if there is to be a winner. Something has to be exploiting something else. It's the law of numbers.'

It's not the law of numbers, as I was taught it back in school in Carlow. But I'm not going to get drawn into a philosophical debate, when there are obvious practical questions which are screaming to be answered.

'Why don't they build some kind of a plant down here?' I say. 'Get a bit of employment going. Surely the real-estate is cheap enough.'

'Because it would expose the social problems that exist, and confront them with their own indifference. This, in turn, would question the whole structure of the Corpo system, and raise too many questions.'

'Like?'

'Like whether we should reintroduce income tax, or corporation tax, or some form of social funding.'

This, I find a bit extremist. Asking hard-working people to pay for bums and layabouts is antediluvian. 'So,' I say, 'not only do you want to rob creds from the workers, but you want to disincentivise the no-boomers into the bargain?'

She grunts again, as though this is the only response my point deserves. We pass in silence through a square, in which a statue of Lao Shi stands decapitated. This, I find more unnerving than the filth and poverty: to have a statue of the mother of Corporatism defiled in such a way, is considered on a par with butchering and eating your own children.

'What the *hell*?' I say.

The Publican lifts her slow eyes from the ground and squints at the monstrosity. 'What do you expect? People who have no stake in society have no respect for it.'

'What kind of a shit-heap is this? How can people live in this . . . shit?'

'Every society has to shit somewhere, and this is where the shit ends up. Shit materials, shit opportunities, shit people. By putting it here, it cleanses the finances and creates a healthy economy coast-side.'

'I still don't understand why you don't do something about it,' I say, avoiding a fan of soapy water whooshed onto the ground by a washer-man. He gives a broken-toothed grin, full of self-effacement and apology, before disappearing back into his hut. 'I mean, you must have contacts in the Corpo.'

'I've tried,' she says, dispassionately. 'Why do you think I'm stuck down here?'

I think of the popular image of Corpo society: of the successful, compassionate, well-dressed female, who finds prosperity through her sense of appreciation for the feelings and needs of others. It's a real struggle to reconcile what I'm seeing, with my previous understanding of the world.

'And I thought the biggest problem we had, was the boredom that comes with excess.'

'It probably is. Far as you're concerned. But if people like you opened their eyes and looked around, they would see the real problems of corporatisation. You're either in or you're out. And if you're out, you're a non-entity: part of the acceptable percentage of loss. Nothing is earned any more, or shared. Money makes money, and the boomers, though they can't spend what they already have, jealously guard the power that money gives them.'

'But what about all the charity programmes? What about the masses of creds that are sent to places like America every year?'

'Cosmetics.'

'I always give my point-five to charity. Where does that go?'

'Goes into making you feel good, to stop you thinking too much. Oh, the Corpo will use some of it to buy a doctor visit here or a coat of paint there, but they're not interested in the real problem. They're interested in the perception of the problem, and the impact of their actions on market sentiment. Lip-service and sticking plasters, that's where your money goes.'

'Fucius' is all I can think of saying, to this particular titbit of treasonous allegation. This old publican is really out there, and I'm beginning to wonder if being with her is enough to get me banged up for a serious cleansing, in some first-offenders refocamp. Stopping to catch her breath with both hands on the handle of her stick, she searches for me in the murk with dim eyes.

'If the Corpo publicly recognised the true extent of the no-boomer problem . . . ' she says. 'If the facts and extent of the problem were to become public, the markets would spiral downward. Trillions would be lost.'

'OK,' I say, walking alongside her when she straightens up and starts shuffling again. 'Supposing we accept that as fact: surely they could work away quietly? I mean, the amount of money they waste covering up the problem would probably go a long way towards resolving it.'

'Ah yes,' she sighs. 'One would think that.'

The moon has risen now, and bathes the shanty in its pale

light. It shines on the corrugated roofs, turning them blue. You can see it in the puddles as we walk, its clear reflection appearing and disappearing. We see it again when we reach the top of a hill, on the river that comes into view below us, where it's splintering on the surface – twinkling like stars from a different universe. Huge and low in the sky, almost white, it frames the silhouettes of the huts, and catches their patchy plumes of smoke. All in all, the moon is putting on a beautiful show. At least the poor bastards have this, I think. Even the Corpo can't sell moonlight.

We come into a quieter neighbourhood, where the only thing stirring is the occasional plastic window-flap. A burst of muffled laughter causes us to turn our heads towards a small house.

'A shebeen,' the Publican says. 'Every second house sells illegal booze or drugs around here. There's a healthy black economy. The Corpo doesn't mind.' She twists her little mouth sardonically. 'The black economy. As long as it stays under 0.2 percent of GDP.'

Further on, in a red-light district, boys hang around corners and look at us hopefully. Most are little more than children. I recognise one or two of them from the print-machine gang. They're dressed in a mixture of mismatched rags, stitched together to display sexuality. Emaciated or bloated torsos are exposed under threadbare belly-tops, while tight trousers cut at the calf reveal swollen or withered limbs. They remind me of the 3D that night at the ball with Emily. But these are not American, these are Irish, and they live less than an hour from Dublin. The Publican seems inured to the whole thing.

I'm about to say something, for the sake of not allowing the sight to go unacknowledged, when she says: 'Most of these could have made a contribution to society, if they had been taught a trade or given even the most basic education. Most will be dead within a couple of years, from drug abuse or treatable disease.'

I'm thinking that it's extraordinary how the Triumvirate let all this happen, when a creepy feeling tells me it's not just down to the Corpo. In what's now looking like a former life, I avoided all forms of social responsibility, as most boomers did. My biggest concern was where to get my hair done, or how to fool Emily into taking me seriously. But that's the boomer class. Our idea of social responsibility was to engage in coffee-shop philosophy about which is the best way to distribute the point-five. The Publican is right: it does ease our social conscience to the point of inaction. We rarely think about detail, and we never talk about Ireland. It's always California or Texas or some such faraway place – as different a dimension as the reality-scapes where we spend leisure time hunting dinosaurs.

'It all seems so pointless,' I say. 'Could these places not be turned to make a profit?'

'Oh, but they are. As you are about to find out.'

17

Down an alleyway, just before the strip turns into a ramp that slides into the river, the huts defy prediction by descending, with the road, into deeper squalor. The insects, which have been busy uptown, become part of the atmosphere here and lose all fear. In the end, I get tired of slapping myself and let them crawl where they want. That's what squalor does to you. Looking around, I realise that even a shanty like Athlone has its very own slum. Down here, makes the plastics and rusting iron of the main strip look architectural: at least it's been battered into something durable. Here is all scrap-wood and canvass, which leaves the alleyway looking like a dump, where rubbish has been bulldozed either side of a walkway. And there's very little light: just one or two weak lanterns, deadened by the corpses of insects, or the swirling mass of live ones.

We stop outside a ramshackle lean-to, whose walls are made of agri-Corpo crates. While I'm wondering if we've stopped for another of her attacks of wheezing, the Publican dips under a flap and disappears. A small hand re-emerges when I don't follow, and beckons impatiently. The first thing I make out is an elderly man hunched over a heating tube. I have to look carefully to be sure he's not a corpse. A slow movement of the jaw convinces me. One of his eyes, I notice with distaste, is a swollen pustular slit, over which a fly is crawling. The other, yellow and alert, lifts as I scrape into the room, then drops again – to the limp hands which shake in the space between his knees.

'Who's he?' he mutters.

'He's with me,' the Publican says. 'He's here to hear your story.'

Lifting the eye again, he considers her steadily, until she takes a parcel of food from her satchel and places it on a table-top, balanced on oil drums.

'I told you everything before,' he insists, moving towards the table and stooping over the package. 'You and your researchers, when you came here with your recording equipment. Why go through it all again?'

'Because,' the Publican says, 'I want you to.'

'*You want me to. You want me to,*' he mimics, while he re-trieves a Tupperware container from under the table. Picking the package open with curved fingers, he places three bread-bars and a sachet of dried noodles into the box. When he has hovered his good eye over the contents, he snaps the airtight lid shut, with a satisfied *cluck* of his tongue. Holding the box like it's a newborn baby, he shambles over to a corner, where there's a metal chest embedded in a circle of concrete. Watch-ing us from the cover of bushy eyebrows, he keys in a number, and the lid lifts. The food is pushed in on top of whatever else is in the strongbox, before he keys again, and clicks it shut. This business concluded, he heads back to the tatty armchair, where he sits and hangs his hands.

'I don't eat much these days,' he explains. 'A little bit does me. Sometimes a boiled egg for me breakfast does me for the day. Smokes?'

When the Publican throws him a packet of endo-smokes, the curved fingers come alive, catching them and working expertly to place one between his colourless lips. Drawing a grateful lungful, he looks me over. 'But I do enjoy an oul' smoke,' he says. 'An oul' smoke never hurt anyone. Did it, son?'

I shrug.

'Sometimes I chews the baccy,' he says. 'I likes to have the choice. Sometimes I'm in the mood for a chew; sometimes I'm in the mood to smoke. And it doesn't matter which one I do. That's what I likes about this place: you can do what you wants. Your time's your own, and so's your decisions.'

'Tell him what age you are,' the Publican says.

'Wha'?' Me age?' What would you say now, sonny?'

I shrug again. I really don't know what to make of this old fuck.

'I dunno. About one-fifty?'

This causes him to cackle – which reveals an archipelago of blackened stumps. 'I'm *seventy-three.*'

My mother gave birth to Zisha at sixty-five, and ran a mara-thon at seventy-eight. This man is in awful condition. Elia, who has ten years on him, looks like his grandson. Then again, they've had different lives. Being late for the manicurist is stressful for

Elia – and his biggest dilemma is whether to drink beer or wine with dinner. This oul'fella would have different priorities. He is a caricature of what we were always told would happen to a man, without the care and protection of a woman. This is what we were warned we would end up like: this shell of a creature who lives in a plywood box and can't look after his teeth.

'Start at the beginning, and take your time,' the Publican says.

The patchy jaw falls, and he half-heartedly wrings a hand. 'I was born not far from here, in the parish of Milltownpass. The fourth of six sons in a family of nine.'

I get the impression this is an old story, one that has been honed and rehearsed.

'Both me parents,' he says, drudgingly, 'were farmers, and for me early childhood, me memories is very happy. Then, when I was about seven, me mother died, in an accident caused by a faulty thresher, borried under the scheme from the Corpo. Me father struggled on for a while, but with no wife to support him, he was on a hiding to nothing. Anyways, the pressure got to him and he turned to peppy pills. He borried from the bank and mustn't have been able to make the repayments, because about a year after me mother died, the Corpo took our farm. He didn't have no choice. The Corpo wanted the farm, and that was that. Me oul' daddy was made to sell.'

'That would have been under the Fair Profit Act,' the Publican says. 'He would have been given the market value of the land, minus the money owed and any outstanding interest. The interest is calculated to the end of the term, so as to avoid Corpo-loss.'

'And with nothing to do all day,' the old man continues, 'he went mad on them peppy-pills. Not one month after the farm was sold, he was a raving peppy-holic. Then he was reported by a neighbour under the Info-for-Profit, and me and me eight brothers and sisters were bought and sent to a nursery to be assessed. I never seen him again, though I heard afterwards he was found floating in the Shannon. Anyways, each of us was given tests to see how we could be used.'

A painful look comes over his face, as though the meaning of what he is saying has just caught up with him, and he stops talking.

'Please,' the Publican says, 'carry on. It's important.'

'Sure, haven't youse heard all this before?'

'He hasn't. Carry on, please.'

'Right, right, right,' he says, summoning strength. 'Where was I, anyways? Ah yes. It was decided that two of me sisters would be best suited to service, and they was sent out to China. I never heard from them since. Another sister, Michelle, who was a bit slow, was sent to hospital for 'further assessment'. I never heard from her either. That leaves six boys. All fine healthy lads, we was. Me two eldest brothers, Terence and Sean, was good breeding stock, and were sent to a repro-farm in Sligo, where I believes their stuff was used to father thousands for women who didn't have time for a husband.'

'The rest of us was sent to an orphanage in Cork, where we was to be reared to work in the factories. We was taught how to work the machine and to obey our line supervisors. We was beaten and starved by the women in that place, if we didn't do exactly what we was told. One of me brothers, Eamonn, died before he was ten years of age. That left three. As we got older, we was sent to separate factories, where we became part of a team of under-workers. We slep' on mats, under our machines, and was responsible for their maintenance as well as working them all day. I was in the sock industry. Very important things, socks.'

Here, he pauses for another suck of his smoke, his eyes bulging as the lower half of his face contracts around the butt. His view on socks is both ironic and pathetic when you consider the double fact of his bondage and his bare ankles. Does he know? Is he aware? His timing would suggest he is. He starts up again.

'It was a terrible life. But I was lucky. Luke, me younger brother, was sent to the meat factory, which was much worse. He killed himself at seventeen, by throwing himself into a vat of boiling sausage meat. I heard from someone who worked there, they didn't even bother to get him out, just cooked him with the rest of the meat and packaged him up to be sold. You never can trust a sausage. There were only the two of us then. Me last brother, Marty, died at forty-three, from heart failure. He had worked seven days a week all his life, with only one week's holidays divided over the year.'

'And all for so-called food and board,' the Publican says, adding: 'Under the Work-for-Upkeep Act. All so that the managers could maximise the number of units rolling off the line: give more to the shareholders.'

The old man opens his hands – as much as he can – over the light of the heating tube. 'He was buried in a corner of a yard at the plant, long with many others. While they poured lime over his skin and bones, I overhears two managers talking. They did not care enough about me to be lowering their voices. They says that he had been the product of the three 'P's – piss-poor planning – and complained to each other about the loss of profit that comes from the death of a unit. I'm not sure if they even knew I was his brother, but whether they did or not, they wouldn't have cared. The only thing bothered them bitches, was profit.'

Dousing his smoke in a depression in the arm of the chair that seems made for the job, he raises his wrist and dabs his eye. He's quiet for a while; sits there lifelessly, save for the hands – which twitch open and closed.

I glance at the Publican, who is rummaging in her satchel. 'Here,' she says to the old man, producing a small tube. 'Put this on your eye. The infected one.'

Grabbing the ointment, he sprays his eye-slit and starts to work the lid, to test the effect. It opens a chink, and a glob of pus oozes onto his cheek. He wipes it away, and stares at the smear on his hand.

'Me and Marty was never allowed to take our holidays together,' he says. 'We would wait outside each other's factories when we was off, so as we could come in after work and lie beside one another on our mats. Them days was the only warmth I ever knew. And there was few enough of them.'

'Fucius,' I say.

'Fucius my arse,' he spits. 'Where was Fucius in them factories? They was full of people. Thousands of them, there must have been. They all had to come from somewhere.'

The Publican puts her hand on the old man's shoulder. 'This is just one story,' she says. 'I could take you through this shanty, and you would hear worse than this. The midlands are full of these towns.'

The old man smirks sadistically, enjoying my discomfort. 'How did you get here?' I ask.

'Oh, they lets me go when I was seventy. They do that. They decrease your functions as you gets older, until you reaches the stage when you're no longer worth the food. Then they just open the factory gates and tells you to get out.'

'These people do not have an ideology,' explains the Publican. 'It's not like they are as noble as Nazis, or anything. They just look at the profit-and-loss statement and act in the "shareholder's interest".'

'But sleeping on a mat under a machine? Sounds like something that used to happen hundreds of years ago. I thought we'd gone beyond that.'

'Then you are misinformed,' she says. 'History is not something that lives in the remote past. It is current, all around us. It constantly reoccurs, from the same constituents which created it before. Like selfishness, greed, fear – and the great mute amorality that comes from profit-lust. It has always been easier to rationalise the consequences than deal with the causes. And you, my friend, whether you care to admit it or not, are part of the cause.'

I want to engage, to somehow convince myself that this is not true, but all I can do is stand still, as my eyes fill. Which lifts the old man's mood considerably. He starts nodding his head and smiling, clapping his arthritic hands – though I doubt that he fully understands what's going on. He doesn't have to. I'm well dressed, and that will be enough. To him, I'm every boomer he has ever hated, every line manager and orphanage worker that has ground him down in the name of profit. As far as he's concerned, I *am* the Corpo. It's a cause of great celebration for him to see my ignorance exposed: to see me humiliated.

18

'Why did you show me that?' I say, when we get clear of the hut.

'Because it's all part of the mess that is a numbers game, in which you are an integral part.'

'What numbers game?'

But she just says: 'We need you now. We need your help.'

A single light-tube hangs from a pole at the end of the alley, where it turns onto the hill that leads up to the main drag. Though our pace is painfully slow, and the insects crawl over my face, I keep it together, by concentrating on the light. 'For what?'

'For something that is vitally important, in not only curing the cancer you've seen today, but for the very survival of our way of life.'

'Way of life? What are you talking about?'

'Society is sick, and it's going to die unless we act.'

'But why me? What possible use could I be to anyone? I'm just a boy-slapper. A Corpo whore – as you were quick to point out, back at the pub.'

'Oh, you might surprise yourself.'

'I doubt it,' I say – and meaning it. My inner self – the one that lives under my skin and behind the bullshit – knows how shallow, and consequently useless, I am. It's not that I want to be, particularly, or that I have some great personality deficit. I'm shallow because I can't be arsed being anything else. Meanwhile, my inner voice – that great protector of this core weakness – is telling me that it's time to get away from here: I can sort out my love-nonsense later. Whatever the Publican thinks she's going to get me to do, is bound to be unhealthy, or she wouldn't be going to all this trouble to get me to do it. To escape the situation, a good sales-pitch is required.

'I've lived with *me* all my life,' I say. 'And believe me, I'm pretty useless. Totally shallow. Nothing matters, unless its immediately gratifying, if we're to be honest. I've never made a sacrifice for anyone, or for any cause, other than myself. I just don't *care* enough. Which might bother me, if I wasn't so shallow. I'm a butterfly who flits from situation to situation, from body to body, taking flight before anything moves on from the initial fun. I'm not what you might call an empathiser or deep thinker. I can't possibly be of use in any grand scheme. I'd only fuck it up on you. There have to be gangs of boys out there who'd be better for the job – whatever it is. I'm a screw-up. Seriously.'

The walnut face locks. 'Nevertheless, you are our best hope.'

'And what about my friend, with the tattoo? I was supposed to be meeting her.'

'Oh, please. You think your little love-feelings have any significance?'

'Well, they do to me.'

We pass the light, and continue to move at a crawling pace through the slum, while she hisses away like an old engine. I could just walk away – but that would mean no Tattoo, and the possibility of Tattoo still seems like something that is worth clinging to. I feel a light grip on my elbow: elderly fingers.

'These people to whom you say you remain indifferent, are suffering . . . in a way you must begin to comprehend. And you are part of the system that creates them. Indeed, you are its . . . epitome.'

'Now hold on a second, I'm not taking the blame for this. I didn't know a thing about any of this . . . .'

'You will please close your mouth,' she says. 'Before too many insects crawl in. And listen. If you want to remain on the right side of Corporatism, then leave here now. Shrug your shoulders at the AGM. When they talk about acceptable loss, pretend to understand the empirical cost of success. Carry on as though people like our friend in the hut don't exist. But you have seen now, haven't you? You've seen real ugliness. Ironic, isn't it?'

'Is it? I'm not good with irony.'

She snorts. 'You've spent so much of yourself seeking out uggos, in order to satisfy a craving for realism, and now that you've seen it, you don't want to look. But it might not be so easy to turn away.'

I wonder how she could know about my sexual preferences; I mean, I haven't made a pass at her, or anything. But this doesn't seem like a great time to cross-question her, and we walk back along the strip in silence. Clouds have gathered by now to snuff out the moon, leaving a dark gloom, in which the huts are ominous shadows. An occasional crack of light from behind a flap, is the only action, until we crest the hill and turn on to the main drag. The doors here are open, and there are people around. Two dogs and a boy are fighting in a gutter over a bone, their bodies weaving and snarling as one. An old man is sitting, bare-arsed, in a doorway, laughing at them.

'You see?' says the Publican. 'What they have been reduced to?'

I go over and kick one of the dogs, send it scuttling down the hill with a whimper. The other lets go of the bone and sprints in the same direction. Picking up a bit of rubble, I chase them for a few yards and fling it in their direction. When I return, the boy is crying angrily, and I have to hold him at arm's length, to fend off his kicks.

'What wrong with you? You could have been hurt. Anyway, you have the bone now.'

'It's only a bone,' he shouts, hitting me with it. 'It wasn't worth hurting them over.'

'We must be careful about interfering,' the Publican says, leading me away by the elbow. 'About the *way* we interfere.'

Looking over my shoulder, I see that the boy has picked up the bone and is running after the dogs.

'I'd really love to know what's going on,' I say. 'I'd really love to give a shit, but I just came to your bar to meet a friend.'

'Oh, she'll be here, when it's time.'

Whatever that's supposed to mean. I stand in her path, and grab the meatless bones of her arms. 'I want to know where she is, and why I'm here.'

I'm shouting at her now, frustrated by my own bewilderment.

'You're here,' she says, removing my hands. 'Because you are part of the Numbers Game.'

'What numbers game? I keep hearing about number games. What the fuck is going on with all these numbers?'

19

Back at the Random Inn, the Publican reaches under the bar and produces a bottle of sake. 'Time, I think, for a drink.'

'I think I would prefer an explanation.'

'Let me try to explain like this,' she says. The bar, empty now, has become eerie, the green light from its single tube pressing against the dark night, which presses back through the windows. Rain, which has begun again, tickles the corrugated roof like a backtrack in a horror-vid. We're sitting at opposite sides of the counter, two chess players.

'I *could* give you a free drink, but I need to pay the rent on this dump. *And* I have a fat husband and three useless kids who depend on me to put food on the table. There's also a father-in-law, living in a hut out back, who would eat the dogs, if I didn't keep him well fed.'

'OK, you don't want to give me a free drink. So what?' I'll buy you one, if it's that big a deal.'

'Ah, now we're getting to the point. You can afford to be nice. I can't. Now, *that's* what builds up resentment.'

'You won't buy me a drink, and you would resent me buying you one. Looks like we're both going to be thirsty. Why do you resent me again?'

'I resent you because you *can* buy me a drink and I *can't* buy you one. Your money places you above me, and me, below you. Therefore, resentment.'

'So, there's resentment. Surely there always was, from the poor towards the rich?'

What she's saying does make sense, but it also makes me uncomfortable. Some moral cause is being unwrapped – which always means trouble. There's bound to be a call for action – which, I keep telling her, I'm never going to give. She continues not to listen.

'Yes, but not to the same extent,' she says. 'The rich are so rich, and the poor are so poor, now, that a huge gulf separates them. They cannot even see each other.'

'So?'

Looking at me like I'm the Down syndrome lady, she says: 'What do you think is happening in America?'

'America? It's a Corpo thing, isn't it? Terrorists are trying to bomb the shit out of the boardroom.'

'That's one way of looking at it. Another would be to say that it's an explosion of resentment. Men, Caucasians, Hispanics and other disenfranchised minorities are sick to the teeth of being patronised and told what to do by super-sensitive elderly Chinese women. They want out of a system which traps them at the bottom of the food-chain. They won't be told they can't buy a drink any more, that being nice means being compliant and grateful. They want their own *nice*: their right to argue over a bone any way they choose.'

She pours an inch of sake into two small tumblers. 'Let's make this one little exception, shall we? Cheers.'

'What about your fat father-in-law?'

'Thing is,' she says, 'there is no father-in-law, and I can afford to buy all the drink I want. And by the way, it was my husband who was supposed to be fat.'

'Who *are* you?'

'The question is,' she says, 'who are *we?*'

'Listen, you,' I say. 'You tell me what the hell is going on. Now. Or I'm walking out that door.'

'Walk,' she says, an indifferent expression on her walnut face. 'And keep walking. But the world is not big enough for you to walk away from what is going to happen. Sooner or later, even you must realise, the walls are coming down.'

I've had it with her frustrating riddle-talk, and bang the counter with the flat of my hand. And yes, I commit the ultimate act of disrespect, by raising my voice to a Chinese.

'What the *fuck* are you talking about?' I say, but there's no fear in her. She's just a bottomless pit of patience and wisdom.

'I think now would be a good time,' she says, in a loud voice of her own.

Haichu and Martha appear from the back room and stand on either side of her. They look different: smarter, more alert. The sight of them fills me with fear, and a well-defined memory of violation comes flooding back, raw and real. I make for the door, but find it blocked by the Swiveller, who smiles the slow smile of a predator.

'Sit down,' the Publican says. 'No one is going to hurt you. If you want to understand, you must listen.'

They shove me into a chair. Haichu brings over my glass of sake, and places it on the table in front of me. 'Have a drink. We've a lot to get through.'

She's looking good: she's has had her hair done, and a tight combat shirt is doing wonders for her baby's-ass cleavage.

'Why? So that you and your henchwoman can get me drunk and rape me again?' I say.

'We did what was necessary.'

'What about you?' I ask Martha. 'What were you doing in Scotland?'

'Following orders.' Her eyes are dull and uninterested.

'OK,' the Publican says, as though she's beginning a committee meeting. 'Perhaps a little clarification is in order.'

'Who are you people?' I demand – though where I find the courage to play the spunky underdog, I don't know. Unsurprisingly, I'm on the verge of losing control of my bladder – and possibly my bowels – an interesting, if unnerving, development. The base things, I have recently discovered, come into play during these intense times. We try to ignore them, to pretend that, as evolved creatures, we are somehow too controlled to fart or have an unwanted erection during an emergency. Truth is, we are the body's slave, not its masters.

'We,' Haichu says, with a flourish, 'are members of the *Kang-yi*. You have no doubt heard of us?'

'No. What the fuck is the *Kang-yi*?'

'The *Kang-yi*,' she says, slowly, 'is a secret society comprised of those board-members who no longer approve of the way the Corpos conduct business.'

'Well, if it's secret, how am I supposed to have heard about it?'

'Most people know of its existence. They just don't know who we are and how we operate,' she says – a little touchily, I think. I shrug.

'We seem to be a little at odds with some of our more conservative colleagues,' the Publican says. 'They have a different view of the Numbers Game and of . . . our problems. They therefore' – she stands up and shuffles about, though why she does I don't know, when it's only going to make her wheeze – 'have different solutions; solutions that might be considered *uncivilised* in certain circles. But there is a group of us, the *Kang-yi*, who are no longer convinced that their approaches are appropriate to the times.'

'Problems?' I say, feeling like a character in a soap. 'What problems? And what's this Numbers Game? You'd better start talking: I've had enough of all this cloak-and-dagger stuff.'

'OK then.'

Haichu is the next to speak. 'You obviously live up very well to your reputation of stupidity. Let's start at the start.' She grips the back of her chair, staring at me and shaking her head. A shard of jet black hair falls over one eye, sexily. The two hench-women stand by respectfully, hands crossed at their crotches, suspicious bulges beneath their jackets. Of the two, the Swivel-ler looks more dangerous – which, when I think about Martha's track-record, scares the crap out of me. Both hench-faces are unreadable, and pitiless.

Haichu looks at the Publican. Finding affirmation there, she turns back to me, the shard swinging dramatically. 'With the birth of feminism and the establishment of the female viewpoint, change became inevitable. It was only a question of time. And in time, those attributes that had given men the edge – like phys-ical prowess and a competitive streak – became redundant, as society became more intricate. The problems facing the world a hundred years ago were very serious. We sometimes forget this.'

'Please,' I interrupt, 'we're not going to start a history lesson, are we?' My gut does a little somersault when I say this. My small intestine is about to disgorge itself through my ass and on to the floor, where I can see it making for the door. I can't believe my own words, and have no idea where I find the stupidity to say them. The Publican raises a finger to make a point, but collaps-es into a fit of convulsive coughing. Haichu, with unexpected tenderness, puts an arm around her and guides her to a chair, where she helps her sip from her glass of sake.

Presently, the Publican calms down enough to say: 'Perhaps if you could see your way to indulging us, just a little, things might become clearer.'

I nod noncommittally, and she leans forward, shaking her head and wheezing wearily, gesturing to Haichu to continue. Though I'm moved, my primary feeling is one of relief: not to be having my head bashed off the table by the Swiveller.

'Really?' Haichu says to the Publican. 'You're going to let him speak to us like that. To *you*?'

'Patience,' the Publican says. 'We're no better than them if we do not have patience.'

'As you wish,' Haichu says, before looking at me in a deri-sory way, before continuing. 'The problems of the world could no longer be solved with physical force or brinkmanship. There came a point when it had all been tried before. Failure after failure eventually caused the penny to drop. Men were ousted and placed carefully on the sidelines, where they could indulge their natures without causing any damage to society. Or so we thought. Now we find new problems arising in the modern world, as a result of over-feminisation.'

When she pauses to gather her thoughts, Martha steps over and tops up her glass. She hangs the neck of the bottle over mine, but I cover it with my hand and look away. I want nothing from her. No matter how well intentioned they say this Kang-yi is, I know what they're capable of. Glancing at the implacable soldier, I can't help feeling a little intimate towards her. In the way you always do towards someone with whom you've bumped uglies. It takes me on a disturbing journey back to that first summer in Carlow: to the seeds of deviance.

'Twentieth-century scientists predicted that the atmosphere of the Earth would have evaporated by 2080,' the Publican, who has by now recovered most of her composure, says, in a rasping voice. 'That did not happen, thanks to the Renewables Revolution. They said the world's population would overrun the planet by 2050. That did not happen either, thanks to the addition of certain chemicals to the water supply of what was then the Third World. Other things, however, happened in the vast noodle-bowl of civilisation, that trumped the women of science. For one thing, communications developed at a far faster rate than expected. The world became one big brain, connected by a network of filaments and waves, binary codes and strings. One thought made centrally, one ideology hatched at a high enough level, could be spewed through this network with unimaginable and devastating efficiency.'

She sits back for a wheeze, and Haichu takes over again. 'Information technology became so sophisticated,' she says. 'With information flowing so quickly in every direction, we were able to collate massive amounts of data about the behaviour and habits of the world's population, in a far more accurate way than had ever been thought possible.'

'So? What has any of this got to do with me getting raped or beaten half to death?' I say – again, against my better judgement. I can't help flirting, it seems – whether it's with women or danger. Maybe it's something to do with binary strings.

'I really do not like your attitude,' Haichu says. 'You make it most difficult for us to be reasonable.'

Hearing this, the henchwomen intensify their attention, waiting for the slightest signal.

'You really should behave yourself,' good-cops the Publican. 'You are in no position to throw your weight about. Not only do we have your friend, but we also have, how shall I say, the upper hand in the physical sense. We understand how difficult it is, from a red-blooded-male perspective, to actually shut up, listen and learn something, but in the circumstances, I think you might at least try.'

I look at the floor, sullenly, not wanting to give them an excuse, but my red blood is making it difficult, especially now that she's let slip that they 'have' Tattoo. Sounds like a hostage situation.

'With the merest indication from us,' Haichu says, 'our friends here could make you very uncomfortable. I can assure you, they are very well trained, and would think nothing of removing a finger, or a testicle, if it comes to it. But we are more than happy to carry on with the exposition, if that is your wish – lengthy and vacillating though it may be – with all your body parts intact.'

'Please,' I say, with a generous wave, 'carry on.'

'If you insist,' she says. 'Where were we? Oh yes. We were able to predict how future behaviour patterns were going to unravel. At first the Corpos used this info for purely profitable purposes. Who buys what colour knickers, all that sort of stuff. But then marketing and advertising became an intelligent, ravenous beast. The wealth and consequent power of the Corpos went nuclear. Profits could be predicted years in advance, and this in turn allowed for complete control of the money markets.'

'The Triumvirates themselves still do not know the full extent of this power,' the Publican says, as Haichu pauses to drink. 'To create *and* destroy. They cling to the principle of maximum comfort for the maximum number. They base their morality, such as it is, on meritocracy – where everyone is entitled to be a shareholder if they earn the right. But it doesn't work that way in reality. There are flashpoints of conflict all over the world. There is brain damage, particularly in America, and we don't know how to control it. We have realised there is something missing from the equation. A group of us happen to think that the missing element is the dispossessed.'

'Dispossessed? What are we talking about here? People who have been cleansed of the devil?' I say, before shutting up politely.

'Amusing,' says Haichu. 'What we mean, is men. Men are the dispossessed.'

'Men? What men?'

'All men, you exasperating fool. And all aspects of men: their opinions, their values, their ideas, their attitudes. We don't know how or why, but we need men in the mix: there is something about them, and their relationship with us, that goes beyond the numbers. Without the male integer, it will be impossible to stop the contagion.'

'But don't you already have that information? I mean, if you have the goods on women, why not men?'

'We thought,' says the Publican, 'we had a grip on history, but the fact is that the dispossessed, the losers, have been air-brushed out. What we have is *our* views of them, not theirs. History has been written by the victors, and a chunk of it is missing.'

The light wavers in the bar, flutters like a heart attack, then recovers, causing the Publican to mutter: 'The bloody generator again.'

Haichu says: 'The Triumvirates don't, or won't, see this. Still clinging to past glory, they are entrenched in their megalomania, and cannot consider their system flawed. But the old methods are not working. Men are out of control, in America, and a group of us feel that if we carry on along the present course, it will only be a question of time before the contagion spreads over the whole planet.'

'Which means?' I say, already dreading the answer.

'Apocalypse,' Haichu says, as though it's obvious. 'The end of the civilised world as we know it.'

There follows a brief silence, which is broken by the Publican: 'Hence the Numbers Game.'

'What is this Numbers Game?' I say, standing up, which causes Martha and the Swiveller move towards me half a step. They are waved back by Haichu. 'Sit down,' she says. 'I am sure that if you can control your hormones for just a little longer, you will find out what you need to know.'

'Let's all have some sake, and relax,' the Publican says, and I sit back down.

Martha fills my glass –without asking, this time – then does the same for the Publican and Haichu.

'And what about Tattoo?' I say. 'Where does she fit into all this?'

'Who?' The Publican looks confused. 'Oh, you mean Daisy? Well, she's one of us.'

'Daisy? Is that her name? Please don't tell me she's the same Daisy who was my childhood friend in Carlow.'

'OK.'

'Well? Is she, or isn't she?'

'Not important.'

'Can you tell me where she is now?'

'Oh yes,' says Haichu.

The rain has become heavier, persistent on the roof, drilling into the wet ground. All over Athlone, the dispossessed will be behaving in predictable patterns: picking washing off lines, plucking children off streets, closing doors and windows, shuddering as they button up raggy jackets. In the bar, we sit and listen.

The Swiveller, walking to the window, looks into the street. 'Why don't we just get it over with?' she asks. 'What's the point in telling him all this?'

'Because,' says the Publican, 'we need him to come in voluntarily.'

'Come in?' I say. 'Come in where?'

'You're part of the Numbers Game. You have vital information, and we need to carry out some tests.'

'What information? And what fucking tests?'

'We need,' she says, obliquely, 'to do a little operation. It won't hurt, and there will be no lasting effect.'

'What type of operation?'

'Nothing much, just a little tap-about with your head. Won't hurt, and you'll be as right as rain afterwards.'

'*Brain* surgery? You must be joking.'

'Why,' asks Haichu, wearily of the Publican, 'do we waste time explaining things? He is only a number. And not a very bright one, as has been clearly demonstrated.'

'I agree,' agrees the Swiveller. 'Why don't we just crack him open and do what we have to do? We'll be in and out of there in an hour. Home in time for supper.'

It's the psychotic calm of their faces which causes me to pick up the chair and throw it through the window: an unpredictable reaction for which they are unprepared. The light starting to blink again is also useful: it adds a supernatural feel to the confusion. Having cleared the window as an escape route, I rush out the door – which sends them running in circles. Martha is the first to get it together, and sprints out into the rain after me. She expects me to keep running, as all women would: I'm a man, terrified and alone after all. But I stop running and turn to face her.

She stops too, when she catches up, with a puzzled look on her face. She can't understand that I'm tired of running, that I have played the odds in my head, and know that my best chance is attack. This type of scenario is so rare in their sanitised fairyland, that women have forgotten what a man does when he's cornered. I wouldn't know either, if it wasn't for my instinct – which is well up on procedure. Launching myself at her, I reach for her throat. The lightness of her bones and the softness of her muscle surprise me, as she crumples to the ground. The paraphernalia of intimidation flakes away. She even gives a little shriek, like a damsel in distress, but I'm too far gone for chivalry, and lay into her with a blind and furious passion. It doesn't take long before her resistance weakens and dies. Breathlessly, I get to my feet and see that she's still conscious.

Leaning over, I grab her face in a pincer grip. 'Who's a pretty boy now?'

And I take a penalty-kick with her head, breaking her nose and knocking her out. The Swiveller, rushing onto the scene, skids to a stop when she sees what's happened.

'You want some too, bitch?' I lurch towards her, and she backs off, palms extended, as if to contain a wild beast. I turn and run through the rain, through the muddy streets of Athlone, snarling abuse at anyone who looks in my direction. I'm a rogue male, and if they come near me, I'll tear them to shreds.

As I near the river, my mind begins to slow. Now that I know what their game is, and am refusing to play, I'm probably expendable. But staying and playing would have posed too high a risk: I would have been expendable anyway, once they'd got what they wanted. I wonder, as I jog down the hill towards the bridge, how many others in the Numbers Game programme have been debriefed; how many others have been lobotomised. The dots begin to join. I'm little better than the human waste the old man in the hut spoke about. I'm just another component in a different type of programme, an acceptable write-off in the name of the numbers.

Important and unique as I've always thought myself to be, I'm a poor boy from Carlow, whom nobody knows or cares about. For a brief moment, I was elevated above the throng by the joy of lovem and was presumptuous enough to think myself prime. But now that I know that this joy was based on fiction, it goes farting out of my heart like a deflating balloon. My hand shakes as I open the car door and scramble in. I'm on a major downer. I know enough at this stage to realise that I've been used and made a fool out of, but this doesn't matter. Not really. Not when you compare it to the sledgehammer of loss and sadness that hits, when I consider that I'll probably never see Tattoo again. I purr up the engine and turn south, assuming they'll be expecting me to be heading east, towards Dublin. As the mall and the shanty recede beneath me, I hear a rustle.

'Hey.' Tattoo sits up in the back and leans her arms over the back of the passenger seat.

The car swerves one way, my heart another. 'Fucius. You gave me a heart attack,' I say, levelling the vehicle.

'Sorry.'

The cabin fills with a resilient sense of possibility, which I try to ignore as I bring us up to international level and open the throttle. We thump forward at three hundred clicks. But I cannot ignore an overwhelming feeling. Everything I've prepared in my head for this moment, every argument and phrase, condenses into a mangled grunt, which struggles past my thick tongue: 'Wha' . . . th' . . . .'

'Say again?'

'What's going on?'

'You're really driving this thing.'

'What's going on? You going to tell me?' I find, absurdly, that I'm trying not to sound intrusive.

'Yes, and you're going to hate me.' She grazes the back of her knuckles against my cheek and whispers: 'We still friends?'

'You really Daisy?'

'Yes.'

The lights of the skyway flash past when we break the clouds. Each one punctuates the growing distance between us. There was a time when I would have read something into the tension, but I'm too fucked emotionally. I therefore sit, slumped over the wheel like a wet rag-doll, waiting for her to say something.

'I think I'd better pull down,' I say.

'Keep driving. I've replanted the sat-track in another car, but it's only a question of time before they realise, and relocate us through our personal devices.'

Sliding over the seat, she takes my hand, and I'm drenched with the actuality of the myth that has been living in my head. I take my hand away. 'Just tell me what's going on.'

'You're in danger,' she says, as if this is news.

'Oh yeah?'

'Not from us. If you think we're a threat, it's because you don't know what else is out there. You're on a list. The only reason you're still alive is because they haven't reached your number yet.'

'Why am I on a list?'

'They want to hijack the Numbers Game.'

'Why?'

The question is meaningless from my point of view, because I don't care, but it bridges a gap as I try to deal with the idea of dark forces *out there*, and her being in here, and my name on a list.

'Because of the situation in America.'

'America?'

'Things are really out of control over there. It's a question of when, not whether, the whole thing goes Armageddon.'

'So your friends in the *Kang-yi* tell me.'

'Are you beginning to get how big this is yet?'

Nobody seems to be understanding that I just don't care. But because she is still the only thing I care about, I play along. 'What I don't get, is why they would want to sabotage the project. Surely it's in everyone's interests to use the intel you get from this Numbers Game?'

'It's amazing how little you understand,' she says. 'It's not the ends, but the means, that's in question. We want to solve the problem systematically; the Triumvirates want a more direct approach. Having the Numbers Game as an alternative is undermining their argument. No matter how powerful they are, being women, they need consensus.'

'And this involves me, why?'

She turns to face me, her expression grim. 'We need your data. You are a data-capture unit. We need all the data in order to be convincing. The fewer gaps, the better for us; the more gaps, the better for them.'

'I'm a data-capture unit?'

'A DCU, yes. There were a thousand of you. We're down to the last 80. I need not tell you: every shred of data is as precious as pure water. Yours more than any other, because in your case, we intensified the tests to accelerate the programme. You're our top priority at this moment.'

'And what makes you think I'm going to walk out of this debriefing the same man I am now? They've already admitted they're going to perform some sort of brain surgery on me.'

'Grow up,' she says. 'They're just going to take out your little device and download, put you through a series of tests, ask a few questions. That type of stuff.'

'What's all this about personal devices anyway? I don't like the sound of that either.'

'Oh, it's quite common these days. Micro-devices in the cranium. And this' – she taps the small hole in her tattoo, where the pheromone implant should be – 'holds a micro-camera and transmission device. It was Haichu's idea to record all external data for continual processing, so that we could react quickly as new information emerged.'

'You mean everything that went on between us, went straight back to Head Office?'

'Well, yeah. Otherwise, how could it be a viable experiment?'

'What about now? Are they switched on?'

'They're always on. There's nothing we can do about it. But I've dolloped mine with Vaseline, which screws up the reception.'

'And mine? My personal device: what does it record?'

'All your chemical responses; the rise and fall in your hormonal levels; your emotions; blood-pressure; what you say and do. That kind of thing.'

The sprawling suburbs of Cork appear through gaps in the clouds. We'll soon be running out of country.

'Who exactly is in charge of this operation?'

'It's supposed to be mainstream. A section of the Corpo is working on it, but half of them are actively sabotaging the results. The real work is being done by the *Kang-yi*.'

'Of which you are a member?'

She hesitates. Her training would have told her never to disclose this information. 'Yes,' she says. 'I'm a member.'

'There has to be a Triumvirate, right? Running this *Kang-yi*.'

'Sure.'

'Haichu, the Publican from the Random Inn?'

'Yes.'

'And the third?'

'I don't know. It's a kind of a spy-cell thing. Helps us protect ourselves.'

'What's the Publican's name?'

'Didn't she introduce herself?'

'Nobody ever introduces me to anyone. And no one ever has the names I think they have. Makes it impossible for me to figure anything out.'

'You always *give* names to people, before they've had a chance to introduce themselves. One of your many strange habits.'

The mention of habits makes me think of masturbation – as it usually does. I get a flash image of that futon in Scotland, and squirm to think that not only her, but a laboratory full of scientists, would have known exactly what I was up to.

Part 2

1

A doctor in Brest scanned my head. After locating the implant, she spent hours removing it with a laser-lance. There are gaps in my memory now – now that I don't have the chip to ground me in the present tense. But I do remember pain: pain, you remember. Like the pain of blood and sweat stinging my eyes. And I remember helplessness, as I tried to move in the head-brace – as I arched my back the millimetre the physical constraints allowed, and bruised my wrists against the leather straps. Slumping back onto the table, I began to think about myself. My previous choices had been driven by impulses, which were probably controlled by someone else, or by the chip. Freedom was coming – that much I knew. It was following behind the pain, bringing its consequences and responsibilities. I thought about consequences, and how they stalk your choices – like the one I made to banish Daisy from my life.

I gave a low groan of regret. The doctor, thinking of a different type of pain, gave me a strip of leather to bite on. Cursing or encouraging beneath her breath, she took regular breaks, re-washed her hands, and asked questions to determine my brain function. What was my favourite number? What was three times three times three? How many people in a room of one hundred needed to be happy to satisfy the basic Corpo tenet of *most happy wins*? She grumbled about the difficulty of operating in deep brain tissue. She chewed solemnly on a baguette, as she stared at the 3D of my brain, then spat crumbs, damning the ingenuity of the Corpo-docs. The garlic on her breath intensified in the heat of the foil wigwam she constructed to fool the sat-trax, until I nearly passed out. She leaned her elbow into the hollow of my shoulder as she worked: then I did pass out, from pain and garlic. When I came around, she was still swearing, but her tone was lighter.

'Which is more profitable, division or addition?' she asked, shining a light into my left pupil.

'Division,' I said. 'Division, because addition is one-track, and division opens up endless routes of opportunity. One of the first lessons we learn in Corpo-school.'

Leaning over me again, she rested the hand with the lance on the other, which was gripping my face, before obscuring my view with a large left breast. 'Your brain seems to be functioning normally,' she said, backing away slowly, until I could see the rigidity of her concentration. 'You're still up to speed on your Corpo mantras.' A faint sound, like a kiss, followed by a definitive clink in a kidney dish, meant that the chip had been sucked out through my frontal lobe and that my head had said goodbye to the Corpo. I was sedated while she re-corked my skull, and was kept under for several hours, while the healing drugs did their thing. When I woke, there was tea and toast – which I could barely taste. Then I was asleep again, then awake: more questions, more scans.

'You'll be fine in a few days,' she said. 'Your brain is functioning within normal parameters, but surgery like this always leaves residual pain. Take these.' She gave me a handful of painkillers, which would also help me sleep. She then led me by the elbow to her desk, where she scribbled her fee on a note and handed it to me. 'Justified, I am sure you will agree, under the circumstances.'

It was not what we agreed but I paid it anyway, too dazed to argue. 'There has been as much theatre as surgery,' I mumbled, as I scanned the amount, causing her to smile. I asked for, and was given, a copy of the chip, minus its tracking device. It was from this copy I was later to put together the first half of this journal, during my first stay at Capri. I sent it to Elia for safe-keeping. Of that, more later.

As an encore, the doctor implanted the original chip in a stray cat, which was in the habit of coming to her window for scraps. We watched as the cat squealed and bolted over a rooftop – though watching made me dizzier. The heat of the doctor's breath, and the weight of her breasts on my back held a familiar subtext, as she sponged the diagrams off my sad, bald head. Too weak to be defiant, I let her pass a hand inappropriately over my ass, to signal that we were done. When she suggested I return in a week for a final check-up, I lied that I would. Edging down that narrow stairway, with her arm clenching my waist, I felt more alone than I had ever remembered feeling. As she pushed me into a taxi, I felt I was being pushed in a small boat into an empty ocean.

#

Following days of lolling around a bed in a cheap hotel, gobbling pills and fainting, I crawled into my car and set off southwards. A no-boomer in Nantes, who dealt in second-hand furniture, bought the Toyota for cash – for a fraction of what it was worth. I let her rip me off, though she was an amateur. My fuzzed, scarred head made her shy, which I could have used to intimidate her into a better deal. But I no longer cared about winning: losing was a demonstration of choice, of freedom. Gradually, my appetite came back, and with it some strength. My hair progressed to stubble in the shop windows, during slow walks of recuperation, and fewer people averted their eyes. Feeling well enough to be impulsive one day, I bought a bicycle and started to cycle aimlessly. I cycled further each day until I left Nantes altogether and made my way from town to town, wanting nothing more than to go where and when I wanted, to enjoy the independence that had been lasered from my head.

The span of sky was endless, and the road seemed never to run out of middle distance. I thought about rainbows, dreamt about colours melting together or exploding into fantastic fountains. I assumed it meant something but, being in no hurry, let the images float free of deconstruction. I thought about Tattoo, and her transformation into Daisy. I thought about Daisy, and her transformation into Tattoo – tried to make sense of betrayal, so I could deal with its pain. I supposed that my feelings said more about me than her: so many unfulfilled longings working themselves into despair. I tried to analyse myself. Thought about my intrinsic disappointment in others, wondered if it came from disappointment in myself.

A wave of heroic resignation hit, and I accepted that, although I had been abused, in different ways, I had been naive enough to let it happen. I saw myself on the far side of experience as an older, wiser person, who would know exactly how to handle Daisy, if I bumped into her again. I ran arguments in my head, where I would rationalise my position and expose her behaviour for what it had been: a mercenary, manipulative, premeditated and heartless exploitation of someone whose only crime had been to care about her. I almost crashed the bike coming up with that one. Yes, you could say I was on more than one journey.

I concluded under a pink sunset, on a seawall in Vendee, that my mind was a chessboard, full of black and white squares into whose shapes I had fitted. Discovering I had been one of the pawns on someone else's board, meant that everything up to the point where I had thrown Daisy out of the car had been pre-destined. Now this had changed, I would have to develop new skills, like independent thought. I revelled in the glory of a post-Daisy independence: I had been shackled for so long to a fiction. Letting her go was liberating. There would be no more heart-breaking or face-slapping.

When I closed my eyes, I saw a heavy ball-bearing, out of control, rolling off the chessboard and onto the contours of an unknown land. I was happy with that thought: it felt free. A maggot crawling out of the cheese in my baguette made me think of emergence. I was really getting my metaphors together as I flicked it away. I felt intelligent, for a while, floating in the ether between numbers.

#

A cold spring mellowed into summer as I wandered along the south-western coast. I stayed in the seaport of La Rochelle for about a month, working as a kitchen porter in a large hotel, swimming every day before and after work. My skin hardened to a salt-watery tan, but my hands cracked from constant exposure to chem-cleaners, so I left and wandered on. I travelled beneath the south-European skyways through the farmlands of Saintonge, picked apples for a spell, and watched with narcissistic detachment my muscles harden to knotty gristle.

I began to smile at strangers, loneliness causing me to reach out inappropriately. I was told to piss off by a woman in a café in Bordeaux, who thought I was a hooker, when all I wanted was company. Catching sight of myself in the mirror behind the counter, I could see her point. I had no right, as a bedraggled, homeless creature in a dirty T-shirt, to assume anyone would want to know me. I followed the Garonne as far as Agen, where I cleaned myself up and spent the winter working in an orchard for a widow called Madame Serres. She fed me sweet prunes and tried to screw me. I let her, after a while – often enough to keep my job and avoid paying rent.

'I know you are in trouble,' she said, one evening at her kitchen table. 'But I do not mind, and do not want to know your past. You are safe here, and I am not so very unattractive, no?

Why don't you stay for a while, where you are safe? I need a man I can trust, yes?'

I stayed for a while, not caring enough to leave. The place did have its attractions, like prunes: for the first time in my life, I was regular. But the following spring, the restlessness returned, and I left. It was early morning: I remember, as I closed the kitchen door softly, her heavy Cognac snores. She would wake in a couple of hours and call my name. She would wander out into the yard, hoping I was painting the barn door, which was due to be done that day, and call again. Eventually, in the barn, she would discover the unopened tin of paint, and my bicycle gone.

Returning to the kitchen, she would sit for a while over a bowl of tea and not care enough to follow me. She would rehearse, in her lonely head, the story of our connection, and add it to the others I had so often endured. There would be a new, updated history to be served up to a future confidant: she would tell them, too, about the father she had loved, and the mother who had left him for another man. The dead husband would be mentioned with a sigh, and his life summarised in one or two fatalistic sentences, as it had been with me. It would not matter who the confidant was, whether lover or friend. The widow was in love with her memories, and needed someone to share them with.

I did not care either, as I pointed my bicycle towards Toulouse. I could have written another journal based on my time with Madame Serres, on our intimate interactions and the development of our relationship. I could have written of the small silences and the messages we read in each other, or of the food we cooked and the times we spent in the kitchen talking. There was plenty of substance, in the time of that relationship, in its own present tense: all the components for an involved narrative. But because there was no love, all of that time – like the times of so many indifferent relationships – will be lost forever. Barn doors will be left unpainted, and no one, other than the owner of the barn, will care. But there would be one connection, I told myself that morning, that would work. There would be one relationship in a thousand that would blossom in the desert and turn into something worthwhile, mean something to someone – be honoured with sorrow and joy. It was a numbers game.

I crossed the Italian border at Menton and saved a child from the sea at Alassio. The father grabbed her, wrapping his incompetence in hostility, afraid I would tell the mother and get him a beating. In La Spezia, I found a public *info-stat* and checked my finances. The money I had laundered from my Credit Union account was not doing so well, now that I no longer had the Corpo to ensure my good judgement, but I still had enough. By July I was making my way down the coast towards Naples. I arrived at the bay a bearded, bedraggled figure, at one with his bicycle, at odds with the world.

4

'Yesterday, Don Pietro, I saw a lizard trying to devour another.'
   'Can you describe it to me, my son?'
   'They were on a baking-hot rock. It was midday. The larger had the smaller's tail in its mouth. They were motionless.'
   'What did you do?'
   'I did like you said: I did not interfere. I observed.'
   'Can you tell me what you observed, my son?'
   'One had the other's tail in its mouth, right up to its hind legs. I stayed for about an hour and neither moved, except for the occasional blink. They seemed very relaxed about the whole thing.'
   'Did you observe anything else?'
   'The lizards were similar – the same arrow-shaped heads. Though their colouring was different. One was a deeper green: the bigger one, I think. Their feet were the same, the same rounded toes – which they spread out on the rock, though it was too hot to touch. I thought it strange.'
   'Tell me what else you remember.'
   'I could see the sea below – deep blue. There were some goats rambling around, further up the hill. Their bells, and the sound of the sea, were all I could hear. My bike was lying on the ground, my backpack open, and I could see my bottle of water and half-eaten roll. The grass was sparse and brown. Oh yes, the sky was completely blue, no clouds at all.'
   'How did that make you feel?'
   'The day was beautiful. That made me happy, I think. It was in the back of my mind that I had to get back to the villa to repair the windows. That made me guilty. I was frustrated, to an extent, by the behaviour of the lizards.'
   'Back to the lizards.'
   'I did not know what to do.'
   'What were your choices?'

'I could have separated them.'

'Why didn't you?'

'Experience. I once stopped two dogs and a child fighting over a bone, and received no thanks for it.'

'How might this have impacted on your attitude towards the lizards?'

'I don't know.'

'You must think in order to understand.'

'OK, firstly, I don't know anything about lizards.'

'So?'

'They may not have been victim and predator. One could have been helping the other, for all I know. They did look relaxed.'

'How probable is this?'

'Not very. It was more likely that one was trying to eat the other.'

'And what would interference have meant in that situation?'

'On the one hand, I could have been saving one lizard's life. On the other, I could have been jeopardising the other's, by denying it dinner.'

'Was there any other possible explanation for their behaviour?'

'Might be something sexual – some kind of lizard foreplay. Perhaps one was collecting the other's eggs, or something else too disgusting to consider.'

'Ah, disgust.'

'Huh?'

'Did anything else occur to you?'

'Time. There was very little movement. I seemed to be in fast-motion. The only other things moving were the goats, and ⁓were sporadic. And the sea, but that seemed very far away. Everything else – the whole landscape, the grass, the rock, the lizards, the sky, everything – was so still, it was like it belonged to another dimension.'

'You must explore this some more, my son.'

'I was taking off and putting back on my hat, wiping sweat from my forehead and the back of my neck. I was walking around the rock, looking at the lizards from different angles. I was becoming agitated, but they seemed content to be motionless, to be at one with their environment. They seemed aware of me, but were unconcerned.'

'How did this make you feel?'

'I'm not sure. Omnipotent, maybe? Irrelevant?'

'To the lizards?'

'Yes.'

'Tell me about the goats.'

'The goats, like me, seemed to be intruders. But they at least had learned to be prudent with movement. I was out of sequence. Though in one sense I was the most sophisticated thing in the landscape, in another I was clumsy and out of place.

'Omnipotent *and* irrelevant?'

Yes, I suppose. But what really made me an anomaly was my wanting to make sense of what was going on. The lizards, the goats, the occasional bird overhead: none of them cared. Only I cared. Only I was curious.'

'What does this teach you?'

'I have no idea.'

'Think it through, my son.'

'Well, I have always believed that our environment can be enumerated.'

'Yes?'

'Yet numeration seemed impossible yesterday.'

'Why?'

'Because I was not capable of understanding the lizards. Because I did not understand the landscape. It was impossible to reduce . . . *things* to components. How can you add up what doesn't have a common denominator?'

'How can you become capable of understanding?'

A coin clunked into a slot in my brain, rolled slowly along a channel, then fell into place. 'You can't.'

'Well, what *can* you do?'

'You can try to learn.'

'How?'

'By observing them. By studying them. By learning to live with *their* rhythm. Only then can I begin to appreciate and understand.

'Well done, my son. You have learned much.'

'By understanding that their time is not my time. Their rhythm is not my rhythm. Their sequence is not my sequence. I felt like picking up a stone and dashing those lizards to pieces. And all because I had neither patience nor the capacity to understand them. I allowed my mind to be clouded by my own attitudes and expectations.

'Excellent.'

'Becoming one with your subject is the only way to understand it – by entering its world, its environment, and respecting the way *it* lives.'

'Excellent. Excellent.'

'By not trying to hammer my own assumptions onto my environment.'

'Your enthusiasm does you credit.'

'By realising that bad things have to happen, and that what's bad to us may not be bad to others, or even to the overall scheme of things.'

'Very good. Very good.'

'By understanding that there is no understanding, just acceptance.'

'Yes, my son.'

'By embracing different perspectives and – '

'That's enough now. Go fix the windows.'

5

Of course, the theory is very different to the practice, and knowing what I was supposed to be doing didn't make it any easier to do it. I was still up to my ass in something else's mouth. Though I wanted to be a better person, I was unsure how, and therefore tentative about a personality overhaul. My motivation was selfish. I had no real interest in helping anyone else – unless by so doing I was making myself happier. Yet my role in the Numbers Game, and the residual guilt associated with it, followed me around the island.

What if Daisy had been right, when she said I was critical to a mission that could help avert war – save humankind, and what-not? At the time, I hadn't given much consideration to the detail, being, as I was, intensely pissed off with the discovery of my identity as shop-dummy. But the guilt that had been tapping my shoulder through Europe had wormed its way into my gut by the time I settled in Capri. It gave off a low hum, which left me emotionally volatile. What if I did have it within my gift to help millions of people? If this was the case, then I had fled from a serious duty. That this duty had been shoved down my throat, didn't make it any less of a duty. And all because I'd been in a strop? Sure, I'd been slapped around a bit, but in the overall scheme of things? Then again, I argued, why should I splay my body on the sacrificial altar for a cause I had no interest in? And surely there were others in a better position to help, regardless of what Daisy said – all the lies *she* told. There was a lot to be worked out as I wandered over the burnt grass and rocky soil, carrying out my various chores, and muttering to myself.

But if I wanted to find myself anywhere, then I suppose Capri was the place. Years ago, it used to be a tourist destination for the very wealthy, when wealth was restricted to about 5 percent of the world population – decimal points of a different planet. Now it was a hill-farm, stuck on the outer hub of Naples, and the world's wealth was said to belong to 80 percent – that is, if you used the stats released by the Corpo, which were generally believed to refer to Asia, Africa and the better parts of Europe. Parts of the world people actually cared about. Capri, unable to compete with the massive pleasure-parks of Australia and Africa, gave itself to its goats and lizards. The only people there now were shepherds, fisherpeople and Don Pietro, a kind of caretaker who looked after an ancient villa on the eastern cliffs. No one knew where he had come from, or who had given him the job. No one was even sure who owned the villa. Some said it had belonged to the Catholics; others, that it had once belonged to an emperor. Either way, the locals I spoke to in the tavern – when I eventually got them to speak – were too superstitious to interfere. One toothless old woman told me that Don Pietro was a prophet, and that he had medical skills. He knew herbal remedies and prescribed cures in exchange for bits of food, odd jobs, and privacy. He never joined me when I went to the harbour to drink wine: he spent most of his time meditating or staring at Mount Vesuvius, simmering across the water on the mainland.

One evening towards the end of my first stay, I found him at the fire – which he sometimes lit in the courtyard in a concrete grate he had had me build for him. (My knuckles still bear the scars from that particular 'odd-job'.) He had a way of getting his money's worth. I sometimes wondered if there was any real difference between him and Madame Serres. Both fucked me in their different ways, just as once I had fucked others. It all comes around, I suppose.

Emboldened by wine, I asked: 'Where you from anyway, Don Pietro?'

It was some time before he answered – which left me wondering if he had forgotten the question, or that I was there. It must have been late September .The summer was dying: there was a chill creeping into the evenings. Standing over him, trying not to sway, I looked at the craggy face, lit by a mixture of firelight and the setting sun, streaming through a portico the ancient architect had positioned westward. There was almost too much wisdom in the wrinkles, in that golden light, and with me half-pissed. But I felt I wanted to know him, to figure him out – to know at least something of what he knew. I needed to go beyond myself. On another level, a bit of gossip would be a big help with my credibility down at the tavern.

'Why do you need to know?' he asked presently, huddling into his tatty cassock.

'I don't *need* to know. Suppose I just *want* to know. Curious, that's all.'

'Ah, I see.'

There followed another silence, in which he seemed as indifferent as I was antsy. With delicate, faggot-like fingers, he placed some faggots into the fire.

I tried again. 'Well, I know you are not a native of Capri. The women in the tavern told me that much.'

'Ah, the locals,' he said, staring into the fire. 'I wonder why they find this interesting.'

'Just curious too, I suppose.' I tried to be casual, and to forget my promise to them to get the old man to open up. 'You're obviously a clever man, but you just sit around here all day doing nothing, achieving nothing. I mean, is there any point to it all?'

'What kind of a point did you have in mind?'

'I dunno, write a treatise on the symbolism of lizards, get some recognition, or even, Fucius forbid, make some money.'

I half expected a philosophical backlash on the evils of Corporatism, but when it came, his reply was as dry as the light wind that ruffled his scant hair. 'Why?'

'Why not? You could add your knowledge to the collective, make the world a better place.'

'Do you really think there is a chance my voice would make a dent in the juggernaut of certainty that prevails nowadays, even if I had something to say?'

'No, I don't suppose there is.'

We settled back to silence, and I visualised imparting these gems to the women in the pub, who were disappointed in me for not having more titbits about Don Pietro. This conversation, sparse as it was, was a breakthrough: our usual communication consisted of me being told what to do, or wrestling with cryptic answers to simple questions. When I spoke again, it was with bravado, as if we had broken through a barrier – like we were comrades in an old soldiers' home.

'But seriously' – I leaned towards him, resisting an urge to slap his knee – 'are you ever going to leave this place?'

The women would want to know. I think one of them had her eye on the land around the villa. Besides, I was tired of being patronised by everybody, and wanted to be thought of as having something useful to contribute.

'Leave? Why?'

'You know, go back to where you came from, see the family, whatever.'

'I don't believe in going backwards, only forwards.'

'You are an addition- as opposed to a subtraction-man?'

'Spoken with the convenient simplification of a Corpo-boy.'

'What I meant was, that you might *add* to experience by seeing other parts of the world. There's not much going on here, after all.'

'There is more going on here, than I can ever possibly comprehend,' he said. 'How can I leave?'

'I don't get it. In fact, I don't get *you.*'

'I know you don't,' he said sadly. 'How could you, when there is so much interference in your head, and so little peace. Now go and bring more sticks from the shed.'

Back to standard treatment, where every fragment of wisdom was traded for some task or other. There were a lot of jobs which, as Don Pietro constantly reminded me, were my personal responsibility. It was my job to tend the small flock of goats, which kept us in milk and stew. Or to fish in the nearby bay, or row across it to fetch lobster-pots. There were a lot of running repairs to be done on the villa, to keep the old place habitable. All this had been explained to me that first morning by Don Pietro, as he walked me around the ruins, pointing out rotten joists and broken window-sashes, while slyly evaluating me. I had been happy, then, to accept his terms, to find routine, and not to be smiling at strangers. I complained later, usually over supper, and usually about the racking effects of hard work. My hands were calloused, my once-manicured nails hacked, and my skin, so soft and desirable, according to so many, like a sailor's knee.

'You told me when you came,' Don Pietro said, when challenged, 'that there was much you wanted to learn. Well, hard work will be your teacher.'

When I pointed out I had expected him to do the teaching, he said: 'I *am* your teacher. My method is work. Hard work will lead to epiphany.'

Epiphany crept slowly behind the chores. Yet I was, I think, improving. I certainly felt in better shape than the night I had arrived on Capri, when I drank myself senseless on the edge of a cliff – which I considered throwing myself off. Cowardice came to my rescue that night – sent me tumbling inland, to have another piss and think things over. And it was into this pool of piss, which had gathered beside the wall of the villa, that I collapsed, to be discovered by Don Pietro the following morning. I had refused to acknowledge my past at first, and he refused to ask me about it. Weeks swinging hammers or saws passed, and I maintained, as I had on my long trip southwards, a crust of pride and resentment. It was all I was left with, when everything else had been taken away. Chasing goats' arseholes and staring at lizards, tempered the intensity.

Finally, one day, as I sat near the cliff-edge, I admitted something to myself: regardless of the big arguments, my life would only ever be half a life without Daisy. While all the stuff about saving the world was far enough beyond my understanding to be ridiculous, Daisy was where it was at, as far as my salvation went. This brought the shadowy prospect of action. For days I wandered around the island, gibbering to the goats that she would have forgotten me, found someone else – or never have cared in the first place. I visualised her withering look. Heard hateful words, spat in my face as my worthlessness was established. Her new lover, a Neanderthal with biceps, would have a quiet word, edged with the threat of violence. My humiliation would be complete with a call to security.

Don Pietro asked me if I had learned nothing, when I sought his advice, then left me to my agony, smiling and shaking his head at my questions. I breezily dismissed his indifference, as if the thing was of no consequence. But under the surface . . . frenzy. Daisy had become more myth than memory, an idealised portrait of everything a woman could be. And she, according to our last conversation, was open to contact. All I had to do was reach out. But there was the problem, real or imagined, of her not caring. And of this new boyfriend. I concocted an approach that would allow me to get my retaliation in first. I would spit the truth into *her* face, beat up the boyfriend with a concealed iron bar, and reduce her to begging for forgiveness – which would not be forthcoming. I would turn away coldly. I would drop to my knee in front of her, as she wandered unhappily out of her apartment, a rose in my teeth. I would bump into her in a café. See her in the street, on the vac. There would be a moment. It was only at this point, incredibly, that I realised I had no idea where she lived, or how to find her. Her vid-number was bound to have been a burner, and everything else I knew, or thought I knew, about her, was a lie.

Days passed. The lizards were gone but the rock remained. The sky stayed blue as the goats chewed scrub. The sea crawled below. A wave of determination came over me. It was pointless to wallow in self-pity, when there was no one to witness it. The goats didn't care. I would have to adopt what wisdom I had learned, and be proactive. Weighing things objectively, I decided that degradation was better than uncertainty: the odds, and the emotions, were in favour of me leaving Capri. Somehow I would find her; I *had* to.

I hugged the old man before I left – to his discomfort – and told him he would have to butcher the goat himself. He patted me dryly on the back, then returned to a pot of fish stew I had prepared, with the fish I had caught, on the stove I had built. I stopped to have one last look at the villa, which had been my home for the best part of a year. There was no one at the doorway to watch me go but a tethered kid.

6

Nobody seemed to notice I was returning to Ireland Inc., and no one seemed to care I had been away. Shuffling through Robinson like a fugitive, I half expected to be hurled against a wall by Security. But the Guards were busy posing or eyeing up better-looking young men, and I wandered unmolested through the terminal, towards the vac-station, to catch a local for Carlow. The place seemed bigger. Then again, the bar in the Marina Grande was the most civilisation I had seen for months.

It took me a while to adjust to the great reckless throng, with its individuals hurling along, bumping into each other or lunging towards empty seats on the shuttle-tube. They reminded me of the goats on Capri, being beaten onto boats by shepherds. There was something familiar about the demeanours – some semi-startled resignation-thing – you see in the eyes of the herded. And still the people-counters passed above the swarm, weaving, flashing, counting. Somebody, somewhere, wanted to know what was going on at Robinson International Vacport.

#

Elia was on his favourite chair in the conservatory, a little older and a little tanner. Having just had some kind of anti-wrinkle treatment, his face shone like a small brown beach ball.

'It's a new technique,' he explained. 'They put nano-cells under the skin, which find and fill the creases from behind.'

'Yeah, it takes years off you,' I lied. 'Laura at work?'

'Retired now. Gone to Dublin to do a bit of shopping. She'll be back for dinner.'

'Did anyone call for me while I was gone?'

'No. Not that I know of,' he said, warily – conditioned towards the negative from years of getting things arse-ways. But as he reached a distracted hand towards his crotch, a deep groove formed on his fat forehead.

'Don't,' I said, 'start mauling your balls. I'll go and make us a cup of tea while you think about it.'

As he moved his hand slowly back to the arm of the chair, his face decompressed into a smile. 'There was that one message,' he said, surprised at his own recall. 'Now that I think about it. Some woman. What was it her name was, now? Rosie? Or was it Lily? No, hold on. Poppy. No. Maybe Petunia.'

'Was it Daisy, by any chance?'

'Yes. That was it, Daisy. I remember now.'

I waited, while he fingered his testicles. 'Well,' I said eventually, 'what did she say?'

'Who?'

'Daisy.'

'Daisy? You mean the girl on the phone?'

'Yes, the girl on the bloody phone. What did she say?'

'Well, I don't know really. You see, she spoke to your mother. But whatever it was, it couldn't have been that important, or else your mother would have mentioned it, now, wouldn't she?'

We sat sipping tea, him watching soap, me watching him, and wondering what went on behind the placid face. Whatever scars experience might have left, were hidden under layers of pertox, without which he might have looked like a haggard crone. Who knew? He might equally have been manicured and beautiful, like Emily's father. The affection I felt for him went deep, beneath my shallowness. It was him, and only him, who knew the food I liked, and the correct temperature for my bath. He was the one who passed the regenerator across my grazed knee when I fell, and fed me dollops of medicated ice-cream when I was ill. It was to him I breathlessly told my nightmares, and from him that bizarre solutions were given to deal with the monsters. *(You are the king of your dreamland, hold out your sceptre and say 'Way, way, go away', quietly but firmly.)* I wondered, as I looked at his distracted eyes, if he missed the young boy I had been, and the closeness we shared. He, like most fathers his age, was living in the cavity that was left when children grew up and went away – or, as in the case of Zisha, worse.

The children did not care – went on to have other lives, as I had, with other distractions and priorities. The dependency pendulum swung the other way. The fathers were not invited into these lives, despite their having nurtured the children on their long journeys. Having served their purpose, they were no longer

part of the equation. They were discarded. The mothers were
excluded too, but to a lesser extent. They would always be useful for their money or their contacts. True, there would be some
eye-rolling at the persistence of an interfering mother, but they
were tolerated, even secretly depended upon. Fathers wallowed
out their lives in comfortable nests, then fell apart like spent
salmon, as Elia was doing. It was another numbers game.

'You're sure you don't remember anything else she might
have said?'

'I'm sure. Now be quiet. I'm watching this.'

I had irritated him, and could understand why. His eyes were
glued to the soap, the pulp of which was obviously a high-point
in what was his life. Now, I was the uninvited. A door had been
closed between us – with a DO NOT DISTURB sign swinging on its
knocker. We sat in silence, like strangers, listening to the mincing
pleas of over-sexualised teenagers. I began to wonder if he knew,
or even cared, who I was anymore. Though he had an understanding of my amorality, he would never know the true extent
of it. Nor would he know about the dangers I had faced, or my
cycle across Europe, or the people I had met who had added to,
or subtracted from, what I had become. I had found other things,
along the road, which had replaced him, just as he had replaced
me, with this soap. About all this, he seemed stoical, judging by
his look of abstract contentment. In his mind, he had delivered a
child to the mystery of adulthood; the rest was up to me.

I realised, staring at him then, that in his world there was
no real difference between me and Zisha. One way or another,
his dependent little boys were dead to him, and would only ever
be a memory for him. If he felt sadness or rejection, he wore it
well. Detachment had become a comfortable state, and he had
learned to live without reciprocation. Like Madame Serres, he
had moved into a new present. His consisted of daytime soaps,
tinkering with old radios, and reliving the antics of lost children.
He looked over occasionally and smiled, as if I reminded him of
someone he had once known, and his smile filled an emptiness I
had forgotten was there.

I went to help Laura when I heard her car powering down.
Her skin, looking tired and grey, hung a little looser around the
neck. She moved with the tentativeness of an older woman, but
stiffened to officer class when she saw me.

'Well ,well, well,' she said. 'Would you look at what's decided
to turn up and honour us with its presence?'

'I'm glad to see you too,' I said.

'Don't be cheeky.' She handed me some bags of groceries, like I was twelve, and proceeded to lecture me in the same vein. 'Have you any idea how worried your father's been? Would it have been out of the question to at least phone or send a mail to let him know that you were all right?'

'It was too dangerous. I'm not even sure if it's safe now.'

We walked into the house together, two lumbering beasts weighed down with plastic sacks and a lifetime of miscommunication. She was wearing an acrylic jumpsuit, into which her figure happily relaxed. Following some immutable law of physics, her trim figure had been put away with the business suits.

'Too dangerous,' she muttered, putting the bags on the table. 'Will you listen to him? Well at least you're all right, I suppose.'

Elia came into the kitchen, robed in concerned curiosity. 'Did you get the Jaffa cakes?'

'Yes, sweetheart.' Unseen by him, she gave me a look, to register what she had to put up with. 'How could I forget the Jaffa cakes, when it's all you talked about all morning?'

He smiled at her foolishly, before transferring the smile to me, looking for indulgence – which I gave, with a little look of my own.

#

'She didn't say much,' Laura said, as she handed me and Elia the groceries to be put away. 'Just asked if we could take a private message to pass on when we saw you next.'

'That's right,' said Elia, as if he had been up to speed all along. 'She just asked us to pass on the message, and hung up.'

Laura made me wait until we had eaten before giving me the phone, arguing that they had waited long enough to see me, and the least I could do was sit down and have a civilised meal with them. I sat quietly and ate dinner, for Elia's sake. It consisted of fried squid, bok choy – and listening to how well my sister was doing, in her new job as a lawyer at a Corpo-bank. Afterwards, I left them sipping sake and eating Jaffa cakes, while I took the phone into what was still, absurdly, my bedroom. It was strange to see her in my old room, all three dimensions of her, standing obliviously among my toys and football posters. The sudden appearance of her image sent a shockwave through me, which re-broke my heart.

'If you're seeing this,' she said, 'you're still alive. If you want to stay that way, you need to listen.' The figurine hesitated, though it had obviously rehearsed what it had to say. The real Daisy had struggled with delivery. 'As you now know, we were both pawns in something big,' she explained. 'Something important. I know we had times, and that we had feelings. Neither of us could deny that. But that doesn't matter now. *We* don't matter. We're only two digits in the overall mess. I wasn't lying when I said lives were at stake – and you can include ours in that. We missed our chance to settle things when you pissed off. Now everything's fucked. Your best chance is to forget. Forget everything: me, all the things you were told, and the people we messed with. I don't need to tell you how dangerous *they* are.'

'You need to disappear. Somewhere; anywhere. Don't tell anyone where you're going. And I mean *anyone*. I've told Head Office you were on the game in Paris and, as far as I was aware, you were killed by an unhappy pervert. It's the type of surreal crap they're inclined to believe. And if they do believe it, you're relatively safe. Your chip was found up a stray cat's arse in Brest, so to a degree at least, you're off their radar. But if you print, or your ID shows up on anything, they'll trace you and kill you. Me too probably, for lying to them. So, do not try to find me, or to do anything heroic. You'll be killing us both.'

And that was that. The message finished, and her image stood transfixed, its last expression frozen on her face – which, without its tattoo, looked naked.

7

When you're out on the street, direction is not important. It doesn't matter where you go or what you do. I sloped into a bar, ordered a bowl of noodles and watched from a window-seat the street drift by. It must have been lunchtime, because there were businesswomen everywhere, talking into spheres and looking like they knew what they were about. But I could see conformity: the sharp suits and weaving bodies were like Roman numerals dancing in the same stream, being dragged to the delta. They probably thought they were in control, that they knew what they were doing, in the tiny portion of the world allotted to them by invisible forces they knew nothing about. They weren't all conformists: a street artist, a woman dressed grotesquely as a man in an ill-fitting tuxedo, stood on a silver box. With bright lipstick, heavy eye make-up and a small moustache pencilled on her lip, she mocked the stereotype.

The suits smirked uncomfortably when she winked at them, and looked away when she grabbed pretend balls. I had no idea what the point of the performance was. Slouching adolescents thought they were different too, when they stopped to talk to each other in clumps. With their spiked hair, hair shaved in coloured patterns, or heads mutating between both. Their faces were pierced at various points with flashing electro-rings, while their eyes, shadowed and lined, flickered with forced indifference. They were parading, promoting particularity, yearning to be appreciated by another number as an individual – and fearing that they never would. They would have these few precious years of nonsense before becoming useful in one way or another to a waiting Corpo.

A bowl was placed before me, of steaming noodles. Picking up some, I watched them slide off my chopsticks before returning my attention to the street. Everything was moving obliviously.

Fixating on the infinity of faces, I zoomed in on expressions in the brief time of their passing. Some walked alone, others in company, talking, not talking, staring stonily ahead, listening to their earpieces, wanting to be left alone, desperate for companionship – searching their spheres for the answer to whatever was troubling them. It was hard to believe, looking at them, that there was an invisible hand, counting their nuances and collating their futures. Their ignorance frightened me. I took another peppy, to make it bearable.

A man with a baby in a buggy and a toddler hanging on to it clattered into the bar. They were quickly hustled out by the waiter. 'No buggies in here. Did you not read the sign?'

He backed, without arguing, out of the door one wheel at a time. I watched them walk away. There was an aura of poverty about them – made them too tired to be embarrassed. The toddler pointed her head upwards to have her nose wiped – which her father did, with a tissue dragged from the pocket of an old tracksuit – and they shambled on. The waiter moved away from the door, to smiled approval from a coven of arty types dipping chocolate fingers into their capuccinos.

Poking noodles around the bowl, I tried to make sense of my situation. It had been weeks since I had read the message from Daisy and left Carlow, with barely a goodbye to my parents. Now living alone, in a small studio in the basement of an old house, I had not spoken to anyone beyond the muttered monosyllables necessary to buy peppies. At first, I tried to find a hidden hope in what Daisy said, but eventually had to accept there was none. The peppies, which had become my new best friend, gradually nudged her to the back of my mind, where her presence hung like the coat of a departed lover in a wardrobe. Having had it pointed out to me just how stupid I was, I decided that nothing should matter to a man who understood nothing. Which meant I didn't have to think any more. One thing I did understand – something that had been made so clear that even I got it – was that Daisy wanted me out of her life. And without her, or at least the promise of her, my deal with nihilism was sealed. The equations in my head were without their main integer. This reduced me. I had no meaning, and therefore no self-respect. The people drifting by outside had other lives: they could do as they wished, and be what they wanted. I would never take another risk, or try to be anything other than an anonymous person, who others ignore.

Forcing some noodles into my mouth, I chewed tastelessly. Perhaps I would meet a nice woman who would take care of me and stop me from being hurt by the world. Yet to be figured out was what to tell her about my past without getting her va-pourised. All that could wait: I would make up some bullshit, as soon as I got my brain working again. There were plenty of nice women out there, I told myself, who would be happy to look after a vulnerable soul – to take ownership of one, whose life would be nothing without their protection. Perhaps. Peppies made everything possible. Placing my chopsticks carefully across the rim of the bowl, I slowly rested my head into my hands. I was so tired. And all I did was sleep. Or shuffle the short distance to the noodle-house or drugstore. Something inside had rolled over, something beyond the understanding of the number-crunchers. It was beyond my understanding too, but whatever it was, it had given up and laid down like a sick beast. Paying for my meal, and leaving the waiter a scowl by way of a tip, I walked to the other side of the plate-glass and became part of the chaos.

8

When you are on peppy-pills, you don't really mind what you do or where you go, as long as you can get peppied there. Time saw me being dragged further and further into peppy-oblivion. When time had used up all my money, I had to configure new ways of sustaining my habit. I begged for a while, mostly from my parents – who, at my sister's insistence, eventually cut me off. I tried my hand at whoring, and was half-heartedly beaten up by a Pimp, who told me to call her when I got myself cleaned up. Eventually, having run out of other places and ideas, Athlone seemed as good as anywhere. The Publican – or at the very least one of the barflies – should be happy to give me something, even just to get rid of me. A lot of people were doing that these days: giving me money to go away. Yes, I thought, as I swayed onto a local, Athlone was my best chance of feeding my habit, for that short slice of the future beyond which I did not look.

The print-machine mob left me alone this time, and I was able to make my way, without interference, to where the Random Inn should have been. The Random Inn was not there. Instead, steam belched from a laundromat in the place where I was sure it had been. Pushing open the door, I saw a woman with red arms shoving dirty clothes into the mouth of a giant washing machine.

'Eh, 'scuse me.'

In loose blue overalls and with a dirty yellow cloth wrapped tightly around her head, she was the picture of androgyny. An endo-smoke dangled from her mouth as though it was part of her face – which was a darker red than her arms. One thing you could say about this woman straight away was, she knew how to sweat. It ran in rivers down her face – which was scrunched up in defence against the three-fronted assault of sweat, endo-smoke and blasts of steam hissing from the washers.

'Wha'?'

'I said, excuse me – '

'I fuckin' heard ye. I said wha' d'ye want?'

Her cheese-ball ass teed up, as she stooped to haul clothes out of a basket. It beckoned to me across the space between my present situation and my uggo-hungry past. It would not have been beyond me, to reach out grasping fingers and work it over, to giggle boyishly and let her do with me what she would. You are never far away from a lurid thought. And proposition was tempting, in a cynical way. I figured a worker like her must be good for a few pills, and my sinews were beginning to tighten with the first, semi-polite symptoms of withdrawal. Convincing myself I had not yet sunk so low, I said: 'Sorry for disturbing and all, but I was wondering if you could tell me where the Random Inn is. I was looking for the Publican.' I decided to just put all the information out there; get it over with.

'Wha'?' The cheese-ball kept bobbing up and down as she filled and emptied the baskets.

'The Random Inn. Didn't it use to be around here somewhere?'

'Wha'? There was no pub ever anywhere near here.'

'Are you sure?'

'Yes.'

She spoke with the absolute certainty of the ignorant. Her mind, either well duped or paid, held no truck with discussion. Stained linen and steam were her universe.

'I was here a while back.' Addiction urged me on. 'And there was definitely a bar called the Random Inn.'

'Look,' she said, 'I've worked this laundromat for fifteen years. There's no fucking Random fucking Inn anywhere in Athlone. Now, I have eight sacks of laundry to get through by two o'clock. So, fuck off.'

Relentlessly, the ass heaved to the rhythm of her labour – if anything, more intently now, because of her irritation. Even my addiction knew that it was pointless to try get more information from her: she was already hating me as much as anything else in her life.

Outside, I walked a few yards, then turned back to look again at the laundromat. I was certain that this was where the bar had stood. A dog with a bone ran yapping past, towards the main drag. Following its echo through the streets, I could still hear it, faintly, at the river, and turned right along the bank to see where the noise would take me. I had no reason for doing this, beyond the fact that you tend to do a lot of wandering when you're peppied. When I could hear the dog no more, I stood stupidly in a puddle-dimpled lane, wondering what to do next.

Throwing myself into the river was a definite option, but it was a cold day, and I was still confident I could find better ways of cancelling my number. An overdose of peppies and alco-pep was still the hot favourite, but for now, I had run out of ideas, as well as options. There was nowhere to go any more. I was about to turn and make my way back towards the river, and from there to the vac-port, and oblivion, when I was struck by something about the hut, outside which I was standing. I tapped at the flap which served as a door, and waited. Nothing. I tapped again, a little harder this time, and the flap lifted a fraction. Poking my head into the gloom, I said: 'Hello? Is there anyone in?'

He was there all right, sitting in his chair, surrounded by the weak green glow of a tube. 'You again?' he wheezed. 'I remembers you.'

'Can I come in?'

He shrugged. I entered, and the flap fell back into place.

'How have you been?'

He shrugged again. 'How *can* I be?'

Looking around, I saw that the room had not changed. The metal chest was still embedded in its circle of concrete, and the old man still presided over it, with his one good eye.

'Can I do anything for you?'

'You looks like you needs more than I does.'

'Smoke?' I had the half-pack I had lifted from the laundromat.

'You could give me a smoke,' he mused. 'Though sometimes I prefers to chew the baccy.'

Weaker and more remote, he looked like he had been patiently awaiting death when I arrived. It felt like we were making small-talk in the waiting room. The infection in his eye, which was still a tightly sealed slit, had subsided, but a rattle from his chest, when he spoke, indicated that the state of his lungs had worsened. I put the cigarettes on the arm of the chair: they would be no good to me in the hours ahead, when my hands would be shaking too much to hold them.

'What about you?' he said.

'Don't smoke any more.'

'Fair enough.'

'Doesn't anyone come by?'

'Man next door come by every now and then, if he want something,' he said, solemnly. 'He be younger than me. Not so near to dying.'

'What about the woman who was with me the last time?'

'She be dead.'

'Dead?' I examined his face, considering the possibility of asking him straight out if he had any peppies – unlikely though this was. 'How do you know?'

The eye gathered me in. 'Because she told me. She came here and gave me money and food and baccy, and told me she wouldn't be back because she were probably going to be dead. She's not been, this long time, and she would never be neglecting the people around here, less than she were dead. Dogs in the street do be barking it, so they do.'

A convulsion overcame him with the first drag of a smoke; nearly toppled him out of the chair. I helped prop him back up; when he raised his head, the eye was crazy from the coughing.

'You OK? Do you want a doctor or anything?'

The laugh that erupted brought on another convulsion, and he slid to one knee on the floor, before I could catch him. Putting him back in his chair was like lifting a bag of oily bones. I thought then how easy it would be to kill him, to get into his chest and rob whatever crap was in there. But I was held back by the same thing that had stopped me jumping into the river, or off the cliff in Capri: cowardice.

'Did she say anything else?' I said, when he settled, probing clumsily for any thread that might lead to a peppy. 'Anything at all?' It was vital, I supposed in my small manipulative mind, to hide the contempt his slow mechanical face made me feel. It wasn't just his fumbling cluelessness that brought this on; there was also a decent degree of self-loathing – that I was so reduced as to be trying, and failing, to exploit an old wreck like him.

'She did say that if anyone came by, to give them something, all right.' He pointed a finger at the chest. 'It be in there.'

Helping him over to his precious box, I stood by as he knelt like a priest. Remembering his paranoia, I turned away, my heart withering a little with shame, as I listened to him messing with the lock. It had to be creds, or at least something that could be sold. There would be more peppies after all. I just had to keep it together a little longer.

'Here,' he said eventually, handing me a sphere. It was different from the standard personal device favoured by the wealthy. Bigger and heavier, its sides were made up of coloured panels. I placed it carefully on the table. I could get a month's high out of this.

'How does it operate?'

'You talks to it. Like any other sphere.'

'Congratulations,' said the 3D of the Publican springing into being. 'You are the winning sperm. We have left thousands of these spheres all over the world in places where we thought our agents likely to find them. You are the first. The rest of the spheres will self-destruct now that this one has been activated. To business. First of all, you are' – a pink laser-flash shot from the sphere and scanned me – 'Ah Li,' she said, pretending to recognise me. 'Digit 2796, Corpo of Ireland. Stubborn factor 6, Determination, Imagination, Intelligence factor 3. Emotional volatility index 7. Penchant for uggos. In love with love. Emotional connection established with liaison officer after third manipulation. I was expecting a more intelligent candidate with a higher determination factor, but as Napoleon said, give me a lucky general. You must be a lucky one. Numbers work in mysterious ways, and it is, after all, a numbers game. We'll have to live with each other.'

Strange, to see that a hologram could look disappointed. She continued: 'I am now going to tell you what your mission is, and I am programmed to answer questions in this regard. Please talk now, to signal understanding.'

'I understand.'

'Very good. Now, let me tell you what is going on. The very fact that you are looking at this, establishes that I am already dead and that the threat to the Numbers Game has escalated. Indeed, we may have already lost the battle. But one way or another, the war will be ongoing. I can only hope that you are as dedicated to our cause, as those great women and men who have given their lives up to now. You must appreciate, at this point, that the principle behind the Numbers Game is to establish solutions to our global problems, in a fair and rational way. If the Game fails, then the forces of conservatism will seek to provide their own solutions – which, I can assure you, will be far more short-sighted and extreme. Their way, will have the interests of an over-moneyed elite at their core.'

'Your mission, on which an entire future depends, is to eliminate Chong-zi. This sphere will provide you with the creds you will need, and is programmed to serve as your identity-scan for cross-border travel to Seattle. Your cover is that you are on an errand to Chong-zi with important info from the European Corpo, which will help her put down the American rebellion. The sphere is programmed as an 'eyes-only' document which will substantiate your story – that you are under instructions to hand it to Chong-zi and Chong-zi only. Once you are in proximity, you will press the following sequence of colours on the sphere; it is important you press in the correct order. The sequence is: red, red, green, blue, red. Once these colours have been pressed, the sphere will arm. Two presses on the yellow will activate an explosion, which will vapourise any living thing within fifty metres. You will have ten seconds to throw the device away and get clear. It should be understood that you are to give your life if the appropriate circumstances for your escape do not present themselves. Any questions?'

I stood looking at the thing dumbly.

'Very good. The hologram chip in the sphere will now self-destruct. Remember: red, red, green, blue, red. And good luck. All of our hopes are with you.'

There followed a small hiss, and the Publican's grave image fizzled into oblivion.

9

Up until the day I met Daisy in the Retro-café, my only real preoccupation had been pornography, of one sort or another. Money was porn, and the accumulation of creds was erotic with the implied possibility of gratification. Mooching uggos was another pornography: an indulgence so obscene, it was delicious. My clothes, my apartment, the latest car, drugs and alcohol . . . all pornography; all revolving around stimulus. Nothing had depth because nothing would be lasting long enough to need it. In my so-called relationships, I would meet the *glamoraty*, fall instantly into empathy around whatever their issue was, then be gone before we had time to see each other without make-up (which in the case of the uggos was probably just as well).

That was the way I had always lived. Indulgence following indulgence. And now, by slow stealth and with a sneer of inevitability, I had become hooked on the strongest porn of all: peppies. I sat, as their slave or victim, in an empty vac and shivered through the blur of rain-distorted light, carving a fluorescent tunnel through the night. The grand words of the Publican were a pale whisper against the screams of addiction. I would sell the sphere as soon as I got back to Dublin. Better to sell straight away and get high, before my conscience had time to kick in and fuck me up.

Remarkably, I got worse. Five minutes into the vac-ride and it felt like my insides had been ripped out and replaced by a sack of maggots. Five minutes later, they had crawled up my neckbone and into my brain. With shoulders bunched and my navel stuck to my spine, I was trying not to vomit maggots onto my knees, when some student-types, boarding at Kinnegad, fulfilled my worst fears of intrusion. They were a group of boys, on their way to Dublin for a midweek night out, judging by their clothes and high tempo. They prattled collectively and grabbed mirrors off each other, touching faces tentatively in small squares. They brought back a memory of baboons, from a visit to the virtu-zoo with Elia. The maggots inside multiplied, and their sucking turned to screaming.

My head fell against the window and I watched hopelessly the rain blast the glass as the lights below screeched past. Dark shapes lurched from the gloom between villages: trees perhaps, or silent farm buildings. We crossed under the western highway, where the laser-lights revealed the startled red eyes of ostrich. Each one would be tagged and numbered. Its exact time and place of death, mode of butchering, packaging, distribution and consumption all pre-planned. Even the handling of the waste they would become was already known: they would be fertiliser to feed the crops that fed their children. I clutched my stomach, groaned, and fell forward in my seat. The students looked over, but none attempted to help me. I was filth, I supposed, in their eyes.

'Oh, my, Fucius,' one of them said. 'Imagine ending up like *that.*'

Somehow, I struggled to a sitting position. 'You'll end up like this all right, you fuck-heads. Your futures are preordained, just like mine was.'

'I *beg* your pardon?'

'You dream of a life like the one I used to have, but you'll end up doing exactly what they want you to. Because you're fucking ostriches. Success is a dream, a fucking wank: the deception of an inner voice telling you how special you are. It's this dream they'll find easiest to exploit. Wankers. You'll be dragged along with their promises until it's too late, and you won't even see it coming.'

My finger rose and swept in an all-encompassing arc. 'You blind red-eyed fucks. By the time you realise what's happened, you'll already be like the old man in the shack. Waiting for death. Knock-knock. (I mimed knocking at a door.) *Death.* You could see the truth if you looked. Yes, it's somewhere in the nasty little spaces between fixes. In those shitty moments when you're alone and the numbers just don't add up.'

I slumped, and a warm trickle of urine hurried down my leg, leaving a dark expanding stain on my trousers. My head began to whir, and I felt myself fainting. Semi-conscious as I was, I heard them break the silence.

'Did he just call us ostriches?'

'No, I think he said we'd be *fucking* ostriches.'

'Oh, my, Fucius. Imagine ending up like that: some crazy, pepped-out tramp on a train.'

'What was he even talking about? And who's this old man?'

'Who cares? Crazy pepped-out drunk. Looks like he's conked. Let's move to a different carriage before he wakes.'

Which they did, silently and quickly.

'Daisy,' I whispered to their backs.

The door between carriages swished shut, and I was alone again. I fainted and was out cold for what must have been minutes, because when I opened my eyes the piss on my leg was cold. I was already talking to myself. 'And now,' I was saying, 'I'm supposed to accept the role of world-saving assassin. Don't they even *know* me?'

I had no intention of travelling to Seattle and throwing a sphere at some triumvir.

'Daisy,' I said again, 'how could you treat me this way?'

The ember of Daisy was the only thing inside me which was not grey and maggoty. It stretched in a glowing thread, which tried to stitch the mess of the present onto something better. With hands outreached, I was trying to touch it, to haul myself to salvation, when suddenly the vac was hissing to a stop at Mary Harney, and I let go. Things had been impossible enough before: now, the only logical thing was to defy the numbers and all their predestination, by dying.

Somehow, I gathered enough energy to fall off the vac and lurch through the station. Far ahead and beyond my grasp, the students dissipated into the city. I missed their noise when they had gone, watched my feet in the aftermath – watched them flop into puddles and explode the reflected light of neon and the sharp green of the people-counters. I would have to go somewhere, whether to my dump of a flat or a cheap hotel. I would have to devise a plan to either die or live. I made it as far as O'Rourke Bridge, where I leaned against the wall, crying in the intervals between pissing myself and dry-puking. I expected to turn into maggots and crawl away. Instead of maggots, I saw ants – a whole army of them, marching from a crack in the kerb, along the gutter, to a drain several yards away, their black backs glistening green. I could see this detail because I had slid, like slime, down the wall and across the pavement, to their level. I got caught in their rhythm, in the accuracy of each tiny step, and the order of the line. They must have had a purpose, something unknown even to them. Was it the same mysterious force which was impelling me? The same un-configurable thing?

My mouth opened in slow motion, urging a puke which was not there: there was nothing left to evacuate. Instead, my body went into a series of empty spasms, one of which pushed what was left in my bowels into my trousers. There are times in life when you approach the line of danger. An inner light goes off somewhere in your better judgement, to protect you against such things. You recoil from the wasp, veer inland from the precipice, mark your distance from the fire. Worse than the sickness or the physical humiliation, was the realisation that I was lying across that line and not caring on which side I might fall.

10

I awoke, not in a wet gutter or hell, but between clean sheets.
'We've kept you sedated,' a voice said.
'He's falling asleep again.'
'That's good.'
I dreamed I was in a desert gasping for water, screaming noiselessly into the hot, empty air. I dreamed I was being eaten alive on a rock by a larger version of myself. I arched and writhed in my dream, and sweated. There were armies of peppy-pills rampaging through my body, like *banditos*, killing randomly. They wore bandoliers of bullets across their round blue bodies, had drooping moustaches and mean little eyes. There was a large ant crawling out of my brain, its antennae quivering. Again, the starchy smell of clean sheets. Light in my eyes. Voices.
'How is he?'
'Semi-conscious.'
'Well, let him rest awhile. See if you can get him to eat something.'

#

When I regained consciousness long enough to realise it, Elia and Laura were sitting beside my bed, with the demeanour of people looking at an injured puppy.
'How are you?' said Elia.
'*Where* am I?'
'You were found unconscious on the street,' said Laura. 'You're in Saint Patrick's.'
An overarching impression of whiteness and a framed picture of Confucius on the wall opposite confirmed this, as did the presence of a man in the bed beside me. As my eyes adjusted to the white light of the ward, I saw he was older than me, a

bit younger than Elia, and smiling benevolently at our family reunion. He waved his fingers politely from under a layer of restraining gauze. I went to wave back, and found my hands similarly restricted by the incredibly heavy, soft material.

'It's for your own safety,' Laura said, seeing me straining with what little strength I had. 'You were threatening to kill yourself when you arrived.'

'Don't fight it,' said Elia, putting a hand on my arm. 'You'll only make them think you're more bonkers than you are.'

'Nurse!' This squawk, which sounded like a pig being spiked, made me and the man in the next bed jump as far as the gauze would allow. 'Nurse, the junkie is awake!'

Raising my head, I saw a toothless old bastard grinning compliance at a nurse, who had hurried into the ward to press him back onto his bed. There are arse-kissers everywhere, I thought, letting my head drop.

'Now, Derek, that's not a very nice thing to say. We're all just patients in here. Nobody's a *junkie*.'

'Is too. State of him when he was dragged in here last week, pissing and shitting all over the place. Took three of youse to clean him up.'

'Derek, that's enough.'

'Me and Henry were nearly puking our rings up, the bleeding smell. That right, Henry?'

'Really,' said the man in the next bed: Henry. 'It wasn't that bad. I've seen worse, dear boy, probably *been* worse myself, if I could only remember.'

He had what I've heard described as a mid-Atlantic accent. His lower lip seemed to be doing most of the work.

'Why thank you, Henry,' Laura was saying. 'It's always nice to meet a gentleman, under any circumstances.' Turning to me, she lowered her voice. 'Have you any idea how worried your father's been? Any idea of the shame you've brought to our family?'

Being lectured by Laura was like receiving a reprimand from a senior executive in a distant Head Office – bureaucratic and badly informed. I did what I had always done since I was a small child, and assumed an expression of thoughtful remorse, while retreating to a secret place in my head until the barrage stopped. Numerous other points were raised, like my wastefulness with money and the history of my bad attitude – until the nurse, reading from the screen above my head, interrupted. 'Blood pressure's normal, heart rate good. His system is clear too, no doubt about it.' Then, to me. 'How does it feel to be detoxed?'

'Exhausting.'

'You will be for a little while. You've been right to the edge, and that always takes recovering from. I'll get the doctor to look in on you later.'

When the nurse had gone, Elia brought his chair closer. 'You *were* in a terrible state when they found you. Luckily some bright spark thought to print you, and they traced you back to us.'

'It's our insurance that's paying for all this, by the way,' Laura said. You'd probably be in a prison hospital being assessed for dog-food otherwise.'

Looking down at my gauze-covered body, I said: 'Are they going to let me out of here?'

'Depends on whether the doctor thinks you're a danger to yourself or others,' Elia said. 'So please, behave yourself when she comes around, and don't say anything loony.'

'That's right,' said Henry, who could overhear everything. 'Make nice with the bastards. That's what I always do.'

He told me afterwards, when the folks had left, that I'd had another visitor.

'Very nice-looking young lady, I'd say. Blonde, well dressed. Told me not to say anything – that she was an old friend who was just checking in on you. That it would only upset you to know she'd been in. But of course, we old junkies must stick together.'

11

I must have made sufficiently nice with the doctor, as we churned through the reasons for my addiction, because the following week she signed me into the care of my parents. We stuck mostly, during our silence-peppered conversations, to my having been rejected by a woman I was in love with.

'That will do it every time,' she said eventually, closing her notebook. Though I think in the end I bored her into signing me out. Other things helped, like me accepting responsibility for my actions and admitting to myself, to her, that I would work on letting go of my infatuation. We both agreed that it wasn't going to be easy, but that every journey began with a single step.

Laura drove home slowly, as if speed would induce me to go back to peppies. As soon as we arrived, I was carried between her and Elia to my bedroom.

'What now? I asked.

'Now,' said Laura, 'you rest, and get your strength back. We talk about later, later.'

And so I lay listlessly in my old room, sometimes reading, sometimes watching old 3DS, mostly lolling around thinking about Daisy. I was watching a vid of King Kong getting the shit kicked out of him by capitalism, when Elia wandered into my room carrying a plate of grapes.

'What are you going to do?' he asked.

'I don't know.'

He sat beside me on the bed. 'When you were a little boy, Daisy was the most important thing in your life. We were not wealthy, and you, like a lot of the kids around here, were treated like any other number in the collective. But Daisy made you different: she was the thing that made you special. No one else had a friendship like that, and it was more precious to the two of you than any new toy or trip to Funland.'

'I don't really remember much.'

'You would take her here sometimes, for tea. Do you remember? You would sit together at the table, leaning towards one another, lost in whatever secret conversations you had going on. You could tell, even then, that there was something special between you, some deep connection.'

'Why are you telling me this?'

He was turning the sod of memory, laying open old wounds across those which were already bleeding. I think he wanted to dig into my past, to get me back to my foundations, so that I could start rebuilding myself. But he was my past; he *was* my foundations. I wanted to rest my head on his shoulder, feel the familiar shape, and fill myself with the smell of crappy aftershave. But there was a distance between us that goes with all the shit of addiction and complicates physical contact. Sensing my inhibition, he reached out a hand and patted the side of my head, as he had done when I was a child – as if I was still a child, as if it was yesterday.

'Judging by what she says, you're in real trouble. You've been played with and manipulated. And it has been going on for so long that you've lost sight – if you ever had it – of what is real. These games of toy soldiers,' he said, waving his hand at my toy soldiers, innocent in their box on the shelf, 'the Corpo are playing, are not real. Believe me when I tell you, they know nothing. They believe their own myths, but none of it is real. And they are only sinister if we allow them to be. History has shown us how moronic these so-called dark forces really are. The great smog, the Kennedy assassinations, the Nazi party, communism, the fall of Israel – all idiots playing toy soldiers, because they did not have the breadth or courage to play the real game.'

I looked at him suspiciously. 'Where's all this coming from?'

'The History Channel,' he said. 'It's not just soap operas that are on during the day.'

'But this myth, this life they've concocted for me, is the only reality I've ever known.'

I started crying, and he instinctively reached for me, drawing me into his shoulder, where I pumped and convulsed, as I had so often done as a child.

I pushed him away and wiped my eyes. 'I'm sorry. This is ridiculous. I'm crying like a big boy's blouse.'

He smiled down at me, his face showing years of patience through fake tan and nano-buffs. 'You must seek out what is real, Li, no matter what she says about danger, no matter how great your fear. If you do not, you will live the type of life I have lived – which is no life at all. You'll become another lost sack of flesh and bone vegetating in front of 3D, while your wife has the real life. Or worse, you'll go back on the peppies and die an addict. Either way, it's no way to live. And when you die, you'll be nothing more than a Corpo-digit. Don't let them do that to you.'

'What else can I do?'

'What do you *want* to do?'

'Find her?'

'Then find her. She's the only reality that counts. No matter what she says, she needs you as much as you need her.'

'But I don't know where to start.'

'Start with that tabloid slapper, William Howe. You'll find he's up to his neck in all this.'

'Howe?'

'Yes. I happen to know his father, and he told me in confidence that his son was involved in some top-secret project with the Corpo, involving numbers. William asked him to ask me if I knew where you were, when you went missing.'

I sat on the edge of the bed and dropped my face into my hands.

'What is it now?' Elia said, putting a hand on my shoulder.

'They're everywhere, these bastards, and I'm afraid of what they might do if I break cover.'

'Ah,' he said, walking from the room, hand on ball-sack. 'What I wouldn't do for a bit of fear. Besides, if they wanted you, they'd already have you. Your cover was broken as soon as you were printed and put into St Patrick's.'

12

'Bill Howe.'

I called him this, knowing how he insisted on being 'William'. Eyes widening at first, then narrowed with recognition before he placed, with thoughtful precision, an assortment of shopping bags into a corner by the door. *Undeez Shop.* Funny how the banal has a way of interjecting into moments of tension. Kicking the door closed with a slow sweep of his heel, he said: 'Oh, great. How did you get in?'

Howe's apartment was even more luxurious than mine used to be. His was right in the heart of where his ego would feel appropriately served, two hundred feet above Grafton and Duke. Rotating at an inch a minute, its large window looked out on a panorama of other rotating penthouses. A black leather couch curved luxuriously into a corner, where it had an unimpeded view. Positioned, presumably, to entertain lovers as he giggled out of his trousers. The walls, floors and ceilings were painted white, offsetting a collection of free-standing Chinese root-wood sculptures. The only other ornamentation was a watercolour of Howe in profile, which hung above the couch. In it, he was wearing a red and white hooped T-shirt, wide-necked in the style of a sailor. The eye had been blued and the lips painted with a flattering intelligence. It must have been done after the adjustments I noticed on his face. Was he was trying to shake the pretty-boy image? The artist's attempt at gaunt intelligence looked like skin stretched over a skull, on which the face was a disconnected caricature. But what do I know?

'I just walked in,' I said breezily. 'Waited until someone else was going into the block, and blagged them about forgetting my key. I had the foresight to bring a towel, so I stripped myself naked, wrapped it around my arse and told the porter I was a "friend" of yours who had accidentally locked himself out of the apartment. It was a racing certainty she would believe you were gay.'

'Interesting technique,' said Howe. 'She must have believed you were gay too.'

I squeezed a tight smile, continuing blithely: 'I retrieved my clothes and made myself a drink, while I waited for you to come home. Nice portrait, by the way: really captures the intensity of the new look. Sick of being pretty, were you? Looking for more gravitas to go with your rising career?'

'Do you want another?' he said, nodding at the empty glass at my elbow. I shrugged, and he made casually towards the cabinet. He was wearing a soft leather half-length jacket and trousers: very expensive and very handsome. At least some coquetry was being held in reserve for the cows of commerce.

He said: 'I suppose at some point we're going to stop circling each other with cutting innuendo?' Clawing some ice into a glass of vodka, he splashed it with orange juice. 'This is what you like, isn't it?'

'Yes,' I said, taking the glass, and worrying momentarily about the places his hand where might have been.

'Well?' he said, lowering himself into the far end of the couch. 'What is it that brings you so unexpectedly to my home?'

I could see the contempt in his eyes and in the curl of his elaborated lip. I could feel it in the tone of the question. To him, I must have looked like a pathetic creature, a one-time competitor who had dropped out of the race. My rough hands, with their broken nails and grimy knuckles, went from bad to worse, when compared to his smooth, manicured fingers. I saw him glancing at them, the faint disgust I engendered playing on his face, as he fiddled with the gold rings on his thumbs. 'You know why I'm here.'

'Do I? Well, just to be sure, why don't you indulge me?'

'OK then, I'll spell it out. There is only one thing I want from you, Billy boy, and then I'll be on my way.'

'It's not money, is it? I suppose I could let you have a few shekels, if it meant getting rid of you.' His fine fingers moved on his knee like tentacles, as if to reflect their superiority.

'No, not money.'

'Well then, let me see. It wouldn't be your old job back, your identity, get the tenants out of your apartment, all that sort of thing, would it? That mightn't be so easy to arrange. The Corpo can't let you continue betting on racing certainties forever.'

'Nope.' I felt myself, despite myself, moving a hand to my head to finger my hair into some sort of shape. Seeing him at close quarters, so well groomed and poised, was reminding me of my old life, and the reassurance that can be found in vanity. It was disappointing to realise that I, despite all recent eye-openers, was so easily corruptible.

'OK, let *me* come to the point. I really do not know why you're here, and what's more, I don't care. I have a busy evening ahead, and cannot sit here chewing the fat, just because you insist we do. I might remind you: we were never really that close.'

'OK, if you insist on playing the cretin. It's about our friend Daisy.'

'Daisy?'

'You know who I'm talking about.'

A smile breaking on his face, developed into a short, contemptuous laugh. He shook his head and looked at me disbelievingly: I was a joke he was sharing with himself.

'Yes, of course I do. Though I must say I'm surprised you are so uptight about that scrawny little thing. What about Emily?' He enunciated the question to an invisible audience: I half expected a gush of canned laughter. 'Now there is a girl with a bit of class.'

'You can have her,' I said, sharply. Though I had anticipated an onslaught, and promised myself that I would maintain control, I was weak and tired and ugly and badly groomed and poorly dressed and sick of being reminded about how inferior I was.

'Oh, don't get snippy.'

'Where is Daisy?' I said, slowly.

'First, we need to talk about Emily. If we're to sort this out, we're going to have to start at the beginning. Otherwise, I'll never get rid of you.'

'If you insist, but hurry it along. I'm as anxious to get on with my evening as you are.' This, despite my not having anything to do for the rest of my life.

'OK,' he said, in that irritating, enunciated way of his, pausing to look me over with an expression that said I was not worth the effort of a lie. 'The problems started when you confounded the numbers with Emily. We profiled you and her in great detail. When we looked at your tastes, habits and personality type, Emily fitted perfectly. I have to admit, you troubled us with your continued insistence of spending the nether-hours of your weekends rutting with the uggos of Dublin. Totally off the reservation.'

'I'll thank you to proceed without unnecessary asides about my character or habits.'

'Bear with me. Poor Emily. She was so upset when you didn't fall for her charms. She tried so hard to be everything you wanted. And you know what hurt her the most? You didn't even attempt to contact her during your adventures. Not once. Poor girl could have been worried sick, for all you cared. We wondered at that. We had not reckoned on you as an insensitive bastard.'

'She didn't care about me, and I didn't care about her. I want to know where Daisy is, so just get on with it.'

'But I thought you called her Tattoo?'

'What difference does it make?' It is possible he may have been the most irritating person I had known in my life. Just looking at him was enough to make me angry. By now, I was sweating to restrain myself.

'No difference at all. You're absolutely right. They are, after all, one and the same Tattoo, Daisy . . . and Emily.'

The penthouse continued its slow loop, but I began to hurtle through space. 'What?'

'Honestly, I thought you would have figured that one out by now.'

'What are you talking about?' I asked again, digging knuckles into my knee to stop both from shaking.

'OK, let me use layperson's terms. I was one of the agents of the Numbers Game. Have you got *that* much?'

I nodded.

'Good,' he said, enthusiastically. 'I was part of the R&D team, and it was my job to liaise with Daisy and make sure she had everything she needed to gather the data from you. It's as simple as that.'

'Keep talking.'

'We reintroduced her to you as Emily, fearing that a resurfacing of the Daisy character might cause complications, because of the untenable coincidence factor, the likelihood of new streams of enquiry and the probability of emotional confusion in the subject. That is, you. You were the subject. When the Emily profile was not working, we doctored her up a bit and tried a different approach. There is always trial and error with new formulae. You know that.'

'But why? I mean, I understand all this data-gathering shit, but why *her?*'

'I dunno. She wanted the gig.'

'But you manipulated my whole life.'

'Don't overestimate yourself. We wanted the data, not you.'

'I want to meet with somebody. I want out, and I want to see Daisy.'

'You poor fool. The people in charge don't care enough about you to put you in or out. They have numbers to crunch.'

'I don't care . . . .'

'It's just numbers. We're all just numbers: you, me and everyone else you see around you. What makes you think you have the right? It is not as if your feelings or opinions count for a grain of sand in the overall scheme of things, now that you're out of the game. You've become randomised and corrupted.'

'It's just a game,' I heard myself saying. 'It doesn't mean anything.'

'To you, maybe. But to those of us who have dedicated our lives to the cause, it means everything. The Numbers Game is not just a matter of a few civil liberties, you know.'

'Very noble. What if I don't believe you? What if I think this is just a pile of horseshit.'

'Nobody cares what you do or don't believe. You were just one of thousands.'

'Do me a favour, Howe. Tell me where the fuck Daisy is.'

'Why do you want to know? What difference will it make?'

I looked at the smooth questioning curve of his eyebrow, and his clean blue eyes. The smirking face knew there was only one logical answer to this equation, and that I was finally realising what it was. I dropped my eyes to the strong funnel of his neck, and saw his larynx move confidently, as he swallowed some of the vodka. He was right, when I thought about it. I was just another cell in a superstructure of cells. There was absolutely no point in my pursuing a questionable goal against ridiculous odds. And in a mathematical culture, it is all about the pursuit of absolutes. I thought of my parents, and Don Pietro. I thought of Scotland and France and the whole shuddering machine of the planet straining to work things out. I added up my options and subtracted my fears. I lifted the portrait off the wall and smashed it over his head. 'Tell me where she is you, you wanker!'

Then I was choking him, digging my dirty fingers into his beautiful neck. I could feel the muscles of his throat rippling against my thumbs like a struggling animal. I snarled, and banged his head off the wall. I surrendered to an unstoppable gush of ecstasy, and abandoned my logical self. It was as though I was seeing the whole thing from the ceiling. The portrait bounced around his neck, his anguished expression in contrast with its smug portrait.

'Just tell me where the fuck she is!' I heard myself shout, as I was lifted and thrown onto the ground. Then Howe's foot was on my neck and he was removing the broken portrait from his head. He was in much better shape than me – a factor I had forgotten to take into consideration.

'There are women, men and children dying by the thousand every day in America. Ask them how important one little obsessive is,' he said, spitting. 'You can do and think what you want. I matter more than you, and believe me, I don't matter at all. Your data has become corrupted, with the removal of your chip and your disappearance off the grid. You are of absolutely no interest or use to anyone any more. Stop being a nuisance. Daisy was doing a job. Take it or leave it: she was a professional acting under orders. She doesn't care about you, any more than anyone else does. The Numbers Game is the only thing that matters to her, me and anyone else who has a brain in their head. Get it?'

'Just tell me where she is,' I wheezed. 'Please. I just want to talk to her.'

#

When I had wandered out of Howe's apartment, leaving him sitting on the couch rubbing his throat and holding his portrait on his lap, I had no idea what my next step would be. Having let me up, he waved me away like an irritating fly and I simply left, grateful I suppose for not having got more beaten up. Nor did he bother to report me to Security – which added to the case for my insignificance. The porter looked me over and smiled as I passed, as if to make the point, perhaps, about her tolerance of gays. I walked through the city, trying to keep my mind off peppies. I walked right down to the Liffey basin and out through the stratified housing complexes of Ringsend. I walked to the open space of Sandymount Strand, where the midnight kite-fliers lit up the sky with strobes and sparkles, like frozen fireworks. Jaded by the time I reached Sydney Parade, I caught a vac back to the city, where I fell into the familiar squalor of my basement flat.

The next morning, slumped over coffee, I realised that the only asset I had left was what was left of my ass. I would have to use it in whatever way I could, to find Daisy. My only other choice was to go back to peppies, and I just could not face the pain and torture of all that again. Difficult though the road to Daisy might be, I was driven by an urge to see her again. I was an engine that would burn its last drop of oil and splutter into flames before I would give her up. Besides, there was the conversation I needed to have about her triple identity, and this alone was enough to entice me to cross a Sahara of hostility. I had been rehearsing it in my head, over and over, like a madman's mantra.

13

'Hi,' I said, studying her reaction. You need to know how to surf a woman's mood and react appropriately. There was a moment of focus, of recognition fused with disbelief – which defused into amusement.

'*Li?*' The glassiness of her stare, along with a too-careful reach for her cocktail glass, told me she was half-peppied – which was what I had been hoping for. I had tidied myself up as much as I could on my budget, had had a haircut, had put on a clean shirt, and so on. The old carcass had been hauled out for duty again, scraped, scrubbed and preened – it was about all I had left, such as it was. The working theory was, I might still somehow qualify as a bit of totty: they like a bit of totty when they're stoned, the cows of commerce. Her clumsy fingers found the circumference of, and lifted to her lips, a busy mojito glass. Taking small, rapid sips, she surveyed me through the undergrowth, big eyes struggling in and out of focus. You had to admire the elegance, though – the sheer stature that comes with being successful.

'What are you doing back in town? I heard you'd emigrated to distant climes. You look awful, by the way. I'm surprised Amy even let you in.'

This had taken a bit of work. Amy had cooled considerably towards me during my junkie period, when I'd had to be thrown out of the club once or twice for begging. She was eventually persuaded to readmit me by a daytime pitch as to my sobriety. There was also a loose overview of my situation with Daisy, and my associated need to make contact with her mother. Amy, like most criminals, was moved by the 'fall and redemption' aspect of my predicament. She was roaming about somewhere in the background now, like the Sheriff of Dance Adonis, and had come into my peripheral line of sight once or twice, as if to remind me to behave. Amy was a rock of dependable corruption who would never have spoken to me as Mianzi was now speaking to me. Her words hurt, fragile as I was. The gimp inside me wanted me to hang my head and limp out of the club, dragging my knuckles on the ground. And believe me, the gimp had a lot to say about what went on with me back there. But another part of me – the part that had nothing to lose – assumed a cavalier posture.

'Thanks, I've been doing a bit of down-and-out.'

'Don't get me wrong,' she said, 'you've still got more going on than any of these.'

Five ringed fingers flapped loosely at the company of studs crowding her table. They could not hear our conversation above the music, but managed to both eye me with territorial resentment and smile enthusiastically at her. She was wrapped curvaceously in lime-green silk, which opened in a generous fan behind her head.

'I didn't think you were the Dance Adonis type, these days,' she said, pulling me towards the bar, where she pressed her breasts onto the counter. 'I thought Retros were more you.'

She was getting it right out there, her participation in my crucifixion. Indolent eyes were taking me in, examining my reactions, seeing if there was to be trouble. In another time and place, and with a different set of priorities – or lack of them – I might have spat something insulting at her. But I had left things like dignity and self-respect behind. I looked around, at the pink feathers adorning the bar and the 3Ds of leather-clad nubiles suspended from the ceiling. At the ubiquitous real-life boys, gyrating around a pole in the corner, cred-pads shoved into budgie-smugglers. At the cows crowding around. Seeing the familiar decadence made me sentimental, for a moment. But that life was behind me now, and there were other things ahead.

'I'm sorry, what did you say?' I said.

'I said, I thought Retros were more your style.'

'They are. Or at least they were, until you're little Corpo-stunt ruined my self-image. I'm realigning my tastes now.'

The nightclub was crowded. Miles Davies – or at least his 3D – was pumping jazz into the buzz.

'You're not going to hold that against me, are you? I was only doing my job, and it was for the greater good and all. And besides' – she cupped the side of my head and drew me close enough to smell her boozy breath – 'it was such fun having you around. Peppy?'

Releasing my face, she dipped her hand into her purse, producing the smooth blue pill, which she rolled between her forefinger and thumb.

'That's all very well,' I said, gently pushing her hand away. 'But the whole thing's left me at a bit of a loose end. I mean, what am I supposed to *do* with myself now?'

'But they told me they left you with plenty of money.'

Eyes opening wide, like two drops of ink exploding in a bowl of cream, her sculpted lips rounded to an expression of dismay. I felt a familiar ping. Pornography.

'All gone,' I said. 'But what good's money to me anyway? Now that my whole life and everything has been screwed up. I don't know what to do or where to go any more.'

I was laying myself at her mercy, like a puppy rolling on its back, or the beta-baboon dipping its head at the alpha. It was the surest way for the male animal, that unconscionable, un-thinking beast, to get attention. I found, unsurprisingly, I wanted to be shagged by her, despite the nobility of my objective. The antenna of my penis had beeped into life, and was plunging me towards her availability. No wonder the women had taken us in hand.

'Come on,' she said. 'Can't be that bad.'

Clicking her fingers like castanets at the barwoman, she pointed to a booth. By the time we had sat down, the Champagne was arriving. Filling my flute until the wine fizzed over the lip, she said: 'Now tell Auntie Mianzi all about it.'

'Well,' I said, accepting her curled toes on my knee, 'it's like I said. What am I supposed to do with myself now?'

'You could always come and work for auntie.'

Putting her hand on top of mine, she continued. 'I couldn't give you a big job, like the one you used to have, but I *am* looking for a PA. You'd be *wonderful*.' As her eyes glistened sympatheti-cally, her evil finger tickled the bone of my wrist.

'I don't know,' I said, turning over my hand and allowing her fingernails to caress its palm. 'It would be humiliating. I mean, everyone would know about how I had been taken for such a ride.'

'Don't be silly, darling. Most of the people who were there at the time were Corpo-plants. You know, part of this Numbers Game. We've a completely different crew there now.'

'But what about Daisy? She'd be hanging around, looking down on me, making me feel naked. I don't think I could bear *her* again.'

Turning my hand over, I entwined my fingers with hers, toy-ing with one of her rings, while I observed her over the rim of my glass.

'Oh, but darling, there's literally *no* chance of that.'

'How can you be so sure?'

'Because.'

Leaning her breasts on the table, she ran a hand through my hair. 'She's over the sea and far away, working as a Corpo-liaison. It's a sideways thing. Not exactly a demotion, but it will keep her busy for a while.'

'You sure?' I said, feebly.

'Quite sure. Had it coming, I suppose. Nasty little ideologue.'

#

'Where's your husband, by the way?' I said, as we stumbled into her quarters in the Bradshaw *Siheyuan*. 'Or was he part of the fabrication as well?'

'Oh no, he's real all right. It's just that he prefers to spend his time in our holiday-home in Clare.'

A top-heavy wooden cabinet balancing precariously on spindly ball and claw legs, reminded me of an ungainly weightlifter. But it didn't budge when Mianzi leaned on it, to half-inch two crystal tumblers with whiskey. She carried them back to the couch in one hand, a bowl of spilling peanuts in the other.

'Seemed like a nice man. Martin. Wasn't that his name?'

'Yes.' She put the glass in my hand. 'He's a nice man. Just doesn't understand the old cut-and-thrust of things, if you know what I mean. Peanut?'

I didn't want a peanut.

'And Daisy seemed so genuinely fond of him. What an actress.'

'Well, she is our daughter. Why wouldn't she be?'

#

'What did you mean last night when you called Daisy a nasty little ideologue?' I said.

Mianzi was in front of an antique mirror, humming and tweezering her eyebrows. 'Hmm? Pass me my slippers, darling. They're under the bed.'

I walked across a few feet of deep-pile and kissed the nape of her neck, as I laid the slippers at her feet. 'Seriously. What did you mean?'

'You know the type.'

Rubbing lotion into last night's make-up, her movements were deliberate and circular. 'Always banging on about how the

Corpo needs to broaden its worldview. Profit would become sec-
ondary to social welfare, if she had her way.'

Wandering back to the queen-sized bed, I lay where my naked body would be cool, and caressed in satin. There was a large
window opposite, with a refreshing view of the mountain and
the city beyond. It added to the opulence of the room, like a perfect painting. I wondered whether the design had been Martin's,
and felt as though I was wearing another man's dirty underwear.
I felt like having a shower, and washing away all the bestial,
post-coital filth.

'Yes. She's more or less a communist, when you think about
it. But the fact that she's your daughter: doesn't that make you
at least a little sympathetic?'

'I love her to bits. What are you talking about? Now be a good
boy, and go down and get me a glass of orange juice.'

She, too, had entered another phase of the pornography cycle. Having made a conquest, she wanted to crown the achieve-
ment with a little light degradation, set me up nice and humble
for the next time.

#

'So, Daisy's in Corpo-liasion?' I placed the juice on the table and
bounced back onto the bed. 'How did you manage to swing that?
I mean, how high up *are* you in the Corpo?'

'High enough,' she said, rubbing hand-cream into her naked
fingers, vigorously. 'But not that high. It wasn't my idea to send
her off. I don't have anything to do with personnel: my main
interest is profit and lifestyle. That type of thing. Now why don't
we' – she walked over and pushed my bare chest – 'talk about the
terms and conditions of your new job?'

#

'And what about William Howe?'

With appropriate deliberation, I placed her tea-tray on a table in the conservatory. 'What about him?'

She was reading a newspaper. The sun shining through the
glass at her back made a candyfloss halo of her pulverised hair.
Unaware, she carried on reading, her boredom growing to irritation. I could see nothing of Daisy in her, but they had both been
so touched up it was impossible to tell. What I could see, was
that she was already regretting her overtures of a PA-ship. It was
there in the curtness of her responses, and the lack of attention

in her eyes. We were at the tail-end of conquest: I was just another body now. Standing behind her, I gave her shoulders a rub. 'Are you seeing him?'

'Don't be ridiculous.' She wriggled away.

'Well, you always seemed to be very fond of him. Bidding for him at the ball, and spending all that time with him afterwards.'

'That's because he was working for me on the Numbers Game project. Pour the coffee, darling, and don't be a bore.'

I poured the coffee. 'But . . . I thought Haichu headed up the project. How come I never saw her knocking about the place?'

'Well, there's a difference between Head Office and the field, isn't there?' She scanned the newspaper distractedly. 'Haichu was chief Field Agent.'

'It's all so confusing. They have all these numbers, and they don't know what to do with them. Hardly seems worth the effort. And they keep changing their objectives. The whole thing sounds like a complete waste of time to me.'

'Look.' She snapped the newspaper down. 'It's very simple. When the results started to come through the system, the powers-that-be realised that the information was far more useful than they had originally thought. That's what Daisy's doing in Seattle: she's working with the Americans to help them build negotiation blocks with the terrorists. It's all about information.'

Stopping abruptly, she took on a look of concern. She had said too much, and was assessing the damage.

'I dunno,' I said. 'It's all imperial to me.'

15

The Doctor in Saint Patrick's said that every journey begins with a single step. Travelling to an American war-zone began with a single step, but there were no doctors on the journey to help me, and no institution to temper reality. The only vac I could find was to Vancouver. From there, I caught a local over the border to a town called Stanwood, where, screeching to a stop, the Seattle Express refused to go further.

'Better get off here, sonny,' an old man pushing past me said, adding, as I handed him his bags off the train: 'Vac don't go into Seattle no more.'

Slinging my backpack over my shoulder, like I knew where I was going, I made my way on foot towards what looked like the centre of town. The good people of Stanwood seemed to be getting on with life, circumnavigating scorched laser-holes in the pavement, as if they were a natural part of the streetscape. They went about with eyes cast sideways or downwards. No contact. Experience seemed to have taught them the value of indifference, but I could see that their incurious faces were clenched with fear. Most of the buildings were more or less intact, though a museum of 'Coke' had had a large slice of its façade scooped out by laser-cannon. 'Museum of ok' was all the sign said now. I walked like a tourist along Main Street, ghosting in and out of hurrying people. Main Street, dying but not yet dead, was still fighting the good fight of commerce. There seemed to be a brisk trade in second-hand or repaired goods, and I could see people bartering with what they had. A woman with two children held up one of their coats and stretched the cloth for the benefit of a dubious shopkeeper. In the next doorway, another showed a boy to three laughing women. She was laughing along, sharing the joke by getting him to flex skinny muscles, while her eyes implored. I turned away and walked on. They might have been my mother, these women, in different circumstances.

The day being bright gave sharp outline to the surroundings, making it feel as though I was walking through 3D, like those waifs at the charity ball so long ago and so far away in Dublin. What the locals thought of me, if anything, I couldn't tell, but it must have looked like I was too ridiculous to be real, in my camo-printed chino shorts and matching backpack. Some bundles of rags leaning against a wall turned into a father and two small children, looking like they'd just walked from Mexico. Purple blotches on bare feet matched the colour of their eye-sockets. A hand emerging from the rags cupped itself and begged in my direction. The father wheezed something as I passed; it sounded like 'Please'.

I supposed I could have stopped: I had plenty of hard currency, acquired with the sphere in Canada. Money might have saved their lives, for a time. But I was pre-programmed with a greater purpose. I rationalised myself in and out of responsibility, with my mind too full of Daisy to care about anything else. Besides, I thought, if I stepped out of my dimension and engaged with them, I might get sucked into their trouble. I was too selfish, too centred on my own dream. I had a plan with which I had been obsessed since I had affected a tantrum and walked out on Mianzi. I tossed my plan in different directions, testing its robustness. It had none. What Daisy would say when she saw me, or what exactly our happy-ever-after would look like, if we even had one, was something I hadn't thought through either. You don't think when you're obsessed, you just *do*, and nothing made sense to do, or think, that wasn't taking me in a straight line towards her.

The practical problem of how I was going to make the remainder of the trip was solved when I rounded a corner and found a dilapidated bicycle shop. Where the Bikey outlets, found all over Europe had shining new machines crowding outside vast gleaming windows, this had three patched-up wrecks, tied together with string and watched over by a one-eyed mongrel. It growled as I approached, warning that I had better be a customer. I thought wistfully of the fifty-speed I had left Don Pietro musing over.

'This all you got?' I asked a woman who wandered towards me wiping her hands, muttering at the dog to shut up. 'These look like they couldn't carry you a click.'

'War on,' she explained, glancing at the sky as if expecting proof. 'We don't get stuff any more, have to make do, best we can. That's a nice accent. Where you from, handsome?'

A cinder of flirtatiousness burned in her sunken eyes. This I appreciated, despite the surreal impossibility of the situation:

you always do. Taking a sly scan at her, I noted that her heavy blue overalls, tied at the waist with bicycle string, gave some indication of a figure. Her sleeves were rolled up from whatever job she had been doing, revealing elegant wrists looped with plaited leather braids: she had not always been a bicycle mechanic. You could see in the battle-fatigue of her demeanour that she needed love – and that I would do.

'Ireland.'

'Ireland? I hear it's pretty. Real green.'

'Oh, it's much like any other place.'

'Smoke?'

What do you do in a situation like this? Do you settle for the immediate fix of an available woman or do you struggle on, into the dark unknown towards the great prize that goes beyond sensuality? I didn't know then, and don't now. But for once, I did the right thing. 'No, thank you. I just want to look at the bikes.'

Shrugging like she didn't give a shit one way or the other, she took me to review the bikes, talking them up with the smoothness of an experienced negotiator. I got the impression that she had previously been something in business, and was enjoying the opportunity to use her skill, like a retired dancer remembering old moves. She had no problem screwing me over. If I had been a local, we would have been talking in fractions of the prices. I didn't care: it was all sphere-money.

'What you doing over here, anyway?' she asked, a little guiltily, as I counted out the creds. 'This is no place for a boy like you.'

'Came to get my girl.'

Wheeling what we agreed was the steadiest of her merchandise towards the road, I waited while the mongrel reluctantly shuffled out of my way.

'Came to get a girl? That's real cute.' she watched me lift the saddle and spin the back wheel, to reveal a wobble. I looked at her equivocally.

'Well, it's not like you going into the Tour de France.' She already had my money, and the dog was on her side. 'Take some advice from inside the heart of a woman who's got nothing to lose or gain either way.' I sat on the saddle and found the pedals with my feet. 'You let the ladies chase you, honey. It don't look good for a man to do the chasing.'

'Is this really the best you can do?' I said, looking down at the bike.

She thought for a second before answering, and when she did the mood was grimmer. 'I can give you some more advice,

see you on your way,' she said, quietly. 'Don't look anyone in
the eye and don't tell anyone which side you're on. And if you do
have to talk to anybody, change with the wind, because either
side thinks nothing of killing the enemy. It's *morally* wrong not
to. And whatever you do, don't tell anyone the truth: truth's a
dangerous commodity these days. Now that's a lot of advice, but
I reckon you paid for it. And,' she remembered, stepping out from
the doorway, 'if you're asked, don't say you're neutral. They both
kill neutrals. Take an informed guess, a fifty-fifty shot: Corporatist or Rebel.'

#

I cycled along the coast road, guiding the front wheel on tarmac
overrun by hairy sinews of weed and scrub. The road snaked
through a dark, deformed forest scarred with raw patches, where
limbs had been torn from trees to provide firewood. The tree-line
was broken occasionally by laser-blasts and on higher ground I
could see the sea to the west, cold and incorrigible. There were
islands out in the bay. I wondered if they were inhabited, or if
their inhabitants could possibly be protected from the war. I
thought of Capri, and cycled on.

   I could see the influence of the Corpo's great morality in the
blackened debris of Marysville and Everett, where war had left
the townscapes scarred and tattered. Here, the behaviour of people was even stranger than in Stanwood. They lurched towards
the shadows or huddled in alleyways, or in any corner that might
offer protection. They were nearer to the war, more acquainted
with death. It may have been this acquaintance, or perhaps a
full-on fear of its inevitability, that made them braver. A figure
from the shadows suddenly emerged and leapt at me. A large
woman in a faded pink jumpsuit. Raising a stick with one hand,
she clawed for a grip on the handlebars with the other. I managed to escape by lashing a foot against her crotch, causing her
to drop the stick and double over.

   I wobbled on. Forced to dismount at the northern outskirts
of Seattle, I wheeled my bike carefully through the intensified
wreckage of buildings and roads. A layer of dusty smoke hung a
few feet above the ground; through the smoke, shadows turned
out to be burnt-out cars, broken furniture or towering lumps of
plaster and brick. A doll's head impaled on a finger of tubular
steel mesh looked like a tribal warning to go no further. I ignored
it and tried cycling on again, adding the bike to the debris when

the back wheel hit a pothole and buckled under my weight. Leaving it where it fell, I tramped on.

Ad hoc bridges, made out of what could be found, were thrown across bomb-craters. The golden arches of a once-famous fast-food empire were melded together with the plastic burger of its redundant competitor, to form a platform across an open sewer. The town must have been called 'Kirkland', judging by the road-sign embedded in the side of a building. Corpo activity increased as I left the suburbs and entered the city. Souped-up people-counters began to whizz overhead, criss-crossing with patrolling armoured cars, which randomly peppered the rubble with laser-shot. Fire, occasionally returned from somewhere in the distance, was deflected harmlessly off battered shields. The cars responded like insects when this happened, suddenly urgent, bobbing and weaving through the wreckage of skyways and buildings to the source of the shot, where they used laser-cannon to blast craters in the craters. I hid under a slab of reinforced concrete until the noise died down, then continued on, guided by the homing beeps of the sphere.

Yes, every journey begins with a single step, and the steps keep adding up until there are more behind than ahead. Onwards I stumbled, through the broken concrete and dust, avoiding the citizens of chaos, when they emerged from the shadows to go about their mysterious business. They moved like rats, quickly along gullies or gutters, or under whatever shelter they could find. Many clutched parcels or bundles – probably food or other basics. The most rudimentary things seemed to have become urgent, like finding of foothold, or successfully crossing an open space. Cackles of what could have been laughter or anguish interrupted unsteady silences: it was as if those unseen people wanted to reassure themselves of their existence, at least once more. They must have known they could have no protection against the random violence from above. The whole city was insane. The numbers had broken down, and hell had taken over. The earth-brain was damaged, and all the calculations and cleverness, all of the collected and collective knowledge of womankind, and their vast computer network, had no idea how to fix it.

'Way it is here,' a young man who joined me at a fire someone had lit in a drum, explained, 'is that no one has a *right* to life. A laser-blast or an avalanche of rubble can get you any time. You got to be lucky to live. Not rich. Not clever. Lucky.'

'Why don't you get out of town?'

'Yeah? And go where? Same all over. Folks in the country

going to get the same treatment we getting, sooner or later. Anyway, ain't no point going nowhere when you ain't got no money.
Some parts, they kill refugees for food.'

I warmed my hands and tried to remember the bike-seller's
advice.

'Fuck,' he said. 'The Corpo say they want to protect our freedom. But that don't mean shit when you don't even have the
basic right to walk down a street.'

'Nothing means shit any more. Except the shit itself.'

'Whose side you on, anyway?' He was withered, half starved
and dressed in rags, and had a plastic bag on his head. There
were two more tied around his shoes. I could have blown him
over, but he might have been carrying a weapon.

'I'm a laser-shot,' I said, beckoning to the dusky horizon,
where the skyline had just been lit up with a blast. 'Aimed right
at the heart of your trouble. I'm here to kill the war. And if you
fuck with me, I'll slice your fucking head off.'

'Hey.' He extended his palms and backed into the mist. 'I
ain't fucking with no laser-shot.'

16

Corpo Headquarters was a giant beehive in the centre of a dust-bowl that used to be rubble, which used to be a Forbidden City. This was, even by the standards of the devastated city, a remarkable sight. Anything that hadn't been razed to atoms had been pushed to a periphery of about half a click, forming a wall of upended buildings and other giant dislocated bits of debris. Corpo cars, buzzing in orbit circles, resumed formation to power beyond the perimeter and zap at anything that looked suspicious – and they were *very* suspicious. A refractor-grid hummed around the building. It cost a fortune to maintain, but was the reason the monolith was still standing.

There were scars along the gleaming surface, where rebel laser-shot had managed to penetrate the shield. They were capable of wounding the beast, but so far only superficially. I had heard somewhere about the polymers they used on these buildings: atoms and molecules fused like strands of a rope, each doubling the strength of the next. It would have all been worked out by the Corpo-physicists, along standard Corpo principles. The rebs were apparently adapting, were probably working with their own experts on a way to beat the shield.

The sky above CHQ was lit by massive 3D skyboards. PROSPERITY IS PEACE, CORPO WORKS . . . DO YOU? REBELS HATE PROFIT, MONEY IS FREEDOM, DON'T SELL OUT, SELL UP. Huge Corpo faces appeared at intervals, filling the sky with their rational expressions, and the air with the thunder of friendly voices. 'Don't sell out . . . sell up! . . . Money *is* freedom. Freedom *is* money. Why hate us? Why hate freedom? Help us fight terrorism today: see how generous we can be. We can work this out at an EGM. Seattle, the city with the *least* number of Corpo-deaths.'

They were relentless, hanging from the sky over the insect rebels, drumming their mindless messages – making subtlety a casualty of war. On and on they pounded, colour, tone and inflection changing suddenly to prevent desensitisation. I visualised the meeting where some bright young thing had stepped up with a pitch that said that if the messages were shouted loudly and regularly enough, a certain number were bound to be affected. And of *that* number, a certain percentage was bound to believe these slogans as truths, and switch affiliation. *This* number might just be sufficient to sway the balance in the Corpo's favour. It is a numbers game, she would explain. If you keep doing it again and often enough, you'll wear them down; create new truth.

I studied from the lobby of an upside-down office building, the open space between me and CHQ; looked with sore eyes at hovering dust, glowing orange with the setting sun, like a layer of poison gas. It had been three days and two nights since I had crossed the border. Though I had eaten relatively well – the power-bars with which I had filled my backpack – I was weak and exhausted. The stench of death will do that to you. The fusion of burning flesh and concrete hits the back of the nostrils and permeates the body. Yet the stench was alluring, in its eviscerating way. It was only a matter of time, it said, before you too will join my accumulating mass.

I decided to get a few hours' sleep before I dealt with the insanity that lay ahead of me, and all around – filling past and future, hanging in the air like poison gas. The morning would be time enough to continue my journey towards death, when, driven by an instinct stronger than myself, I would scuttle on, like an ant towards a drain. But in the meantime, I could sleep. It would probably be my last luxury. Climbing up an inverted stairway, I crawled into an upside-down reception desk, and curled up in relative safety. The nights were tropically alive, with moans of pain or manic laughter, interspersed with hisses of cannon and shot. The slightest shuffle could have been a cat-sized rat, replete on human flesh, or a starving reb hunting it.

Lowering myself out of the desk the following morning, I stared through a hole in the wall as I pissed, at the huge crystal uterus the Publican had sent me to inseminate. The morning had whitened the dust, and the ominous air of the previous evening had evaporated into the plain danger of broad daylight. There was something monstrously beautiful about CHQ, something in the brilliant blue of its shield and the smooth ellipse of its perfect shape, against the grey of its setting. There was no doubting the Corpo's ability to build a monument, but it looked like a giant tombstone on a great, dusty grave. The fear with which it filled me made me think, for the thousandth time, of flight. I calculated a ten to one chance, at most, of surviving a retreat to the border, where I would probably be refused entry by the same Canadian authorities who had been so quick to usher me out of their country.

The hole in the wall beckoned like a portal through which I could crawl towards a ridiculous future. On the other side of the hole, the numbers became too bizarre to calculate. The chances of me walking ten steps across an open area this close to CHQ, without being lasered, were remote. There weren't even coordinates beyond that: no numbers with which to calculate outcomes. Still, the morning light streamed like a beam of hope through the hole, and drew me onwards. There were wastelands in Carlow, where Daisy and I had reigned as children. Pebbles on the ground were buildings, and puddles lakes, patches of scrub-grass forests or jungles. We strayed over our domain, our eyes the glass bottoms of cars hovering on the *outer-strat*. We covered great distances this way; yards became clicks; fields, countries. We ran in circles, or sped forward to explore great new worlds, all the time humming like solar engines, our arms extended like hi-speed stabilising flaps. We were safe, high in the sky of our eyes, safe enough to enjoy the beauty in simple things, like a monster frog lurching over a landscape, or the storm of a plume of dust kicked into the air. Insects were people; ants, ritualistic tribeswomen; flies, drunken drivers. I was the insect now, tribe-less, mate-less, an insignificant speck of flesh to be squashed.

Crawling through the hole, I made my way into the abyss, where, stumbling forward, I counted two steps, then three, then four. I stopped and stood with my arms out, blinking in the sun. Nothing happened, and I stumbled on, one step more, then two, then three, and still, nothing. As I walked up to the outer cordon, a pod hovered over me, lazily. Slowly, I brought my hands over my head and locked my fingers together. A voice crackled from the pillbox portico surrounding the base of the building. 'Identify yourself, and your reason for being here.'

'I am a courier from Euro-Corpo.' I repeated the numbers which had given to me by the Publican's hologram. 'My mission is confidential.'

I waited in silence for them to decide what to do. They could have done anything: I could have been anyone, making anything up. For all they knew, my blood was filled with undetectable synthetic explosives. By my calculations, it would make as much sense for them to slice me in half and take their chances, as to do anything else. As I stood and sweated, I believed that, one way or another, my journey was almost over. That whole fiasco of deception and materialism, which had been my life, was coming to an end. Penitently, I looked down at my grimy sneakers, covered in the dust of commerce, or dead rebels, or fuck-knew what else. All had been reduced – deconstructed, broken into component parts – just as the building in front of me had been constructed from those very same components.

Atom to atom, dust to dust. Everything was compiled from atoms: the same atoms which had been begotten from the star that created us – all of it a component in the digitisation of infinity. I was about to lose my life; somebody inside just needed to push a button. All those memories and sensations, those little pleasures, like masturbation or grilled tofu, would be blinked away. I would become atoms, to be reconstructed, or to blow as dust over the wasteland. I found, disturbingly, that I would be sorry to lose everything, reasoning that even a lousy life was better than no life at all. What sickened me most was the possibility of losing my latest and greatest acquisition, love. I had bet the house on it, and now I was praying to Confucius that Ameri-Corpo would decide that no one in their right mind would try to fool their security system. Computers were probably calculating this outcome, now, as I waited in the cool, motionless air. No one would ever know, or care, if I was squashed.

A door on the front of the pillbox opened. 'Step into the doorway please.'

I stepped into a bunker, giddy with borrowed time. The door I walked through had to close before the one in front opened, leaving me to be ogled by a series of cams protruding from high in the wall. Eventually, the door in front opened, and I stepped into a large antechamber. Two security guards entered, followed by two others, who held me in their laser-sights. I could see red spots dance around my head and heart, in a glass panel – obviously a one-way mirror. A voice echoed through speakers. 'Clean?'

'Clean.'

'Number two, clean?'

'No plastic or biological explosive, sir. Clean.'

They circled me as they spoke, and looked tense enough to blow me apart if I twitched. A sudden kick on the back of my knee sent me sprawling to the ground, where I was held immobile by two of the guards, while another rummaged through my pack. My power-bars and dirty tightie-whities had to be scattered on the ground before the sphere was discovered by the fourth – which she held triumphantly in front of one of the cams. 'Found this, sir.'

The cam took its time observing the sphere, but eventually said: 'Let him up.'

17

I was thinking about Carlow again. Maybe it's true what they say: that your life flashes in front of your eyes before you die. This time, I was in the kitchen of our module, watching Elia and Laura at their dinner. They wouldn't know where I was, or the danger I was in. Elia might have a guilty suspicion, seeing as how it was him who gave me the pitch about saving myself through heroism and love, and all that other noble crap. Though I couldn't hear what they were saying, in my imagination they were probably talking about the garden, or planning a shopping trip. Or whether to invite friends for dinner at the weekend. Both of them gathering whatever enjoyment they could, from the scrag-end of lives they had slaved away for the opportunity to devitalise in peace.

I both loved and missed them, as I stood trembling in that concrete bunker. More than I realised I could. Right then, I would have done anything to see them just one more time, to tell them I was sorry, that I loved them, whatever. In the meantime, they were far away and safe – unaware they were about to lose another son.

A tall woman walked into the room, dressed in the combat uniform of a commander. 'Stand down.'

The guards, following some metallic clicking of their weapons, took three steps back and stood in pairs on either side of the room, the butts of their cannons resting on the floor in front of them. The Commander took off her helmet, to reveal a hollow-cheeked face, reminding me of the bike- shop woman and everyone else I had seen since crossing the border. 'You going to blow us all up, sweetie?'

'No.'

'How can I be sure?'

'You can't.'

She shrugged. 'Welcome to Seattle. It's good that our associates in Europe haven't forgotten us. Now give me the sphere, sweetie.'

'It's a private message for the Triumvirate. I am under orders not to allow anyone else access.'

'Well then, this situation has become awkward. *I* am under orders to shoot anyone who refuses to comply with security regulations.'

'Be very careful,' I said, handing the sphere to her. 'It's programmed to implode if it travels more than a few yards from me.'

She passed it to one of the guards, who, having stamped her foot respectfully, began examining it with an infra-scanner, looking like a jeweller peering through a loupe at a dodgy diamond.

'I need to talk to you, privately.' The tone with which I said this was louder and more demanding than I had intended, causing the Commander to look up quickly and raise an eyebrow. Expecting to be sliced in two by a laser-shot, I found, gives you the insane courage to get as far as possible before it happens. This was what Daisy would have called 'cavalier male behaviour'.

Thankfully, the Commander was a battle-hardened pro with no feathers to ruffle. 'Of course.'

The guard handed the sphere back to the Commander. 'No trace, sir.'

Slipping it into the leg-pocket of her combats, she led me into a small room, whose furniture consisted of a table and two chairs. 'Coffee? Synthetic but drinkable.'

'No time. I have urgent information for your Triumvirate, and need to confer with our agent. I must proceed to her immediately, with the sphere.'

'Her name?'

'The name I've been given is Emily Bradshaw, but she uses different identities. I've been told there is only one Euro-agent in Seattle at the moment, so whoever you're thinking of must be her.'

'We have to be very careful about who we permit into HQ. I'm sure you can appreciate this.'

'I understand, but I am under strict instructions, and time, as we all know, is a key integer. It's your call, but if we don't move it, the whole reason for me being here will become pointless.'

I detected the faintest bleep from her earpiece.

'Of course. Follow me.'

The soft whirring of moveable eye-cams followed our journey along a concrete corridor, until we came to an elevator, where she thumbed a security pad, showed her eye to a scanner and breathed onto a breath-identifier. 'I've been told to take you upstairs.'

Whizzed upwards at stomach-dragging speed, we stopped suddenly to step into another corridor, this one carpeted and filled with pan-pipe music. The walls of the room were partitioned with glass, through which vast open-plan offices of frantic workers played like silent movies. The Commander retina-scanned, thumbed and coughed her way through a series of glass doors into a room, where senior-looking types stood away from sat-images they were studying, to salute her. A man at a desk stopped typing, to usher us through to a small back office, where an elaborate cough slid away the wall to reveal the doors of yet another elevator, which shot up a few storeys before opening into another small office.

'We must wait here,' she said.

I wandered to a window and looked out at the perimeter, dwarfed now, and uninspiring. Beyond, the rubble reaching to the horizon was all that was left of what had once been one of the world's great cities. The true extent of the damage could only be appreciated from a height. Dust, ubiquitous and permanent, lay like graveyard mist in every direction, consuming the distance. Stumps, which were once skyscrapers, protruded randomly through the layer, giving the city the look of a shallow bay of shipwrecks.

'Nice job you're doing here,' I said.

'We do our best.'

She joined me at the window. When I glanced at her, the light revealed a lattice of broken veins and tiny scars on her face. Her whole body was probably the same: broken and put back together so many times that there was more scar than skin.

'How are the wounded being treated?'

'We have an infirmary on the twenty-sixth.'

'I meant out there.'

'We're not concerned with how the rebs deal with their problems. Probably with a laser-shot to the head. Few of them are exactly the Medi-Corpo type.' She took a moment, before adding: 'They're used to stepping over each other where they fall in the street.'

'How did all this start? I mean, I know the history of the uprising of the no-boomers, but how did it get this bad?'

'The rebs refused all reasonable approaches at reconciliation. They insisted on threatening our way of life, and we were bound by our self-interest to protect it. We will not be intimidated or bullied by terrorists who have no respect for freedom or human life.'

'Look out the window. It can't get any worse than this. Don't you think it's time you people stopped mouthing that tired bullshit?'

Walking to the far side of the desk, she poured a paper cup of water from a dispenser. 'Want one?'

I shook my head.

She drank a sip. 'It is very unusual for them to send a man to do a woman's work.'

'They thought I would be less conspicuous. You know, look like less of a threat.'

This was carefully considered.

'You seem nervous, like you might be hiding something.'

'Oh, I'm nervous all right. And I'm hiding plenty. But my orders are to give the message I have to Ching-zi, and no one else. And I need that sphere in order to fulfil those orders.'

'You mean *Chong*-zi, of course.'

'Yeah, whatever.'

'You don't seem very respectful or well informed. Not exactly what one would expect from an agent of the great Euro-Corpo. Wouldn't you agree?'

'I wouldn't know, but I think my expendability was important to them. I'm not what you would call a trained agent or anything. More of a courier. Nobody gives a shit what happens to me. But the message I have . . . . Now, that's a different matter. So I would treat me with the greatest care and attention until that's delivered, if I were you.'

'That is the obvious thing for you to say.'

'OK, it's obvious. So what?'

I waited for her to answer but she remained silent, staring at me, trying to read something in my face. It was a poker moment, as we used say in the marketing business: first one to talk loses. I said: 'What are you looking at me like that for?'

'Maybe I don't believe you. Maybe we could pay a little visit to the interrogation chamber. Maybe a few choice drugs would make you blab the truth out of your pretty little face.'

'Yes,' I agreed. 'We could – but who would activate the message if you fucked me up?'

'I think we could get the sphere to work without you.'

'Maybe.'

'I'm sure we could torture you into activating it.'

'Why bother? I'm happy to activate it.'

'We could detain you, in very uncomfortable circumstances, until we were entirely satisfied that you were being truthful.'

'Do we have the time for that?'

'I don't know.'

'Neither do I.'

'There's something about you that doesn't add up. I don't trust you. You should know this. I will be watching you very carefully. I would also advise that you keep your opinions to yourself. Especially in regard to what you term 'tired bullshit'. People around here have had their families wiped out for our beliefs. Our freedom is sacred.'

'Hey.' I held up my palms, then waved them towards the apocalypse below. 'I didn't crap up your city.'

What I really wanted to say was 'What freedom?' but you can't argue with these ideological types. They never realise that, by destroying their enemy, they're destroying themselves. There needs to be a strong moral reason for war to work out, not a makey-up one like theirs – which wouldn't fool a twelve-year-old of average intelligence.

'You really are a most awkward and opinionated boy,' she said. 'That may pass for sexy in Europe, but it's considered a pain in the ass here.'

'Add it up,' I said, while pondering the implications of her bringing up the word 'sexy'. 'The rebs must have a point of view, or they wouldn't be dying for it.'

'Their point of view is of no importance. It is backward, crude and anti-freedom. Anti-*profit*. Nothing they say could be of interest.'

'As I said, it's your business. I don't actually give a crap.'

She fixed me with a look which was halfway between disdain and curiosity. 'You're very forthright. I suppose that's a European thing too.'

If only these women got laid more often, I thought, when she had left the room. If only they at least factored sexual frustration into their decision-process.

18

The young Chinese man who entered the room an hour later was slight and eye-avoiding. He looked like he was carrying a thousand secrets in his finely shaven head.

'You will follow me?'

This might have been a question, or it might have been a command; it was hard to know from his voice, which was as distant and grey as the smoke curling around the horizon. Once outside, we were joined by the Commander, who followed us, with a hand on her holster. There was another door, and then we were in a boardroom, in which three elderly Chinese and a young European sat at a large polished table.

'We were expecting William Howe,' said Daisy.

And there she was: the thing that had been living it up in my head for so long. I had to convince myself she was real. She looked too good to be real, like some super-defined hologram of a movie star. A sequence flashed in my head, of the different places where I had loved her. By the lake in Scotland where, as Tattoo, she had wolfed the food I cooked and laughed in my face for asking her to help with the dishes; as Daisy, in the wastelands of Carlow, where we had played together as children; or as Emily, in the trendy bars of Dublin, where the do-gooder had sipped alco-free martinis, while lecturing me on how to do good. It all merges together. The emotion explodes in your heart, and your brain kicks into gear, tries to rationalise it all. This woman had been different women, who had belonged to different parts of my life. I had loved them all.

I wondered then, as I stood like an idiot, whether I loved all women, or at least all women who showed me any serious attention. Was it a 'man thing'? Had this susceptibility been the reason men had been destined to submit? I had loved my model-car collection as a child, had fingered and polished each tiny replica.

I hid them from Zisha, terrified he would touch my sacred, secret things with his clumsy hands. I once threatened to kill him – and meant it – if he dared to even think about touching my cars. They were under the bed at home now, as far as I could remember, neglected, forgotten. Their potency faded with the arrival of adolescence and the desire for all things fleshy. The model cars, with their neat corners and shiny detail, became slightly ridiculous then, and I told Zisha he could have them. Now, he too was lying under a bed.

Daisy was dressed in the same high-collared business suit as the Chinese. Hers was blue, theirs red – the official colour of the Triumvirates. One of them, stabbing me with a look, said: 'You mean, this is not our friend with the money?'

'He has brought this,' said the Commander, placing the sphere on the table, where they had been examining 3D charts, which, in the absence of input, began to bob up and down impatiently, fulfilling some pre-programmed instruction to demand attention.

'Perhaps we should do some introductions,' said another, waving her hand vaguely around the table. 'I am Yingtao, and these are my colleagues Sha-yu,' she said, referring to the angry one, 'and Chong-zi. You are . . . ?'

'Here to deliver a message,' I said. The woman I had come so far to murder was smaller than her colleagues, and older. Though her face was set in an implacable expression, her eyes flickered constantly. This could have been a sign either of intelligence or of insanity. It was hard to tell. The rest of us waited for her to say or do something. Eventually she stood up and shuffled around the table, ponderously dragging her fingertips on the polished surface, sliding them over the off-switch to the bar-charts. Picking up the sphere, she examined it by holding it close to one eye against the light of the glass wall. Placing it back on the table, she walked one or two steps closer, then stopped to consider me, as the others continued to consider her. She took her time, oblivious to the vacuum her silence had created, as she squinted up at me. Now that she was near, I noticed that one of her eyes was slightly off centre, and seemed to have interests of its own over my left shoulder. I wondered why she had not get corrective surgery.

'They were expecting Howe,' said Daisy. She told me afterwards she had felt the need to interject – to direct the great woman away from a possible 'Off with his head!' moment. 'They were told he was coming with funds.'

'I am here as a courier,' I said. 'To convey the following message – and I'm quoting, so don't get pissed off with me: *There will be no funds until you incompetent morons can explain why you are so pathetically incapable of suppressing this uprising. Details of Euro-Corpo's position and requirements are contained in the sphere.*'

Sha-yu stood up, and slapped the table. 'How *dare* you.'

Her colleagues looked at each other, a little awkwardly. She in turn looked at Chong-zi for support – which she took from an indolent eye. Spitting indignation, she said: 'The impudence. Take him outside and have him shot.'

I felt the Commander's hand tighten on my elbow. 'By all means,' I said, 'shoot the messenger. That will do you a lot of good with my superiors. Yes, that will fit nicely with your catalogue of well-judged decisions. It'll really help you decode the sphere too.'

'You must forgive my colleague,' said Chong-zi, considering me from beneath at least one of her hooded eyes. 'We have all been under a degree of pressure lately, and we are not used to being spoken to in such a manner by anyone, let alone a . . . boy. Sit.'

The grip on my elbow vanished, and I was pushed onto a seat beside Daisy, with our elbows almost touching. 'Please, tell us what you have faced such great danger to come to say.'

'You are not going to take this stripling seriously?' Sha-yu said this with an elaborate groan, accompanied by a wave of her arms in my direction – in case anyone might be unclear who the stripling was.

'We must use our heads,' Chong-zi said, with the quiet authority of one who did not need to elaborate. 'We have nothing to lose by listening. There is obviously *something* going on, and the boy strikes me as being too foolish to be practising a deception.'

'Thank you,' I said to Chong-zi, 'for your vote of confidence.' I had lost all fear, for some reason, and was slipping along in a stream of adrenalin. 'You are of course correct. They couldn't risk sending Howe, or any other half-respectable individual. The message I have to relay is relatively simple, and I am relatively expendable.'

'You won't mind,' insinuated Yingtao, 'if we confirm your status with our counterparts in Europe?'

'Oh, please do,' I answered. 'There's every chance your communication won't be intercepted and my presence here exposed. The rebs probably won't be surprised at all to hear that

Ameri-Corpo needs handouts from Euro-Corpo, just to keep the lights on.'

Her frozen smile twitched. 'Idiot,' she said. 'We are well beyond the stage when we care about what anyone thinks, and besides, you might be surprised to learn that we have the capability to communicate without fear of detection.'

'Perhaps,' said Chong-zi, 'the boy might bring us some tea. I have found that there has rarely been a problem that cannot be solved over a bowl of tea.' The shaven-headed boy, who had been hovering in the background, like a bar-chart, withdrew. When he had gone, Yingtao turned to Daisy. 'You might be considerate enough to inform us of the source of his authority?'

'My instructions come from an agent called "Mianzi",' I said. 'Who is based in Dublin. Where her instructions come from, I am not aware.'

Chong-zi looked like she was straining to hold her patience – like she wanted to swat. 'I was not addressing you,' she said, with painstaking politeness, before turning back to Daisy. 'Are you familiar with such an agent?'

'Yes, and I can confirm that she has been involved in the Numbers Game.'

She did not mention that the 'agent' happened to be her mother.

'Very well,' said Chong-zi. 'Let him continue . . . . Oh yes, and your own name . . . ?'

'Call me Li. Now, if I have your attention?'

'Li?' said Yingtao. 'Let us hope that it is not literal.'

A snort from Sha-yu indicated that this had been a joke.

'Let him continue,' said Chong-zi.

The 'boy' appeared with tea, but was signalled from the room by Chong-zi's fingers before he could pour. Bowing graciously, he left the tray on the table and retreated backwards. I followed his path out of the room; my gaze stopped at the Commander, who was sitting quietly by the door. She remained cold in her obedience, an extra on set, though her lips, chapped and thick against her drawn face, held the line of her commitment.

'You have been asked,' said Yingtao, 'to explain why exactly you are here. Perhaps when it is convenient?'

The tea-set consisted of, among other bits and pieces, a clay pot and five cups. The tray, the pot and the cups were all hand-carved with the same simple yet intricate monogram of the Ameri-Corpo logo. A clay bear and bull sat on either side of the pot, which Yingtao picked up, to dribble a thin stream through a sieve into the first cup, which she handed to Chong-zi. They love their rituals, the Chinese. It was ritual that underpinned their ideology. It was the ritual of hierarchy – of Yingtao giving Chong-zi the first cup – which justified everything they did, and the way they lived. These rituals were their attempt to impose order on a disordered world. It was for rituals that so much blood had been spattered on the rubble. And on the burnt-out cars, upended shopping trolleys and doll torsos – on all the broken toys of capitalism in that great dump that was still being called Seattle.

'There is coded information in the sphere,' I said, 'that will help you use the Numbers Game to crush the rebellion. I am to recode the sphere with your response and your plan. If the plan is considered viable, then funds will follow. There are to be regular visits to assess progress against key criteria.'

'The Numbers Game was never designed to *crush* the rebellion,' said Daisy, with a nervous laugh. 'The intention was to help us understand it.'

'Silence, fool!' I shouted. 'You are to return with me after this briefing. You're usefulness here is at an end.'

A malicious glint passed from one triumvir eye to another. Daisy had been their main contact with Euro-Corpo and the principles of the Game, but if what I said was true, she would become expendable. And they loved to expend.

'There is obviously a lot to be considered,' Chong-zi said quietly. 'I suggest we break for lunch, and reconvene later to consider the situation.'

'Excuse me, sir.'

The Commander, still standing erect by the door, would have stood there all day if Chong-zi had not waved her magic fingers to allow her to speak. 'It's the sphere, sir. The courier says it will implode if it travels more than a few metres from him, sir.'

'And have you examined the sphere?' asked Chong-zi unenthusiastically.

'Yes, sir.'

'And do we not have the most up-to-date systems on the planet for detecting implosives?'

'We do, sir.'

'And what did your examinations uncover?'

'Nothing, sir. It's just a basic sphere with the usual holographics and memory components.'

'Then what are you worried about? Go and have your lunch, Commander.'

19

'Are you completely insane?' Daisy said, as we walked down a pan-piping corridor. 'Coming here and spouting all that bullshit. These people are no fools: they're the most powerful people in America right now.'

'It's amazing,' I said. 'You hear about these people all your life. You live in a kind of awe of their distance and status. Yet when you meet them . . . they look so ordinary. They're scared shitless, if you ask me. I think they're totally out of control. I'm not impressed.'

'You're not impressed? You've completely lost your marbles, haven't you? I always knew you were out there . . . . But this . . . . Oh Fucius, we're both dead . . . .'

In the canteen, there was a line of employees having food ladled onto plates by American boys with bandanas wedged on their heads and smiles hanging from their faces.

'But I don't like potatoes.' The Chinese boy was complaining to one of the serving boys, whose plastered smile began to flake.

'It's America Day, sir. We have an American theme today.'

This was backed up by throbbing rock-and-roll music, which had replaced the pan-pipes as soon as we entered.

'Do not argue with me. I would not care if it was Shangsi Day. I want noodles.'

'I'm sorry, sir, we don't have any noodles. Would you like hash-browns? Everyone else seems to think they're pretty good.'

There did seem to be a lot of hash-browns on the trays being carried to tables by the shuffling throng. The Chinese boy's fine forehead crinkled. 'What else do you have?'

'We have hot-dogs,' the server said hopefully. 'Hamburger. Waffles with or without syrup. We have French fries, fried chicken, fried eggs, fried ham, fried beans. We have corn-dogs, baby-back ribs, egg salad, bean salad, tomato salad, hummus, biscuits and baloney. For dessert, we have apple pie, blueberry pie, ice cream and fruit salad.'

'Synthetic?'

'Most of it. But it's still good.'

'Pig-swill,' said the Chinese, half to himself. 'Give me a banana.'

'Pretty high maintenance,' I said to the server, when it was my turn at the trough. I nodded in the direction of the Chinese boy, who was sitting at a table looking at his banana. Laughing awkwardly, the server dropped his eyes to the fried chicken. He seemed to have been more comfortable in the previous exchange.

'Dickhead,' I said to Daisy as we sat down. 'Deserves all the grief he gets. Servile gobshite.'

'And you're such a big-shot,' she whispered, leaning over the table towards me. 'Have you any idea how deep the deep shit we are in is? Of the danger you have caused for the Numbers Game?'

'I'm sick to my teeth of this Numbers Game.'

This caused her to urge me to keep my voice low – with a look that managed to both stab and seethe.

'It's all you ever think about,' I said, in a smaller voice. 'The whole thing's more trouble than it's worth.'

'That is not for you to say. There are other, slightly more intelligent people who might have a different perspective. Some might say – if they dared to disagree with you, that is – that the project's conclusions might still have some small use for the greater good.'

'Daisy, the Publican is dead. She was killed in Athlone.'

'Impossible. She's too important.'

'Not any more.'

She crushed hash-browns with the side of her fork. 'She can't be.'

'I wouldn't say it if it wasn't true.'

Searching my face for a sign of deceit or a thread of hope, she found neither. 'She will be a great loss. But if there was one thing she taught me, it was that none of us matter. Not really. Not to the overall scheme of things.' Dragging her fork across the battered mess of her food, she added, wistfully: 'The project's the important thing.'

'I'm sorry.'

'What are you sorry for? Did you kill her?'

'No, of course I didn't bloody kill her. But I knew her too, you know. And she's one of the reasons I'm here. She's sent me on a mission.'

I don't know why I said that. I think I was trying to big myself up in Daisy's eyes, to include myself in her grief, or involve myself in that higher world of hers, from which I was always excluded.

'What are you talking about? You come over here with some freaky sphere, spouting out of you that there's info on it that will help them crush the rebellion. What info?'

'*I* don't know. I was just bullshitting, telling them what I thought they wanted to hear.'

'Oh, great. The future of the world is in the hands of a moron.'

'Look,' I said, putting my hand on her arm, 'I'm not a complete moron. The Publican did send me here to do something, and once I'm finished, we can make a run for it. Do you know a way out of here?'

'Yeah? What did she send you to do?'

'I can't tell you right now.'

'Well, whatever your reason, it had better be worth it. I was making progress before you stuck your stupid head into that room.'

'You *know* the real reason I'm here,' I said, taking her hand and looking into her eyes.

'Please.' She pulled her hand away. 'Don't start.'

'They are going to kill you,' I said, grasping her hand. 'Mianzi as good as told me herself. You were a dead woman as soon as you left Dublin. You're a disciple of the Publican. Do you really think they'll let you live? You are an idealist, and they have to root out ideology before they can prevail.'

'And that's another thing. What the fuck has Mianzi got to do with this? And why would she tell you anything?'

I tried to look calm, as my mind raced for an answer. 'We've been . . . hanging out a bit.'

'Oh, sweet Fucius,' she said, removing my hand like it was filthy. 'You've been fucking my mother. And do you know what? I'm not even surprised.'

'OK, OK, so I shagged your mother. I did what I had to do. It wasn't easy for me when you just disappeared. I didn't have that many options.'

She pointed her fork at me. 'You've been an indiscriminate slut for years. But we don't have time for that now. What we need to concentrate on is our current situation, and how the hell we are going to get through it.'

The Chinese boy began, finally, to eat his banana, chewing it with resigned tastelessness.

'We have to find a way out of here,' I said.

'We can't *leave*. Not until we find out what they're planning.'

'Who cares? They're going to do what they're going to do any-way, one way or another.'

'Look, you might be happy to dismiss the Game and every-thing it stood for, but I can't. I can't allow these women to deal with this uprising in their own way. Fuck knows what they'll do.'

'OkaOKy then.' I churned the numbers in my head. The best chance I would have of both surviving and winning the girl would be to play along, for now. 'Let's hear what they have to say.'

'Agreed.'

When she began to eat, laboriously, her face said that the food had no taste. I chewed on the fried chicken, which was de-licious compared to power-bars.

'Are you really not afraid of them?' she said. 'Did you mean what you said earlier?'

'Sure.'

'Do you really think we can make it past those three witch-es?'

'I think they're frightened. They're out of their depth.'

'Even Chong-zi?'

'Cross-eyed fucker,' I murmured, stirring my synthetic milk-shake with a straw. 'She doesn't scare me.'

'You guys finished?'

The serving guy was at the table, clearing plates. I was not sure how much he had heard.

'There's a launchpad on the roof,' Daisy said, when he had left. 'They've got strato-pods up there that would get us home in a couple of hours.'

'Could you get us up there?'

'I think so. One of the guards is a sympathiser – or so she says.'

'Might be worth the risk to just go for it now, get the fuck away from here in one piece.'

'Yes, but what then? Even if we did make it, we'd spend the rest of our lives looking over our shoulders.'

'I know a place we could go. And a doctor who puts ID chips up cat's arses. We'd have a chance.'

She looked at me with her cool blue eyes. I should have per-haps mentioned that she looked like Tattoo, without the tattoo, and blonde. This was how she really looked, she said later, and cool blue was the natural colour of her eyes.

'Were you not listening? We can't. There are too many other

things at stake. We need to play this out, find out what they're planning, and then do whatever it takes stop them. Now, are you ready to step up and be something more than a slag, for once in your life?'

'Fuck it,' I said, using the opportunity to squeeze her hand. 'Let's rock and roll.'

20

'The servant from the canteen told us everything,' said Sha-yu when we reconvened after lunch. We had been followed into the room by the Commander and the Chinese boy, who quietly closed the door and sat either side of it, like Egyptian dogs at the entrance to a tomb.

'Yeah?' I replied, smiling broadly, as if to acknowledge some private joke. 'About the hash-browns, all that crap? We heard the whole thing. Got into a row with your boy there, who wanted noodles. He said the food was pig-swill, if I remember correctly. And to be fair, he had a point. I'd reconsider this America Day if I were you, I really would. I mean now, Italy Day or French Cuisine Day . . . that might be something worth considering. Mind you, the chicken wasn't actually that bad . . . .'

'Silence, fool!' Sha-yu shouted, thumping everyone to attention. 'You were overheard plotting against the Board by the servant.'

I heard myself speaking – which was unfortunate, in a way, because I hadn't consulted myself about what I was going to say. 'Yeah?' I said. 'And you're going to listen to a, you know, crawling underling who can't even butter his waffles?'

Sha-yu continued to look at me with the contempt of a cross-examining barrister, while Yingtao's expression of incredulity fixed itself for the long haul. I didn't look at Chong-zi.

'Fucius,' I continued. 'You guys really take the biscuit. This is all baloney. Hah.'

'He has been a reliable source of information before,' said Yingtao – mild, in comparison to her histrionic partner. 'Which, when added to this recording he made of your conversation, makes for compelling evidence.'

A reco-button was placed onto the table and pressed. The sounds of the canteen immediately filled the room. Background babble phased into mine and Daisy's lunchtime conversation. Though initially faint, it became clearer: he had obviously moved closer to our table.

No Numbers Game . . . More trouble than it's worth . . . Then Daisy's voice: *The project's the important thing.*

I snorted. 'Yeah, well, you know. That could, like, mean anything. Matter of fact, far as I remember, we were chatting about the Round-Ireland Rally. Yeah, that's it. We were thinking of entering the Round-Ireland Rally when we get home. And that waiter is, like you know, just trying to, you know, make trouble. He's so pussy-whipped, he has whiplash.' Then, confidentially: 'Wouldn't surprise me if he was working for the other side.'

'Oh, it gets more specific,' said Yingtao, pressing the button again. Glancing at Sha-yu, I saw her demeanour morph into that of a cat, with its paw on the tail of an injured vole. This time it was Daisy's voice first, and the reception was crystal clear: *What are you talking about? You come over here with some freaky sphere, spouting out of you that there's info on it that will help them crush the rebellion. What info?*

I don't know. I was just bullshitting, telling them what I thought they wanted to hear.

Oh, great. The future of the world is in the hands of a moron.

'So?' I said. 'I'm not going to, like, tell *her* why I'm here, am I? You can hardly call that anti-establishment.'

'Oh, and we picked this up from your conversation in the corridor. You will allow me?'

Yingtao, who was being gratuitous, pressed the button anyway. Out came my incriminating voice. *They look so ordinary. They're scared shitless, if you ask me. I think they're totally out of control. I'm not impressed.*

Her eyelids rose slowly. 'So sorry we have failed to impress you.'

Forcing a smile, I tried to make it look like I really appreciated her sense of humour. 'You girls. I was putting Daisy at her ease,' I said, with an enormous sweep of my arm. 'Trying to, you know, find out what she knows. Fucius, this is so frustrating. I came here to deliver a simple message, and I find myself embroiled in some kind of, you know, moronic game of . . . subterfuge and what-not, with people who are, like, supposed to be, like, in control of a continent. No wonder the whole place is falling asunder. Ha-ha.'

I pointed at the Chinese boy, making him start. 'Ask him. Ask him what he thinks of your Mata Hari.'

'It is true,' he confirmed sullenly. 'He is an idiot, that servant.'

'Thank you for your opinion,' said Yingtao. 'It provides no helpful insight whatsoever.'

He stood, bowed, and sat down again.

'So,' she continued, to me, 'you are saying you were *pretending* to be plotting against the Board, in order to establish Miss Bradshaw's credentials? That the servant in the canteen is an idiot, and that you are in fact working in the interests of the Ameri-Corpo? So, what did you discover? Is Miss Bradshaw an enemy of the Ameri-Corpo?'

'That's *exactly* what I'm trying to establish,' I said, hoping that the relief I forced into my voice would, at least, suggest credibility. 'We're all on the, you know, same side here, approaching the same problem from different angles. As it were.'

Daisy could have said something, but she just stared at the floor as if she were in a different place. It made me think of a captured soldier preparing for interrogation or torture, or worse.

'Well then, you must have a high degree of respect for the Seattle Triumvirate?' Yingtao was saying.

'I most certainly have. Abso-fucking-lutely.'

I could feel Daisy's discomfort now. Something was making her tune back in to the conversation. Yingtao nodded and looked at Chong-zi, who had moved to the glass wall. A security car sliding silently by, left a thin white wake, which dissipated into the blue haze of the refractor-grid, more visible now, in the rising dust of the afternoon. Eventually, Chong-zi nodded back and Yintao reached a slow thumb towards the button on the table.

Did you mean what you said about them, out in the corridor?
Sure.
Do you really think we can make it past those three witches?
Sure. I think they're frightened. They're out of their depth.
Even Chong-zi?
Cross-eyed fucker. She doesn't scare me.

We looked at each other in the space that followed another click of the annoying button.

'Hardly the words of a loyal follower,' observed Yingtao.

'More like the words of treacherous terrorists,' shouted Sha-yu.

'Girls, girls,' I said, affecting weariness, while desperately bolting around my head for a way out. 'You obviously misunderstand our Irish accents. We had been talking about which one of you we fancy the most. It was a private conversation: the type of banter that goes on between old friends. Daisy – Miss Bradshaw, – as you no doubt know, is as gay as Christmas, and it's no secret that I'm fond of a bit of *older* myself.'

'Do you take us for *complete* imbeciles?' Yingtao said.

'Look, what Miss Bradshaw said was, you'll never make a *pass* at those three.'

Their faces stretched. 'And *witches* is a term we use for sexy, and yes, I'm going to say it, *older* ladies back home. I can see how you could misinterpret the next sentence, what with all the pan-pipes and everything. What I actually said about Chong-zi was: *Of course I'd fuck her.* We're Europeans, for crying out loud, we like, you know, bang on about this stuff all the time. Who we would, or wouldn't, give a good seeing to . . . . Look, I know we talk a lot of nonsense and everything, but believe me, we're, like, very committed to, like, the cause, and everything. And what matters is – '

'Well, what about this then,' Yingtao interrupted. 'As an indication of your . . . commitment?'

We sat and listened to me and Daisy talk about screwing up their plans, then making a run for it in a strato-pod. I smiled weakly when the conversation came to the part where I had screwed Mianzi. *You've been fucking my mother. And do you know what? I'm not even surprised.*

OK, OK. So I shagged your mother.

Daisy let out a small sigh.

Chong-zi was actually smiling now, though this seemed to be causing some pain. 'Your level of stupidity is amusing,' she said.

'Smile away,' I heard myself say, unhelpfully. 'I'll pay for the stitches.'

The smile disappeared.

'But of all the little insights we've gleaned from these recordings,' Yingtao said, 'regarding your general stupidity and sexual depravity, which I suppose *could* be possible, there is one little snippet which stands out as being particularly unambiguous. May I?'

She tapped the button, and we heard first my voice, then Daisy's. *I know a place we could go. And a doctor who puts* ID *chips up cat's arses. We'd have a chance.*

Were you not listening? We can't. There are too many other things at stake. We need to play this out, find out what they're planning – and then whatever it takes stop them. Now, are you ready to step up with me and be something more than a slag all your life?

Fuck it. Let's rock and roll.

Following a silence, which killed all ambiguity, Yingtao said, in a calm, measured voice: 'Can anyone give me a reason why we should not decapitate these rebels and throw them into the hamburger mince, for next week's America Day special?'

A murmur of assent indicated that this was probably the best way to proceed. Chong-zi, who was still by the glass, turned her back to us and gazed over the city. The episode was surreal to me. I was standing in the middle of a soap, up to my earlobes in stilted lines and a bizarre plot.

The Commander stood up slowly, and seemed on the point of saying something, when Daisy spoke into the void. 'Look,' she said, 'I think we all need to dislocate ourselves from our egos for a second, and use common sense. Whether or not myself and Li were having a conversation about the Triumvirate is not the issue here. And if we were thinking of getting the fuck out of here, well, you could hardly blame us. Of course we think you are "witches" and "dangerous bitches": what else *could* we think, under the circumstances? And yes, I am a disciple of the Numbers Game, and am committed to its mission. But you knew that already. We don't have to love each other, to work together. And we all still share the same problem. The rebels are getting more desperate, more organised, and nearer to hitting this building with a mass assault. And if Seattle HQ falls, then the war here is lost. And it will spread to the rest of the world. This problem does not care about our differences. It is going to steamroll through all of us, and everything we've ever believed in or cared about, if we don't act together. Now.'

'A noble speech', said Yingtao. 'But I would be very interested to hear what value you can bring as a solution to this *problem.*'

'Why don't we get the sphere and hear what it has to say,' Daisy said. 'Either it will be helpful or it will not. If it is, you can compile a response and we can take it to Europe to request funds, as planned.'

'And if not?'

'Well, then we're back to where we are now, but this was the original plan, and unless anyone has a better idea . . . .'

'Go,' said Chong-zi tonelessly to the Chinese boy. 'Bring the sphere.'

21

A distant crackle of laser-shot started below us: the alien wasteland was coming alive. I looked at Daisy, who was staring at the floor again, probably crunching, weighing up options. She could never escape her conditioning: there were always odds to be considered. The Triumvirate had gathered in a huddle near a corner of the room, moving there by strange sequence, together. They began to mutter; Yingtao and Sha-yu seemed to be pressing Chong-zi about something, while she stood with her back against the wall, hands hidden in the wide sleeves of her jacket, looking over at us from time to time. Daisy began to rock in her chair, tapping time on the floor with her toe, while the Commander, still coiled by the door, caressed, absently, her holster with a fingertip.

When the boy came in with the sphere, he placed it quietly on the table before resuming Egyptian dog duties. I thought of making a lunge, and wondered if I would have time to code in the colours, before being sliced in two by the Commander's pistol. If I did manage to trigger the explosion, I would be killing everyone in the room, including myself. I decided to sit quietly and think again.

The Triumvirate, who had glanced at the sphere when it arrived, were more interested in their conversation. Nothing happened for several minutes and I began to feel listless – wishing something would. I raised a defiant look at the Commander and was met by her vacant face. Inconveniently, I found myself fantasising about her. I wanted her to drag me from the room and push me against a wall. I wanted to be strapped into a chair and questioned, to be slapped and cajoled – the centre of her attention. I wanted her chapped lips to whisper from behind my head that I was a dead man if I did not talk. I wanted to stand up to her, with dignity, to repel her and control my impulses in the face of her overtures. I wanted to lose and regain control – to encourage and reject, to imply then deny. To dance the shallow salsa of seduction. It was strange to be in the middle of such a fraught situation and find myself absorbed by base impulse. But it was base impulse that had made me what I was, Daisy said, during her Emily period, and what I always would be. The laser-shots below cackled away, like background laughter.

'We have decided,' said Yingtao, 'to tell you about Sixing 6.'

Producing a projector-button from her pocket, she pressed it onto the table and was immediately surrounded by a graph of what looked like chemical formulae. Sha-yu sat to watch; Chongzi remained at the wall, dark-blue and diminutive.

'Sixing 6,' said Yingtao, blinking against the light of the projection, 'is the key to the Passover Project. It is a gas with several special qualities – one of which is to settle at ground level and not rise above a height of ten feet.'

She tapped the disc, and another set of graphs and figures sprang into the room. I did not understand any of it, but Daisy seemed to be trying to work something out. It looked like she had seen this before somewhere.

'Another, is that it is completely invisible and has no detectable scent.' Yingtao pointed to a row of figures. 'But its most special quality is that it causes a new strain of tuberculosis, an antique disease thought to have been eradicated many years ago.'

A swallow waltzed by outside, diving and ducking after an invisible insect. It was late in the year for swallows. she must have been feeding up for the long flight south.

'What do you intend doing with it?' I said, daring them to say that the whole thing was just a joke. Horrors such as these could not be real. Yingtao said, in a voice that was slightly bedroom: 'What we intend doing, my sweet, is exploding some canisters of it in the rubble.'

I smiled, responsively, grateful for the flirt, before realising what she had just said.

She carried on gravely. 'It will look as if a natural epidemic has broken out in the unsanitary conditions. The disease, though immediately debilitating, takes three to four months to kill, after which point the gas will have dissipated to tolerable and undetectable levels.'

'We, in the tower, will have been *passed over*,' explained Sha-yu.

'We move in with the bulldozers,' said Yingtao. 'Burn the bodies, provide antidotes for survivors, and emerge as heroic matriarchs. It's all planned: the publicity, the media. News broadcasts will go around the world about the terrible epidemic. About how the Corpo is doing everything it can to help a beleaguered population.'

'After a year, we will have won the public-relations war,' said Sha-yu, slapping the table. 'And the war in the rest of the country will be a fait accompli, with us dropping a canister here and there, and generally turning the continent into a triage centre. The rebellion will deflate, its leaders will be dead in the rubble, and the world will realise that the Ameri-Corpo is a caring and powerful force to be respected and obeyed.' Having worked herself up into a frenzy, she fell dramatically silent, her eyes glowing warmly.

'In five years, the country will be rebuilt,' Yingtao said, rationally. 'As will its financial and business institutions. We'll form some kind of a liberal quango, which will include representatives from the disenfranchised groupings. It will of course be toothless, but we will pay its hand-picked members sufficiently to win and lose the correct arguments.'

'How many?' said Daisy, quietly.

'Excuse me?'

Yingtao had heard, and only asked for the question to be repeated in order to emphasise its audacity. These old girls were full of their own self-righteousness.

'How many will die?'

'Oh, no more than absolutely necessary. The numbers will be important, though. We will orchestrate a minimum quota, in order to allow the project to assume the status of **a** global catastrophe.'

'How many?'

'Well, if you're looking for specific numbers . . . somewhere between 5 and 10 million would be expected from the initial phase.'

'It's crazy,' I heard myself say, aloud. 'You're all lunatics.' It should have been obvious to me – I was an insignificant speck in the present company – it seemed to be to everyone else. I wondered if by this outburst they would think me even more of an idiot than I had already established myself as being. Strange to be insecure at a time like this, but then again, it's difficult to escape the human condition of human conditioning. Well, it is when you're a shallow bastard like me. Even in this nightmare, I couldn't help my vanity. I looked around. Chong-zi had raised the eyebrow over her bad eye, and was scrutinising me with the other.

Her colleagues were openly sneering. They were amused by me. I was their clown – which was possibly the reason I was still alive.

'This is unnecessary,' Daisy said. 'We have already established several other options, which can be looked at before we go to Armageddon. We must look again at the Numbers Game . . . at what it can tell us.'

'In order to compute, you must have uniformity of constituents,' said Yingtao. 'The Numbers Game is useless in this respect. Human beings cannot be digitised, at sub-levels. Oh, it is easy to be misled. There are many, many common denominators – as any marketeer will tell you. But for every area of commonality, there is a variety of contradictions. We were arrogant enough to fund this project over the years because we thought it would be possible to break the code, to define people in measurable components. We now know that this is impossible. And we are no nearer to understanding why the rebels behave as they do, than we are to answering the great questions of what was before the beginning, or why we are here.'

'Would it not be an idea,' said Daisy, 'to initiate contact with the rebel leaders, to at least *try* to develop a dialogue?'

'We do *not*,' said Sha-yu, sharply, 'negotiate with terrorists.'

'And besides,' said Yingtao, 'such an approach would have little chance of being successful in the current climate. Time has run out. We did consider your approach, but it would take too much time and expose us to too many potential pitfalls. Even if it did work, it would take generations. We are more interested in the profits we can provide in *our* lifetimes than a possible peace that would take years to establish.'

'You have a point.' Daisy was straining, like me, to hold her composure, and made this concession in order to appeal to their glorious female rationale. 'But surely we can do better. Can we really be responsible for the deaths of millions? We would be no better than the most brutal men in history. We *could* initiate communications with the rebs. We *could* try to find a way to negotiate.'

'We do not negotiate with terrorists,' repeated Sha-yu, slapping the table.

'We can use the intelligence that has already been gathered,' said Daisy. 'There are a hundred different ways we can approach this problem, before we revert to Sixing.'

'Like what?' asked Yingtao. She, like Daisy, was drawing on her self-control. I was reminded of an old spy-thriller where the villain tells the hero that the two of them are more alike than either cares to admit.

'Like,' said Daisy, 'an international conference. It could be attended by representatives from all the Corpos and reb factions. We could put together an independent, international body, like the old United Nations, to give the thing credibility. It could agree global incentives for investments in reb-inclusive Corpos.'

Yingtao leaned over the table on her fists, pushing her focus right into Daisy. 'It would take too long,' she said. 'We'd be blown to smithereens before it had a chance to work. And besides, no one would buy it. Human nature is too consumed with short-term gain to ever think in such a lateral way. Surely you gleaned that much from your Numbers Game.'

'You don't know that,' said Daisy. 'It has to be worth thinking about, at least.'

'You are a very idealistic young woman. We' – she gestured towards her fellow triumvirs with a thumb – 'We, on the other hand, have many years of hard experience.' We have dealt with idealists before. For millennia, humankind has given attention to idealists and their view of our . . . struggles. Philosophers, scientists, priests, artists of every type. Self-aggrandising, cut-price gurus, the lot of them. Shakespeare . . . .' She stretched the word disapprovingly, before continuing, singsong: 'The constant struggles we have had to deal with: guilt, regret, loss. What does it all mean? Nothing. Or how about the poets? What wonderful images of refinement and complication they paint, to cover up our base, human, undeniable *meagreness*. Oh yes, we could spend another fifty years at the Numbers Game, trying to understand why we see ourselves in one way and behave in another. Or we could spend a hundred sitting around a table with a group of ill-smelling males, trying to understand their feelings. It does not amount to anything. It does not pay any bills or feed any children.'

She looked at Chong-zi, still lurking by the wall, and I wondered if perhaps she had gone too far, had gone off-message in some way. It was hard to tell from their expressions, what went on between them. They never like to expose their emotions, the Chinese, unless you can call contempt an emotion.

Yingtao, following an almost imperceptible nod from Chong-zi, concluded: 'There is no *profit* in it.'

Daisy said: 'But to kill so many . . . .'

'That's as may be,' said Chong-zi, her quiet authority filling the room. 'But we have a greater urgency now. Many millions, and more, will die all over the world, unless we come up with a swift and effective solution.'

Thinking about it afterwards, I remembered her ready use of the pronoun 'we'. She was acknowledging no direct responsibility, though she could have stopped everything with a single word. She was hiding in the collective, using the numbers.

'But why this solution?' Daisy looked at Chong-zi blankly: she couldn't find the rational. 'What about using the metadata we've collected? We already know that they would be prepared to compromise in return for medical assistance. Why not use that?'

'No time.' Sha-yu's voice came out as a hiss. 'We need to initiate Passover.'

I could see the next thought descend over Daisy's face like a shadow. 'Why are you telling *us* this?'

Sha-yu looked at Yingtao, who was at the ready with her pointer. She started prodding figures on the chart again. 'We will need money. For the orchestration of the rescue efforts, for equipment and supplies. And we will need to know that the money is there to rebuild the country. We have prepared a requisition. We suggest a fifty-year loan at 2.5 percent plus 0.01 percent of GNP for the same period.'

'How much you looking for?' I asked, resuming my charade of courier. There was hardly any point at this stage. Still, a man has pride in his work.

'Two hundred quadrillion.'

'Fucius,' I said. 'I didn't realise there was that much money in the world.'

'They'll never agree to it.' Daisy's voice was hoarse now.

'Won't they?' said Chong-zi from the wall, from the thick laser-proof polymer and refractor-grid that separated her from the filth of reality. 'I think they will, when they talk to bimbo-boy here and he gives them a first-hand account of how desperate things have become. How desperate they might become elsewhere.'

'You really think they'll take him seriously?' said Daisy. 'Why not send me?'

'You are much too dangerous,' Sha-yu said. 'What with your idealism and independent thought. No, much better to keep you here and threaten the love-sick puppy with your execution if he doesn't do a convincing job.'

'He's nobody – just a random body picked out for his responses to the Numbers Game. Why not just let him go, and leave the job to me? They'll never listen to him.'

'They will listen to everything and everyone.' Yingtao's voice snapped like a trap. 'They are Corporatists. They weigh up evidence, and first-hand testimony is the most powerful evidence of all.'

'It doesn't add up,' said Daisy. 'It's not even the money. The plan itself . . . is too barbaric. They won't go for it.'

'I think you'll find you are wrong there,' she replied. 'This was their idea, put together from the metadata from the Numbers Game. We will merely be giving them an update and asking for permission to launch.'

'You mean,' Daisy said, 'that all this time the Numbers Game was being used . . . for *this?*'

Chong-zi, shuffling over, put a hand on her shoulder. 'Yes, my dear. I'm afraid so.'

#

We had reached a critical point in the drama. The characters stood around waiting for something to happen, to advance the narrative. Down below, the laser-shot stopped, as suddenly as it had started. I may have been uncomfortable in this silence, or just looking for attention, as usual. It may have been that I was pissed off about having my destiny discussed in the third person, or at being called a bimbo-boy. Or – and this was the part that frightened me – I may have seen, finally, the opportunity to do something useful. They had forgotten about the sphere, in all the excitement, but I hadn't.

I lunged and grabbed it, holding it above my head. 'Anyone doesn't want to die today, should proceed slowly towards the door.'

There were a few moments of blank-faced confusion, before I explained. 'It's a bomb.'

The Commander looked at Chong-zi, who shook her head. 'Let's indulge this lunatic one last time,' she said, before taking her place at the back of the queue which had started to file bemusedly out of the room.

'Blow it, Li!' shouted Daisy, grabbing me by the arm. 'Or give to me, and I will.'

But the Commander had grabbed her and, twisting her arm expertly behind her back, pushed her through the door.

'Not you,' I said, as Chong-zi passed. 'You and I have something to discuss.'

22

All of it, the whole damned mess, pivoted on one moment, as far as I'm concerned, and Don Pietro agrees with me. That moment was when I convinced Chong-zi to allow me leave with Daisy. This happened during the conversation we had after I had cleared everyone else out of the boardroom. Following some monologue on her part about the fragility of history (recorded at the beginning of this journal), we got on to the subject of departure. At first, she was intransigent, but I used sales techniques I had learned at Ningbo. Closing questions, as any decent salesperson will tell you, are like a magic trick: they work.

'OK,' I said, 'you want me to give a pitch to Euro-Corpo, and I want to leave here with Daisy. Right?'

'Yes,' she said. 'That much is established.'

'Well, if we could both find a way of getting what we want, would it not make sense to just go that way, do what has to be done, get on with the rest of our lives and so on? Instead of killing each other or screwing everything up, or whatever.'

'It would make sense, but you are forgetting that I don't trust either you or her. And I trust her far less than you.'

'So, is it just a matter of trust, or is there some other obstacle?'

'This is exasperating. But no, there is no other obstacle. If you could convince the Euro-Corpo of the validity of our timing, I would be satisfied.'

'OK then. If I could satisfy you on the trust issue, would you let both me and Daisy go?'

'No.'

'Why not?'

'Whatever about you – I could threaten you with her, or your family or whatever – but she is a fanatic. Nothing would dissuade her from trying to sabotage our project.'

'But if there *was* a way, would you consider it?'

'I am at heart a pragmatist.'

'Then bring her in. I have an idea.'

The boy – that indolent, indispensable servant – was called, and sent to find Daisy, who entered the room at the point of the Commander's pistol. Though suspicious of Chong-zi's weary instruction to stand down, the Commander knew her place in the ordinal, and sat quietly by the door, as I explained the situation to Daisy. I told her the Numbers Game had stalled but was still viable. I told her the Passover Project was the lesser of two evils, and that one way or another people were going to die – were already dying. At least, I pointed out, if she played along, both she and I would live to keep working in a stable rather than a revolution-torn world. She argued, but in the end relented. The logic of the numbers was too compelling. Chong-zi walked with us to the strato-pad, advising me to hold the sphere above my head threateningly: she felt that it would be more politic. When we had been projected skywards, Daisy reached into her bag and brought out one of Elia's transistor radios.

'Where did you get *that?*' I asked stupidly.

'It was a present from your father.'

'And what are you doing with it?'

'This.'

She turned a dial. 'Look,' she said, and I followed her finger to CHQ, in time to see the refractor-grid fade, then shut off.

'What?'

'It's simple,' she said. 'This old remote, and a wad of plastic, were the only things I could get past their security. I stuck the explosive and a radio-activated charger in the refractor control room. Just a small explosion really, but enough to take out its central control unit.'

Reb fire was already beginning to rip into the building, and there were lumps of polymer and steel splintering everywhere. Daisy revved up the pod and we hit the stratosphere, leaving the scene behind.

'It'll all be over in a couple of hours,' she said.

'And what then?'

I was numb. To think of the thousands of people in the tower we had just left. To think of the death which would be ripping through the corridors, the screams and the terror – the knowing that this would be their last day. America Day.

'Who knows?' Daisy said. 'But it's the beginning of the end for the whole rotten system.'

'And us?'

'I'm going to join my unit. I'll drop you where you like.'

'No, I mean *us*.'

'There isn't time for an *us*. There's a war to be won.'

She may have had some scrap of humanity in her after all, because she added, in a softer voice: 'You did great. You're one of the bravest people I know, and I know a lot of brave people, living and dead.'

'Everything was just bullshit,' I said, faintly. 'You pretending to have feelings for me. You pretending to buy my argument in front of Chong-zi. Fucius, you're good.'

'Honey, I do have feelings for you. How could I not have? But with the whole world in upheaval, do you really think our feelings count for anything?'

'And how did you get Elia to help? I suppose you lied to him as well. It would be just like him to be innocent enough to believe you. You people.'

'No, I didn't have to lie to him. He's one of us and always has been. One of our most effective operatives. How do you think we got access to you?'

Through the devastation, through the sucking of air from my lungs and light from my life, one question demanded an answer. 'Are they even my real parents?'

'No,' she said. 'You were hatched on a repro-farm in Sligo. Just like me.'

#

She dropped me in Capri – the only place I could think to go. I half expected a laser-shot to the back of my head as I walked away from the pod. Instead, I heard her shout, and turned to see her running towards me. Then her arms were around my neck, and her lips on mine.

'Hey,' she said. 'You know I love you, right?'

'Well, no. Not really.'

'Well I do. We're ingrained into one another – always have been. You feel it too.'

'You know I do.'

'But I have to do this. You understand that, right? There's too much at stake for too many people. I just don't have a choice – not right now. But if you wait for me, I'll be back. I promise.'

'You can't promise that.'

Drawing away from me, she held my face in her hands.

'Maybe not. But you need to know I'll do everything possible to come back to you.'

I could see tears in her eyes when she gave me one final kiss and hurried back to the pod, leaving me to wander in a daze towards what used to be home. When I looked back, she gave me a salute, before closing the door and shooting upwards. I stood and watched until the pod disappeared into the blazing azure of a summer sky, and the island settled into its immutable calm. Don Pietro was walking towards me as I crested the hill near the old villa, having seen the pod land and take off.

'You've come back?'

'I had nowhere else to go.'

'I see.'

'It's over, Don Pietro. Everything I've ever known or loved never existed. Everything is over.'

He put his hand on my shoulder, and I started crying.

'No, my friend,' he said. 'Nothing that never began can ever be over. No, nothing is over, but something can begin, if you have the courage not to measure it.'

'What does that even mean?'

'I'll explain, when you've slaughtered the goat.'

Shortly afterwards, my concentration was taken up by a discussion between me and Don Pietro about how to slaughter a kid goat, which the old man held by the scruff of its neck with one hand while gesticulating with a large knife in the other. I think I wanted to stun it first, with a claw hammer, with which I gesticulated back.

#

The sun sinks, slowly, behind the horizon of the Mediterranean, leaving a seam of darkening amber. It flames on to the sea, makes a relief of the Vesuvian skyline. I sit by the lizard rock – though they have long slithered off to their mysterious lives, or deaths, somewhere else. It is strange to be here, to be staring at all this beauty and having no one to share it with. I lie awake at night, on my cot, breathing the warm breath of the Mediterranean. I listen for the drone of a pod but hear instead another zanzara, and cover myself with the sheet. Only the females bite: they waltz by your breath, to be sure your blood's what they're looking for. Fucius knows what the males do, if anything.

Time passes, and its passing allows me to work through the mess that was left in my head by those who, for one reason or another, saw fit to fuck it up. I've gone through disbelief and anger, but struggle with acceptance. The war is still at the raging stage, somewhere, far away. We hear about it at the Marina when we go to trade. Something's going on in Greece, something else in Lombardia – I think that's about as near as it gets. Ireland was bombed a few times, but I heard that the deaths were still only in the thousands.

I've phoned Elia and Laura. Told them everything I knew. About how they manipulated my whole life, and reared me like a goat to be slaughtered. They protested that they had never really known what was going on – had been duped as much as I had. They had just been happy, they said, to have such a beautiful baby boy to adopt. And yes, the help the Corpo gave Laura with her business went a long way towards giving us the standard of living we all enjoyed. What did I want? That they live like no-boomers in some no-boomer shithole? It was only then, with all else denuded, that Elia admitted that my brother Zisha had somehow found out what was going on, and this was enough to get him killed. The day following our conversation, he went into the garden and tried to hang himself. The branch on the tree broke and he ended up in the carp-pond, where Laura later discovered him unconscious, the fish nibbling pertox from his leaking neck. When Laura rang to tell me about it, I begged her to keep an eye on him. She assured me she would, and I think we had our first honest conversation.

They're going to come for a visit, as soon as the war leaves Euro-land alone long enough to allow international travel. Most of the war seems to be going on in the Americas, India and Africa – places too distant to be real. No one's sure who's winning, or even what difference it will make when somebody does. Daisy's out there somewhere in the chaos – if she's still alive – trying to impose her coordinates on an impossible landscape. I can't let her go, not yet: she's living inside me in the innumerate emotion that makes me what I am. I'm still hoping, irrationally, that when this war ends and the chaos inside her calms, she'll come back for me. Soldiers do that, I tell myself: they arrive unexpectedly a little older, a little wearier, and scarred with things they can never talk about – things they can never add up. But they come back. They come back to the people they love because, after all, what else is there? There's always hope, slender on the horizon: a slip of light as the sun goes down.

ACKNOWLEDGEMENTS

The following read the manuscript of this book and provided helpful advice and guidance: Sarah Davis-Goff, Carlotta Galimberti, David O'Dwyer, Adam Pritchard, Vanessa Fox O'Loughlin and Christine Dwyer Hickey. I would like to sincerely thank these people for giving me their time and senses.

Seán O'Keeffe, who edited the book, gave me critical guidance and enormous support. To him I am also extremely grateful.

A big thank you too, to Cormac Kinsella and Sarah Connolly for their support with the publicity.